Of Lake Land and Liberty

The Battle of Plattsburgh in the War of 1812
Copyright © By Joseph Bebo 2012

Foreword

Though little remembered in the great scheme of American History, a mere tussle as battles go in a war that was hardly a war to speak of, the Battle of Plattsburgh during the War of 1812 was as stirring and important as any battle where American blood was spilt in defense of our country, especially since it was one of the few fought on our own soil against a foreign invader.

Overshadowed by the great events at New Orleans just a few months later where "Old Hickory", Brigadier General Andrew Jackson, defeated 7,000 of Wellington's battle hardened veterans fresh from their victories against Napoleon, the 1500 regulars and as many volunteers, raw militia and convalescents, in a little border town in the northeast corner of New York, faced a similarly formidable foe of over 10,000.

Although not as well known, Plattsburgh had the same strategic importance as New Orleans. A successful British drive down the eastern part of New York State might have split the fractious, antiwar New England states from the union, just as a defeat in the south might have split the entire Louisiana Territory from the fledgling nation.

While Jackson had an army comparable in number and some of the best artillery in the country, the enemy had a formidable task just getting to the battlefield through the myriad of bayous and lagoons. General Prevost's 10,351 troops at Plattsburgh could march down a flat, wide valley without so much as a hill or brook to obstruct them, fed all the way by hard-strapped and unpatriotic farmers on both sides of the lake in Vermont and New York.

There are a lot of parallels between the events in Plattsburgh and New Orleans. Both brought stinging defeat to an over confident, over ambitious foe. If the Battle of New Orleans had not occurred – the war was already over when it was fought – that other battle in the North Country might have become better appreciated and a bigger part of American lore. In the hearts and minds of those who fought it, however, the farm boys and tinkers, soldiers and merchants, lake men and hunters, who faced those overwhelming odds, it had all the intensity and glory of any battle ever fought.

Those facing those odds had one thing in common, an overwhelming love of their country and the land that bore them, the mountains and forests, the lakes and streams where they grew up, and a resolve to keep it from the hands of the British who had just burnt the nation's capital. It was a small battle with a huge consequence for the nation at a turning point in its early struggle for survival.

This is the story of that battle and the men and boys who fought it, who grew up on the shores of that lake hearing tales about earlier wars from their fathers. It stirred their hearts and imaginations and is still being told today, the story of the greatest battle that almost was.

Chapter 1

Village of Plattsburgh, NY, June 1812

As they usually did on a Saturday, Sam Turner and his cousin Jesse Lebow were walking the twenty miles from their small hamlet of what would one day be Dannemora, to the village of Plattsburgh nestled in the valley next to Lake Champlain. They lived in the foothills at the northern tip of the Adirondacks, and they did not know it at the time, but it was a day that would change their carefree lives forever.

Although it took almost half the day to get there and half to get back, they enjoyed the adventure and the excitement of the village, where they could get news about what was happening in the world from people who had actually seen it – the grand ships of the "blue water fleet" leaving their ports for the open Atlantic; the goings-on of Congress as they decided the young country's future; the hustle-and-bustle in the great cities of the fast growing nation. There were cute girls there as well, which was another incentive for the tall, lanky, blue-eyed 16-year-old Sam, with his long, curly, light-brown hair.

"What are we going to do when we get to town?" asked Jesse, who was short and wiry, with black hair and dark eyes.

"I don't know," said Sam. "Maybe hang around the barbershop, see who comes in. Or go down to the docks. There might be a gunboat at the pier."

Sam was the youngest of three. His father owned a farm and had once been the county sheriff. Now semi-retired, he helped Jack, his eldest son, run the place. Sam's sister, Mary Jane, was already married with a child of her own. They also lived at the farm where her husband, Jerry, worked as a hand. Everyone was busy and had little time for young Sam, and that suited him just fine. Once he was through with his chores he loved to wander about the countryside alone or with Jesse, fishing, or shooting the hand-me-down muskets their fathers had given them.

Mostly they shot at targets. Sam wasn't particularly fond of killing harmless animals who were just minding their own business, although hunting was in their blood. But you had to go deep into the mountains to find any real game. Shooting little critters just wasn't much fun as far as Sam was concerned, so he curbed his younger cousin's enthusiasm for killing, as best he could. They were careful for the most part and knew how to handle guns, having fired them even as small children with their papas standing behind them, hugging them with the muskets pressed in their hands. Jesse could shoot the head off a snake swimming in a choppy lake thirty yards away. Today they had left their guns at home, since there was not much need for them in the village and they were too heavy to lug all that way.

Jesse was the only family member near Sam's age that he had to play with, although there were plenty of other boys at school and in the area. It was just that he and Jesse had a special bond, having grown up together. They could always make each other laugh. Where Sam was easygoing, always smiling and slow to anger, Jesse was a hothead, with a mean streak when provoked. When his little cousin got riled, even Sam, who was two years older and a whole head taller, and twice as strong from working on the farm, kept his distance. He'd seen what Jesse could do when he was mad.

Sam was just too mild-mannered for fighting. Although he was bigger and stronger than most kids, there were plenty of boys meaner than him who could beat him in a fight, but with Jesse by his side, few bothered to try.

They walked along the Saranac River, where it ran wide and swift from the mountains, close to the road, eventually emptying into Lake Champlain. The road itself was hard-packed dirt, but wide enough for two buggies to pass, though they hadn't seen a cart since they started out earlier that morning. It was a clear spring day, the sky so clean it seemed to shine. The leaves radiated every shade of green you could imagine, and were already so thick the eye could no longer penetrate the trees that hugged the road on the side across from the river.

They chatted as they walked, joking and commenting on the things they heard in school or around their hamlet. There was a lot of talk of war in the air, but that was the furthest thing from their minds.

"My Dad says there's an Indian uprising out west," said Jesse. "They're killing settlers all over the place. Do you think the Indians will start killing people here, too?" Jesse Lebow always had Indians on his mind. Daniel Boone was one of his favorite heroes.

"I doubt it," said Sam. "There are hardly any Indians around here anymore. They sent them all away."

"What about that Techum, Techema, you know? Miss Kathy told us about him."

"You mean Tecumseh, out in Tippecanoe?"

"Yeah, Tippecanoe and you too," said Jesse, pushing Sam off balance and laughing. Sam pushed him back and they tussled for a little while in fun, along the fast rushing river.

"I don't know," said Sam, giving his cousin a final shove after catching him as they ran. "My Dad says we took a lot of their land and the Indians don't want to give any more of it up."

"My Pa says we should wipe them out, but I like the Indians. They get to run around with no clothes and scalp people."

"I'll scalp you, if you don't watch out," laughed Sam. They ran the next mile or so, taking turns chasing each other down and pretending to scalp one another. In this way, they made their way down to the village of Plattsburgh by the lake.

As they reached the outskirts of the village, they meandered down a broad dirt street that descended from the last of the western hills to the lake valley. They could see the tall steeples of the churches in the distance. There were broad fields on each side of them, fencing in cows and some horses, which alternated with wide rows of corn. The surrounding hillsides were covered with fruit trees of all kinds. Soon houses started to appear on both sides of the wide road.

The cluster of buildings making up that part of the village on the near side of the river soon came into view. Sam and Jesse stopped for a while at a large church and looked up at the bell tower, the tallest structure in town, but were afraid to go inside.

There was a lot going on in the village, which was the central hub for traffic flowing north and south on the 100-mile long lake, from New York via the Hudson River, to Montreal and Quebec. There were farmers bringing their produce to market, and a depot where coaches brought people from neighboring towns and distant cities. The docks were crowded with barges and boats of all description, full of goods, which came and went at all hours of the day and night. Furs, tar, and timber flowed south; beef, wheat, and cotton headed north. There was even a newspaper, *The Plattsburgh Republican*. The village had it all. There were people of all kinds and colors, even soldiers from the nearby camps, as well as sailors from the gunboats on the lake. It was a regular metropolis compared to the small, one-horse hamlet they came from, one among many making up the District of Champlain.

Sam and Jesse walked along the dusty main street, past a saloon and an eating-house, then a boardinghouse with stables and a craftsman's shop. There was a shoemaker, the town's only Italian, and a dressmaker from New York City. Past the smithy's stood a general store and an outdoor market where you could get almost every kind of fresh produce grown in the area, as well as beef and venison, and even buffalo meat. There were peddlers and sutlers, where most men bought their whiskey. Tinkers of all kinds wandered the street, selling their wares, from patent medicine to bananas. There was even an itinerant man who sharpened knives and scissors.

They made their way down a side street that ran to a new wooden bridge that spanned the Saranac shortly before it spilled into Lake Champlain. They crossed the bridge behind a herd of cows being led to the docks to be ferried across the lake. They were at the eastern extent of their domain, neither having been to Vermont, although Jesse had gone with his father across the border a fair distance, almost to Montreal.

They came to part of town where the Platts lived, the founding family of the village. The big brick houses of some of its leading citizens lay clustered in a shaded park across from the depot, where coaches came and went in all directions. They made their first stop at the barbershop, to look at the magazines and listen to the men talk. If they were lucky, a soldier or a sailor might come in.

"I tell you, those British don't know when to quit," said a man sitting in a chair waiting for a cut and waving a broad piece of paper. "They didn't learn their lesson from the first war. Now we'll have to invade Canada and teach them good."

"They say they're inciting the Indians out West to kill whites," said the man in the barber's chair. "They're scalping women and children. It's terrible."

"Quiet, Bill," said the barber, motioning at the two boys who had just sat down in his chairs. "You boys want a haircut?"

"Sure," said Jesse. "What do you think we're here for? But take your time. We ain't in no hurry."

The men continued their conversation.

"Well, they've gone and done it now," said the man waiting for his haircut. "They've been taking our citizens off American ships right in sight of our own harbors. They've killed innocent men, who have done no harm to them, on the pretense that they might be English deserters. It's disgraceful and had to stop. Now the President's declared war."

"Who cares if they've stopped a few of our ships?" said the man getting the shave. "What of it? They're at war with Napoleon. They pay most of our trade and import revenues. So what if a few sailors get taken off our ships and forced into the British navy? It's not worth going to war over."

"Yeah," said another man, a farmer by the look of him. "First thing they'll do is tax us."

"That's what this country needs," the man in the barber's chair answered, "a national bank and a sound revenue-gathering process, but not for war and certainly not to invade Canada."

"You sound like a darned Federalist," said the man with the long whiskers, waiting for his haircut. All of them wore the latest cut suit, except the farmer, who wore old-style britches and waistcoat.

"Gentlemen, I'll have no politics discussed in my shop," pronounced the barber. He pointed to a sign that said the same, and another one that read, "Federalists and Republicans stay out". The barber had a good sense of humor but he wasn't joking now. He didn't need his customers fighting one another.

"I still say we should invade Canada," said the first man, leaning his chair back and spitting into a can positioned squarely on a barrel for just that purpose. "We could march on Montreal, no problem. It's only sixty or so miles away. Why, there's not a hill or creek between us and the border. There can't be more than a few thousand troops in all of Canada."

"You're all talk," said the man in the barber's chair, who was just about finished. "You'd be the first to say no if someone asked you to fight."

"Yeah, well I'm an old man. I have a family."

"Well, the young ones would have to fight and die, and they have families too. What about these boys here?" he said, standing up and dusting himself off. "You want them to die for your insulted pride?"

"You boys want to fight in a war?" asked the first man.

"Hank, must you?" said the barber, as Hank got in his chair.

"There's no harm," said Hank. "Well do you, boys?"

"Sure," said Jesse. "I hate the dirty redcoats."

"My Dad says it would be hard to fight the English again," said Sam. "We don't have an army or navy, while they've got the biggest army in the world, and over a hundred warships."

"Your father's right," said the Federalist, as he left the shop.

"Ah, their army's tied down in France," said the man now in the barber's chair as the barber started trimming his long sideburns. "Bonaparte's kicking their butts. And ship for ship, our navy's the best in the world. We just need to build more ships, that's all."

A short time later, two men in gray military uniforms walked in from the army camp a few miles away on the south end of town. All talk of war ceased. The barber joined the farmer in a conversation about spring planting, crops and livestock, relieved to have the topic turn to something other than politics and war. He was distressed by the talk of conflict with England. Where would it all end? Although it could be good for business, especially if there were a lot of solders in town, talk of invading Montreal unnerved him. Just the opposite might happen, and the thought of an English invasion frightened him.

When he finished with the others, the barber turned to the two boys and asked, "Who's first?"

"Not me," said Jesse, getting up and giggling. "I don't want to get scalped."

"Me neither," said Sam, laughing even louder and running out of the shop after his cousin.

They ran down the street laughing.

"Wow, war!" shouted Jesse. "We're going to fight in a war. Whoopee!"

"Don't be so happy, Jess," said Sam. "War ain't so great. My father fought in the last one and he says war is the worst thing you can imagine. Lot of people die and stuff."

"Ah, don't be such a sissy," said Jesse, who literally hated the English. His father was half French-Canadian, along with a few other nationalities. He carried his own father's animosity with him, all the way from 1763 when the French had lost almost everything they possessed in North America to the English. "My Pa says the English still act like they own us. We licked them once, now we have to do it again to teach them some respect."

They walked down to the boat dock, hoping to see a big two-master bristling with cannons, but all they saw was a broken down gunboat among a couple of flat-bottom scows. That was enough for Sam and Jesse, however. To them the old gunboat was just about the most fantastic thing they had ever seen.

They hung around there for the rest of the afternoon watching the men work, and listened to them talk as they cleaned the ship and loaded and unloaded supplies, a couple of them in navy uniforms. The ship had a large, 12-pound cannon in the bow, facing out but clearly visible in profile from where they stood on the shore. It was the biggest gun they had ever seen, its mouth the size of a boy's head.

Their goal was to get as close to the gun as possible. Making their way to the end of the pier, being careful to stay out of the way of the working men, they were soon overlooking the large naval cannon, only a dozen feet away. They stared in amazement.

"Boy, I bet that makes a loud boom," said Jesse.

"Yeah," said Sam. "Bam!" he yelled, lunging at his cousin and making him jump.

"Bang!" screamed Jesse, even louder and laughing.

"What are you boys doing out here?" rang out a voice behind them. "This is a restricted area, gentlemen. How do I know you're not spies?"

They both spun around in alarm.

"We ain't spies," yelled Jesse. They both stood speechless, their mouths open, looking up at the tall man in the uniform of a

United States Naval officer. They had never seen one this close before.

"Sorry, sir," said Sam finally. "We just wanted to get a good look at that boat. Is that your boat, mister?"

"There you go asking questions, just like a spy," said the man, the commander of the navy's small lake fleet. "It's a ship, Sir, and if I tell you any more I'll have to shoot you."

"What?" yelled Jesse, not getting the joke.

"Really, Mister," said Sam, not quite sure himself. His own sense of humor inclined toward pranks and practical jokes. He was always ready to laugh at someone else's expense, but wasn't so sure he liked it when the laugh was on him. "We're really not spies. Honest."

"I'm sorry, boys. I was only kidding you. You both look like you're about ready to jump in the lake there." He laughed, a big, good-natured, hardy laugh that made both boys breathe a sigh of relief. "Here, to make it up to you, how about a peace offering?"

He took out a handkerchief filled with several chucks of rock-candy, and gave each of them a large piece.

"Here, you boys take these. They're for my fiancée's younger brother but he won't miss a couple pieces. Beside's he's a little overweight. Not like you boys. Remember, if you ever want to get in good with a girl, give her candy. And if she has a little brother, it doesn't hurt to give him some candy too."

"Gee," said Sam. "I wish you had courted my sister. None of her beaus ever gave me candy."

The navy man laughed again. "Sorry boys, I'm happy to know you like my ship, but you can't stay here. It's not safe. We're at war now, you know. And that means we all have to be on our toes and alert and ready for anything the enemy might throw at us. What would you do if one of His Majesty's 34-gun frigates came around the 'Head' there and started blasting?"

"34-guns?" echoed Sam in amazement. He had read that word in story books and history books, but had never heard it used here in Plattsburgh. "On this lake?"

"You bet. And if they don't have one, they soon will. Anyway, I have to be ready for things like that, and if an enemy ship does come into the bay, I don't want you two lads standing on my dock. So off with you now and have a good day."

11

What he didn't tell them was that such a possibility was a constant nightmare to men like Lieutenant Sidney Smith. It had been even before war was declared. The British enjoyed an immense and overwhelming naval superiority not only here on the lake, but on every body of water in the world. It would take more than a few gunboats like the ones he commanded and President Jefferson had staked the country's future on to stop them if the English decided to attack. If anyone could stop them, however, it was the officers who had commanded that small navy during the Quasi-war with France and the wars with the Barbary Pirates. By Lieutenant Smith's estimate they were the best commanders in the whole darn world.

Sam and Jesse thanked the man and scampered off the pier, sucking their candy as they went. It was a rare treat for the simple farm boys, though Sam's father had brought home candy now and then, mostly for Christmas and other holidays.

It was getting late, almost school quitting time, around three. They would have to hurry if they wanted to make it home for supper.

On the way out of town, they passed a wagon full of apples, the horse that pulled it hitched to a post. Looking up and down the street and not seeing the driver anywhere, they jumped up on the wagon to snatch a couple of red, juicy apples. Just as they were about to jump down again with a plump apple in each hand, an angry voice called out.

"Hey you boys! Get out of my wagon! Drop those apples!"

Jesse jumped off the wagon with his ill-gotten gain and started to run away. Glancing back, he saw Sam standing in the wagon, collared by a big, wide-shouldered bearded man, who was shaking his cousin like an old dust rag. Jesse froze in his tracks, horrified. His cousin and best friend was about to get murdered, for that's the kind of look the man had in his eyes.

Sam tried to push the man away, but lost his balance and fell backwards and almost off the wagon. The man knelt over him and grabbed him by the front of the collar. Pulling his right arm back, he delivered a blow to Sam's head as he lay helpless on his back. Jesse covered his eyes in horror and missed the first punch. He heard it though, and opened his eyes in amazement.

12

The man's first blow landed hard, right between the planks on the floor of his wagon, cutting his knuckle. Sam had darted his head to the side at the last moment, missing the blow by a fraction of an inch. He was laughing at the man for missing and hurting his fist. This made the man even madder. He bent over Sam, holding his shirt even tighter and delivered another thundering right that just missed Sam's head again, as he slid it to the side at the last moment. Again and again the man tried to hit him with hard rights, each time missing and hitting his hand on the hard wagon floor, until he hit it so hard that he startled the horse, which moved forward a few steps, throwing the man off balance. He would later learn he had broken his hand. When asked why he kept trying to hit the kid with straight rights and hadn't used both hands to hit him, he said he hadn't thought of that.

Sam had clearly been lucky, but to him it was just a big joke. He hadn't stopped laughing from the first punch on, but when the big man fell backwards on his behind, Sam laughed so hard he couldn't get up. Jesse had to grab him and help him down from the wagon, making sure to grab a couple more apples in the process.

"Wow!" said Jesse, looking at his cousin in a new light. "I never seen anything like it. He couldn't hit you. How'd you learn to do that?"

"I don't know," said Sam. "I'm so used to having my older brother sit on me and punch me I guess I just got good at dodging."

"That was good!" Jesse laughed again, slapping his older cousin on the back. "That big jerk couldn't hit you for all he was worth. Ha ha!" He darted his head back and forth in imitation of Sam's movements."

"I guess we shouldn't have stolen his apples," said Sam.

"Ah, he had a whole wagon full of them. They was last year's apples anyway. I hope he broke his stupid hand. That was great." He laughed again. "Wait 'til I tell my pa."

"You better not tell your pa. What do you think he'd do if he found out you were stealing apples?"

"He'd whip me 'til the cows came home."

"Right, so you better not say anything. Even about us going down to the docks."

"Ok, but it's a great story," said Jesse, still laughing.

They made their way back home, enjoying their apples as they walked. They didn't talk much the rest of the way, both thinking about all they had seen and heard, but most of all about the war, which spurred their imaginations in different ways. Jesse saw himself shooting redcoats and becoming a hero, covered with medals and ribbons like he'd seen in the paintings; riding a big white horse with his men behind him. He thought only of the glory of war. Sam had other thoughts, also spurred by the paintings he had seen, of young men lying dying and bleeding on the ground. He had no hatred of the British like his cousin, just the opposite. He admired them in many ways, especially the stories of their navy men like Cook and Nelson, who he had read about. Still, he was just as patriotic as the next fellow, and if his country was invaded he would fight to protect it like his father had. When he thought of war, however, he thought of ships standing toe to toe, blasting each other with broadsides.

They ran the last ten miles to make it home just before dusk, where they split up and went their separate ways, both late for supper.

Middleton, Connecticut, June 1812

30-year-old Thomas Macdonough had been agitated ever since he heard the news that Madison had declared war on England. Although he thought the declaration was warranted to uphold the nation's honor, he was well aware of the odds. He had been schooled under the tutelage of the first Secretary of the Navy, Benjamin Stoddert, along with a cadre of celebrated officers that included one of the most celebrated of all them all, Edward Preble. Macdonough had served in both the Quasi-war with France and on the coast of Tripoli against the Barbary Pirates. There he had earned his reputation as one of Preble's boys, taking part in the famous storming of the captured USS Philadelphia. He was at his family home in Middletown, Connecticut, and had finally, against his father's advice, written to the Secretary of the Navy to be reinstated at his former rank and given an assignment.

"I only hope they give me command of a good ship," he said to his father when he told him of his intention to reenlist. "I hear the Constellation is available. That would be a fine ship to command."

"You're crazy," said the old man. "There are plenty of other good men. Anyway, the war will be over quickly, as soon as the British blockade our coasts."

"They won't if I have anything to say about it," said his son, more certain of his decision despite his father's objections. "That is why I want my commission back. The war will be over soon, and others are already achieving fame and glory."

"And dying. Why they'll have our whole fleet bottled up in port soon. You won't be able to sail out without encountering three or four ships of the line, all of them with more guns than you. While we've spent 20 years tearing down our navy, the British have been building theirs up. They have hundreds of ships, some of them with 74-guns."

"It takes more than guns to win a battle."

"Don't tell me what it takes to win a battle," said the elder Macdonough sternly. "I know first hand."

"So do I," said his son just as emphatically. "There will always be a way to slip out of port, especially in the winter storms. It's just not possible to stop every ship, at every port, all of the time. Just a few of our ships on the prowl will cause them to restrict their offensive operations and go on the defensive. It gives us the initiative. At least in the early stages of the conflict, and initiative can often times make the difference. Anyway, I cannot stand by idly while my country is at war, especially against such an adversary. It is my duty."

"Your duty is to stay home with your family and help them in their old age. You will be getting married soon."

"How can one think of marriage, of the future, at a time like this?" said the young ex-navy man. "They need every able-bodied officer they can find."

His father gave up trying to give his son any advice. Throwing up his hands in disgust, he left the room, shaking his head and muttering. Thomas sat by the fire and stared at the dying embers, thinking about the future and the war.

That night, as he lay in bed with his bible in his hands, he prayed fervently for himself and his young country. "Dear Lord, grant that I may see glory. Help me defend my small country against this aggression, against those who would do us harm and make us their slaves."

He didn't care where they sent him, to what ship or squadron they assigned him, as long as he could be of service to the country he loved and uphold the memory of those who had given their lives in its cause. He prayed that whatever task he was assigned he would do honor to himself and his flag, fervently hoping that it would be in a position of real command where he could make a difference. He was extremely confident in himself and his ability to overcome all odds, if only the country was behind him and had the will to do what was needed.

Chapter 2

Mountains West of Plattsburgh, District of Champlain, NY, June 1812

Sam's father confronted him as soon as he came through the door. "Where have you been, Samuel?"

They lived in a simple, two-story, white farm house, framed between two wide, plowed fields with a barn in the back and wood-covered mountains in the background. "Your mother had dinner on the table an hour ago. Where you been?"

"Me and Jesse went into the village. My chores were done. I told Ma."

"You were supposed to be back by dinnertime," said his mother, who already looked grand-motherly at 48, plump with grey hair and glasses. "You promised. That's what I get for letting you go off with your cousin. He's no good, just like his father. I don't know why Augusta had to marry that good-for-nothing."

"Now Catherine, don't go speaking ill of the boy just because you don't like his father," said her husband. "Mike's all right, if you don't get him riled."

"Yeah, and if he's not whiskied-up."

"We went down to the boat docks. We saw a gunboat and met the captain." Sam decided to change the subject, hoping his news would make up for his tardy appearance. "At the barbershop they said there's a war, and the captain at the docks said the British might have a ship with over 34 guns on the lake."

"I wouldn't be surprised," said his father.

"War!" said his mother in alarm.

"I was going to tell you earlier, but I wanted to wait until Sam was home," confessed his father.

"Oh dear, don't tell me you're going to go off to war again," said Sam's mother. "You're too old for that."

"No one's going off to war, Catherine. It won't affect us way up here. It's all out on the ocean, far away from here."

"That's not what the lieutenant said," interjected Sam.

"Never you mind what the lieutenant said," replied his father. "That's no excuse for coming home after dark and missing your supper. You won't be allowed to go to the village if you can't be home on time. Next weekend you're going to help your brother and I take some vegetables to the market in Malone."

"Ah, Dad, the navy chap said the whole fleet will be there next week. I just gotta see them."

"Not next week you're not. Now eat your supper," said Mister Benjamin Turner.

"I'll heat some soup up for you on the fire, and there's some bread," said Sam's mom.

"Thanks mom. I'm starving," answered Sam, sitting at the table.

Later that evening to Sam's delight, a few friends of his father's came over to share a few pipes and trade gossip and stories. Sam was not allowed to participate, a boy having no place, like women, in men's company. But he was just as content to sit on the stairs leading up to his room and listen as the men talked and laughed in the smoke-filled living room below. Even more to Sam's delight, they talked about the war.

These weren't just any friends, but his father's old war buddies, soldiers he had fought with in the Revolution, men with whom he had shared victory at Saratoga. They didn't waste any time getting down to what concerned them, and it wasn't crops.

"The same thing's happening again," said Bill Carlton, Sam's uncle by marriage and one of his father's closet friends. They had gone through the war together. After the war Sam's father had brought Bill home and introduced him to his younger sister. They were married soon after and lived just across the lane. "They'll try to come down the valley from Canada and cut off New England from the Union. Sooner or later, you'll see."

"They already tried that once. They'll remember what happened," said Sam's father.

"That's right, they won't be stupid enough to try it in winter," said Carl Philips, another old comrade from the regiment.

"Bill has a point there," said John Fisher, a successful physician from Boston and their old commander. "The New England states are not too happy with Mister Madison's war, if I may say. It wouldn't take much to split them off. It's the very disunion of the country that has brought this war upon us. The Governor of Massachusetts, the Honorable Caleb Strong…"

"Ah, he tain't so honorable," said Carl Philips, spitting and making everyone laugh, including their old commander. Carl was a man known for his bravery under fire, as well as for his fiery temper.

"That may be," continued John Fisher. "But that didn't prevent him from calling for a nationwide fast to protest the war."

"Damned Federalists," spat Carl again.

"It'll be hard to fight a war if we split the country apart," said the ex-colonel.

"You think it will come to that?" asked Sam's father.

"It could, Benjamin" answered John Fisher. "Some of the more extreme newspapers in Boston are calling for just such a thing, especially if things go badly, and they haven't been going well. We only have 20 men-of-war. Not much of a navy. The British navy has over a thousand war ships, some with over 70 guns."

"Ah, I'm scared," said Carl, eliciting laughs again.

"We got, what, maybe 12 or 15 thousand in our army?" continued John Fisher, unperturbed. "They've got over ten times that many, trained regulars, not militia."

"We did all right with militia," said Carl. "We licked them once, we can beat them again."

"Most of their troops are tied down fighting Napoleon in Europe," observed Sam's father, echoing what the man in the barbershop had said. Sam was proud his father was so smart and kept up with world events through his far flung contacts and friends.

"Yeah, for the time being," said their old commander. "That's what the President is counting on, obviously. But it is a risky gamble. Things can change so fast on that front. What coalition is fighting Napoleon now? The second, third, what? Things change from day to day over there."

"That's all far away and out to sea," said Sam's Uncle Bill. "Who cares if a few sailors get taken off a few ships. Is it worth fighting a war over?"

"Impressment is a big thing to some people," countered John Fisher, the 'Colonel' to most of the men when he wasn't around. "To see free Americans taken off our very own ships, ships serving your needs, right in front of our eyes, right off our own shores. Well, that can be hard to take."

"When you look at it in that light, there is all the more reason to go to war," said Sam's father. "To stand up for our rights."

"I'm all for it," said Carl. "So why are all those damned New Englanders so afraid to fight?"

"It's not that, Carl," replied Sam's father. "Despite the way they treat our seamen, the English are our best customers. At least they are to a majority of people in New England, and down South too. They don't want to bite the hand that feeds them. Who's going to pay for this war anyway? It takes money to fight a war."

"Like we paid for the last one," said his brother-in-law, Bill Carlton.

"I don't think the French are in any position to lend us money, even if they wanted to," said John Fisher, laughing.

"We can give them the Louisiana Territory back," spat Carl, making everyone laugh again. "Tain't worth a damned nickel."

"Ben is right. It takes money to fight a war," said the Colonel ignoring Carl's joke. "We can't borrow our way through it like we did the last time. If we go to war with our biggest trading partner and our only income is from custom duties on imports from that country, well, things can't turn out very good. We'll be up a creek without a paddle."

"There's militia," said Sam's Uncle Bill. "We can raise 100,000 in New York and Pennsylvania alone."

"They wouldn't stand a chance against hardened British regulars," said John Fisher

"I wouldn't be too sure of that," replied Carl, eyeing his ex-regimental commander with a hard look.

"Gentlemen," said Sam's father with a soothing gesture. "We all know the merits of the prospective armies and navies. We've all been through war and know how horrible it is. I know I don't wish it upon my sons, but it isn't a matter of who's tougher or who's better. It's a matter of who can do the best with what they have at the critical moment and that can only be determined by

God's Divine Providence. So let us pray God is with us in this struggle."

They all agreed with knowing nods and murmurs, and the conversation drifted away from talk of the current war to wars past. They started trading stories of their days in the Great Rebellion, until finally they drifted back to the present conflict again, which still weighed heavily on their hearts.

"We are weak almost everywhere," declared the Colonel, trying to make them see the reality of the situation. He knew the only answer was raising taxes, which the wealthy new nation could easily afford to do. But to these farmers and steadfast Jeffersonian Republicans, the very word tax was anathema. "The British not only have a naval superiority on the oceans, they have it on the lakes too, including your own Lake Champlain here."

"So what?" protested Carl defiantly.

"So they can land as many troops as they want anywhere they want, right along our whole seaboard, from Maine to Louisiana, from Plattsburgh to Lake Michigan."

"That's why we have to strike now," said Carl. "There can't be more than 5000 people all totaled in Montreal, not more than a few thousand of your famed British regulars, as you call them, in all of Canada. We can raise the militia from all the bordering states, tens of thousands of them. Take the whole darned worthless country."

"Even if you could raise such an army," said John, "We have to have officers who can train and lead them, not to mention uniforms, and muskets and ball and powder, and cannons. All that takes money."

"Anyway, Carl," replied Sam's father. "You can't take the militia across the border to invade another country. The Governors of the states won't allow it."

"Well now, Benjamin," said John Fisher. "Carl here might not be too far off the mark. I've already heard rumors in Boston that Madison is planning just such an attack on Montreal from Plattsburgh."

"Now you're talking," said Carl.

"But you can't invade another country like Canada without money," persisted the Colonel, hammering his point home.

21

"Ah," replied Carl Philips still unconvinced, his fighting juices flowing, although when all was said and done, he trusted his old commander's judgment and would have followed him anywhere.

John continued, as if lecturing the men on their next objective. "First thing you need to do is build ships on the lakes. The gateway to Canada is through her waterways, Lake Erie and Ontario, the St. Lawrence and Lake Champlain. Get superiority on the lakes and you'd be able to ferry an invading army of any size you want, but not militia. Why waste men who aren't trained for war with incompetent generals who have never seen it. Congress has raised the bonuses and inducements to enlistment, as well as the limits of the army to 30,000. A regular, well-trained army of half that size would do, but they would need heavy artillery and plenty of ammunition, and all that takes money."

Sam's father looked at the ex-colonel with concern. "John, I know where you're going with this. The Republicans haven't stayed in power for going on 12 years now by being stupid enough to tax the populace. They didn't have taxes during the war with Tripoli or the so called Quasi-war with the French, and they sure as heck aren't going to start imposing taxes on people now. They'll do it on the cheap like they've always done."

"Then I'm afraid we're in for some rough times," answered John. "The Federalists may be a bunch of self-serving, unpatriotic blowhards, but at least they know you can't fight a war or have a strong country without a bank and taxes. We can well afford it. There's plenty of money flowing around."

"Oh, here we go again," said Carl Philips. "Speak for yourself John. I don't see any specie flowing around here. Now you wants to go and take our hard earned money and give it to a bunch of stock-jabbers and bankers. Give me a good leader like we had in the last war, like the great General Washington, and a few good men like the ones around me here, and point me to the enemy and you'll see what a group of freemen can do."

"Here, here!" shouted everyone around the room, including Sam. That got him scolded by his mother and put to bed in no uncertain terms.

"Speaking of that, Ben," said his brother-in-law Bill, after Sam had been sent to his room. "I hear Woolsey's forming up a company of Veteran Exempts to aid the war effort. He's been appointed General of the militia. He's got Judge Newcomb and John Stevenson working with him."

"Yes," said Sam's father, checking the door and making sure Sam was no longer listening on the stairs and his wife had gone to bed. "Peter told me when I was last in the village," he said, speaking of Peter Sailly the local revenue agent. "He said they called up Thomas Miller's regiment and the 7th NY militia. They got 'em all out at Champlain and Chateaugay. He asked me if I was going to join the Exempts."

"Well, are you?" asked Carl Philips.

"I don't know, Carl. I'll have to talk it over with Catherine. It's not like last time. We're not exempt for nothing you know. We've all done our duty. It is only with the gravest consideration and under the most dire conditions that I would take up arms again and go to war. I would advise you to give such notions, if you so contemplate them, careful consideration as well."

"Sounds like an excuse to me," said Carl.

"No one is questioning Benjamin's courage or patriotism," declared John Fisher, looking at Philips sternly. Carl instantly felt embarrassed and knew he had spoken unfairly. Ben Turner was the bravest and fiercest fighter among them.

"Anyway, it may not matter," said Sam's father. "Lieutenant Curtis down in the village was telling me the recruitments are picking up. Maybe the new inducements the Colonel was telling us about are having an effect. They might not need the Exempts, and that would be a good thing. After all, none of us is getting any younger" They all laughed and agreed.

The conversation continued long into the night, after a bottle of whiskey was opened, and more tobacco drawn. John Fisher had made his point and Carl Philips raised their fighting spirit, and the rest of the night was spent trying to outdo one another with funny stories, to see who could make who laugh the loudest. It was well after two am when the last of them, Ben's brother-in-law Bill, left, long after Samuel had fallen asleep and dreamt his dreams of glory and adventure.

* * * * *

Unlike with Sam, there was no fire on the stove, no candles burning in the window when Jesse got home. The house was dark. His father and mother both worked at the tavern. His mother cooked. His father Mike ran the bar. His brothers and sisters had been fed hours ago, and were either with relatives or at the tavern, playing on the floor in the back of the kitchen. Jesse decided to go there. It was a risky proposition, depending on what kind of mood his father was in and if he'd been drinking, but the chance of getting a warm meal from his mother outweighed the risk.

It was busy as usual by the time he arrived, many patrons still eating their evening meals. There were mostly men, but a few couples were seated at the tables as well. The bar was lined with regulars and a few out-of-towners, mostly drifters or salesmen. He avoided his father, who was tending bar with another man, and made his way directly to the kitchen where his mother was cooking. Mostly she made stew and meat pies, and sometimes soup and sausage like tonight. There wasn't much variety but the food was good and hearty, and warm.

"Where have you been, Jesse?" asked his mother, Augusta, who was the sister of Sam's Mother. "I've been worried sick about you."

"I went to the village with Sam. We saw a gunboat. It had the biggest gun I've ever seen."

"You didn't tell me you were going to the village. You can't just go wander off whenever you like without telling me."

"You wouldn't a let me go if I told you," complained Jesse.

"You know it's not my decision. You'd have to ask your pa. If he finds out you ran off without saying, you'll be in a thick of trouble. You'd better stay out of his way tonight. Maybe he'll forget about it in the morning if you're good."

"Gee Ma, you don't expect me to stay around here all day when there's a war with the redcoats."

"Never you mind about the redcoats. You got your pa to worry about, and if he sees you here after missing supper and me feeding you, your hide will be red."

"Ah, Ma."

"Here, have some of the sausage soup before it's all gone, and try to stay out of your father's way. I saved a nice piece of bread for you. Go over there by the table. I have some cold milk iced up for you under the cloth. Then you can play in the corner with your brother and sisters 'til I leave. You can escort us home. Your father has to stay and close up the tavern. At least that's what he says, but you and I know he wants to stay and drink and cuss and spit with his drunken buddies."

They both laughed as Jesse sat at the small table and ate his dinner greedily. Later that evening, after the kitchen had been closed up for the night, Jesse led his brothers and sisters as they walked behind their mother the short distance to their house down at the end of the hill. His mind was filled with the events and news of the day, and thoughts of war.

Chapter 3

Village of Plattsburgh, NY, August 1812

There were over 5000 troops in town now by Sam's reckoning, volunteers and regulars, with militiamen from two states thrown in, more than enough to handle any trouble. Sam wondered what they were all doing here in the village.

"Are there any Indians around here?" he asked his father, wondering if his mother's fears about the massacres out west happening here had any merit. They were sitting in the 'Ark', a tavern on River Street where his father was conducting business with a local merchant. The man had left, but Sam and his dad had stayed to soak up the atmosphere of the bustling establishment. Sam's dad wanted another draft of ale before hitting the road, and Sam was thirsty as well. Not quite old enough for alcoholic beverages, he had a ginger-water and vinegar sweetened with honey, a local concoction called a switzel.

"Not many," said his father. "The great Iroquois nations are mostly gone now, moved out west or to the reservation. They didn't fare too well after the Revolution. They backed the wrong horse."

"What do you mean?" asked Sam, taking a long swig of his switzel.

"They sided with the British in the last war and fought against the Colonies. The New Yorkers would have killed them all if they had their way, but Washington, General Washington that is, made the colonists see reason. There's only a few hundred living around here now, maybe a few more hundred along the border in Canada, living just like us in cabins, wearing the same clothes. They aren't going to cause any trouble."

"You mean they don't dress like Indians?"

"No, most of them dress just like you and me. As a matter of fact, see that gentleman over there, sitting with the Major?" He pointed discreetly to a well-dressed man sitting across the room at another table.

"Yes," said Sam, looking at the man casually.

"He's a full-blooded Caughnawaga Indian."

Sam looked closer at the man, staring almost rudely across the room. He wore a dark waist-coat and a white shirt with a high starched collar. He had well-formed features and was clean shaven with a high forehead and dark wavy hair cut medium length. "He looks like a preacher man," said Sam.

"He is a preacher man. His name is Eleazer Williams. He also works with the government. See him coming and going all the time, hobnobbing with the generals."

"What's he do?" asked Sam.

"I don't know. Works with the Indian scouts I guess, probably spying on the British."

"He's a spy?" exclaimed Sam loudly.

"Quiet. Not so loud. I didn't say that. I don't know what he does. And quit staring over there like a jackass. It's not polite to gape like that, especially not at an Indian. He's liable to take offense and do a war dance on your noggin. Even if he is a spy, you don't want to be blabbing it about. We're at war, remember? And he's on our side, so keep your mouth shut. You got that?"

"Yes, Sir," replied Sam. "So what do you think they're going to do with all these men? There must be over 5000 of them."

"8,259 to be exact," said Mister Turner, having seen the number on a recent bulletin. "I don't know, but there's more men than they need for defending the town and policing the border. They're up to something. I hear they got a new general coming up, just been appointed, General Bloomfield. He's on his way here now. He's in Whitehall, I believe. He'll be here by Friday."

"Maybe they're going to attack Montreal like Mister Fisher said," conjectured Sam.

Before his father could reply, there was a small commotion, as a tall, trim man with light-brown, short curly hair, entered the tavern. He wore the insignias of a colonel, and just about everyone in the place stood and shouted hello when he came in. There were three men with him, all officers. They made their way to the table where the Indian preacher and the Major were sitting, and after greeting them, sat down.

"Is that the General?" asked Sam, not having seen one that close before.

"No, that's only a Colonel, but probably the most famous man in the whole U.S. army. That's Colonel Zebulon Pike, the man who discovered those mountains way out west."

"Who?" asked Sam again, not recognizing the name.

"Didn't they teach you anything in school? Those mountains out west in Colorado territory, there's snow on top of them even in the dead of summer."

Colorado sounded vaguely familiar, so Sam pretended to recognize the name.

"Oh," he said. "If he's so famous, what's he doing here?"

"He's the commander of the 15th Regiment. They're camped out in the western part of town, by the river."

"Oh," said Sam again, suitably impressed, although he still didn't know who the man was or what it was he was supposed to have discovered. He made a mental note to take a hike out to see if he could find the camp and learn more about this Colonel Pike.

Western Mountains, District of Champlain, NY, August 1812

A few days after Sam's visit to town with his father, he and Jesse built their own version of the gunboat they had seen on their visit to Plattsburgh back in June, complete with a cannon. Using the stone foundation of an old chicken coup as an outline, Sam nailed a few boards expertly around it to form the sides, bow and stern of the ship. A large log served as the cannon. Jesse was the Captain, of course, and Sam the first-mate and crew. They even let some of Jesse's younger siblings join in and a couple of the girls who lived down the lane, much to Jesse's dismay. Sam, however, kind of liked Julie May, Carl Philip's daughter. He thought her father was about the funniest most interesting person in the hamlet, especially his cussing and spitting. Sam had never seen his father spit or cuss, though he didn't seem to mind his war buddies doing it.

They were all playing together, enacting an intense battle scene where Sam and the girls manned the cannon and Jesse steered the ship and barked out orders. In the mayhem that ensued while boarding the enemy vessel, Julie May fell and cut her knee badly on a shard of slate from the old chicken coup. It was a bad gash and bled profusely. Sam was the first at her side and immediately told her to lie still and not look at the wound. He knew she'd be sorry if she did, and didn't want her to get hysterical and start screaming, as girls were apt to do. Though he had never seen anyone tend an injured person before, he seemed to know exactly what to do. All of a sudden, Sam became the commander, barking out orders.

"Jesse, go get my brother Jack. He's in the next field." He was the closest grownup in the vicinity and had a horse and wagon, which Sam realized immediately would be needed. "Tell him to bring the wagon."

He looked around for the cleanest article.

"Becky, tear the end off your petticoat there, we need a bandage."

"But my ma will kill me," objected Becky.

"Tell her you had to do it to help Julie May. She'll understand. Now do it!" he shouted.

Becky hurried to obey, ripping a large strip from the bottom of her mostly clean white petticoat. Sam applied it gently but firmly to the wound, wrapping it while he pinched the cut together to stop the flow of blood, and quickly had it bound.

He kept her lying quietly, and talked soothingly to her about ships and battles at sea, and the men he admired most in the whole world, Hull and Porter and Rodgers and the others. His brother Jack came a short time later. They carried the unfortunate Julie May to the wagon and brought her home, where her mother tended the wound. Her father got the local doctor, who was able to sew up her leg with only six stitches. She recovered well enough and was soon back on her feet as if nothing had happened, though she carried a small scar on her right knee for the rest of her life, a reminder of Sam her hero.

Chapter 4

Western Mountains, District of Champlain, NY, October 1812

A lot had happened since the opening days of the war the previous June, most of it bad for the fledgling nation. In contrast, the lives of Sam and his cousin Jesse changed not at all. School had started and they were a quarter of a year older, but as far as they were concerned, time stood still in their little hamlet and life passed by, totally ignoring them. Jesse had not been back to the village since his last visit in June.

Madison had delivered his terms for ending the war in August. One of them, the Orders of Council, had already been repealed by the British government. Another, the ceasing of impressment, would never be agreed to. In the end, attempts at ending the war early came to naught. As a result, the British had taken all of Michigan territory in the early fighting and now controlled the entire northwestern part of the country. It would be the largest occupation of U.S. territory in the nation's history and the country's response was feeble at best.

All of this was known to Ben Turner and his friends, and to Sam and Jesse as well. The reports of the debacles out west fueled their anger toward the British. Talk of invading Canada was rampant. To Jesse and Sam however, it was the stories of the Indian massacres that riveted their attention and imagination the most. Stories of how Tecumseh and his warriors would come out of the forest painted and whooping to decimate well-armed soldiers in superior numbers with surprise and ferocity. Jesse wondered why the white men didn't fight like that. Their fathers said it was incompetent and cowardly generals, and bureaucrats in Washington who were responsible for the whole thing.

It was the tales of the war at sea and the "blue water fleet", however, that most captivated Sam's imagination. The exploits of the *USS Constitution* and *Essex* and their commanders, along with the rest of the squadron, gave the country its only taste of success in the early days of the fighting, against overwhelming odds. News of the *Constitution's* decisive victory over the British frigate *HMS*

Guerriere electrified the country and Sam. The fact that his father's friend, the Colonel, actually lived in Boston where the *Constitution* was birthed and could see it any time he wanted, impressed Sam beyond reckoning.

Colonel Fisher had come up from Boston again and brought great news, which he delivered when he came for dinner one night.

"The president has decided upon a plan of action exactly like we were talking about, Ben," announced the Colonel. "He's sent Captain Isaac Chauncey to build ships and obtain naval superiority on the lakes. His man, Lieutenant Elliot, arrived in Buffalo just last month."

"Yes, I've heard something about that," said Ben Turner. "But words are cheap. Where's the money coming from?"

"Congress has agreed to increase the naval budget. There's still a lot of custom revenue, most of it from trading licenses with the British. Much of New England is still selling grain to Wellington's army in Spain." He laughed.

"So much for patriotism," said Sam's father.

"Speaking of patriotism, they need shipwrights and carpenters out there in Buffalo. They've got the right idea, now they just need to carry it through. They need volunteers to do that. I hear you're still a good carpenter, Ben."

Sam's father was not only a farmer, ex-soldier and one time sheriff, he was also a carpenter by trade and had earned most of the money he used to buy the farm building homes and barns for other people. Both his own house and barn were built by Ben and his father, who was a carpenter before him. They had built many of the neighboring places as well. Sam had learned the trade, though he was still too young to go out on his own, or so thought his parents, even though he had finished the eighth grade last year. His father didn't have the means to send him into the village to further his education, and the little schoolhouse he and his cousin had been attending since the first grade only went to the eighth.

"I'm too old for that kind of work now," said Sam's father, "though I've worked on a boat or two in my time."

"I want to go," said Sam excitedly.

"You're too young," replied his mother in alarm.

"You promised your Uncle Bill you'd work for him this year, learn the trade proper," interjected his father, who wasn't much more than his son's age when he went to war.

"Helping them build ships to win the war is a lot more important than working on old barns and houses," reasoned Sam. "I'll be seventeen in a month. I want to help win the war. Tommy Johnson just joined the army."

"He's eighteen," said his mother, "A whole year and a half older than you."

"Well Sammy, that's nice of you to volunteer," interrupted the Colonel. "But what can you do?"

"I'm just as good a carpenter as my older brother Jack. I can learn what I don't know."

"I sure do like your boy's spirit, Ben," John Fisher confided to Sam's father. "We could use a few good lads like Sammy here."

"Maybe next year," said Ben, looking proudly at his son and using any ploy he could to forestall the inevitable. "He promised to help his uncle. A promise is a promise. Anyway, you don't know enough yet, and you've never built a ship. That's why you need a year working with Bill. He'll teach you everything you need to know. You go off half-cocked and you won't be a help to anyone, let alone those men out there building ships on Lake Erie."

"I wouldn't be too sure of that Ben," said John Fisher, looking at Sam's father with a grin. "You never know where life's path will take you. Sometimes you just got to do what your instincts tell you. Oh, by the way, I have some other news you might be interested in."

"I must say John you certainly are a fountain of information. You should come by more often. Keep us poor backward country folk up to date with what's happening in the world."

"Well, this news affects your neck of the woods directly. Lieutenant Thomas Macdonough is coming to take command on Lake Champlain. Madison is finally getting serious about this war of his."

"I've heard of him," yelled Sam loudly and earning a reproachful look from his father. "He's the hero from the war with the pirates. One of Preble's boys," he continued softly before his father silenced him with another stern look.

32

"That's right Sammy," replied John Fisher, trying to take some of the heat off the lad. "He's quite a distinguished and famous naval officer and he's going to be running things right here on your little lake. How do you like that?"

"I like it a lot!" yelled Sam, making everyone at the table laugh, except his father who looked at his son with disappointment. Sam's outburst only confirmed his conviction that Sam had a lot to learn before he would be ready to go out into the world.

Whitehall, NY, October 1812

Lieutenant Thomas Macdonough surveyed the thin strip of water that formed the South Bay at Whitehall, New York, a small hamlet nestled between the southern tip of Lake Champlain and Lake George. He had just arrived from Albany after a harrowing ride along roads that were no more then rutted paths, all the way from Portland Maine. He had recently requested re-instatement, and was honored to be picked personally by the President for the assignment. He was worried, however, about the challenges he faced and the fact that he had never commanded anything like the fleet of dilapidated sloops and gunboats he was inheriting. He wasn't too pleased with Whitehall either, located only thirty miles below Fort Ticonderoga. He had faith in the Lord, however, and the love of his bride-to-be to keep him going.

"It was not easy getting here," said Macdonough to his second in command, Lieutenant Sidney Smith, who had commanded the lake fleet before his arrival. Smith wasn't happy about being replaced, but he respected Macdonough's reputation even if the man hardly outranked him in seniority. Reputation was everything in the new navy however, and Macdonough had a very good one. "The roads up from Albany were atrocious. I thought I was out west or something."

"Yeah, except we don't have any Indians to speak of here. They've all been pacified and are on our side now. We've been getting a lot of information from them about British movements along the St. Lawrence."

"We don't have any Indians in Connecticut either, Mister Smith, but at least we have decent roads," said Macdonough, brushing himself off as if to emphasize the point.

"Oh, is that where you've been, Sir? I thought you might be out chasing English frigates like Porter and Hull."

Even though there might have been a little sarcasm in Smith's words, Macdonough took no offense, his good nature coming to the fore even in the most trying of times.

"Like you Mister Smith, I come and go as the navy commands. I have just recently been reinstated and ordered by the President to come here. And while I am here I am going to do my very best to carry out my orders."

"Yes, Sir, I meant no offense, Sir," said Smith. He may have envied Macdonough's command but not the task he faced in trying to defend the lake from the British with two under-manned sloops and two decrepit gunboats. They looked out at the lip of water, the steep sides of a rocky hill on their right. A cow pasture rose up a gentle slope on their left, studded with boulders and trees. The end of the lake shimmered in between.

"Not much of a place is it?" complained Macdonough, used to slightly larger bodies of water.

"Oh, the lake's big enough and hard enough to defend. It's the gateway to Canada."

"As are all the lakes," replied Macdonough. "They can be doors to our country as well as theirs. Look what's happened out west. That, I suppose, is why they sent me here."

"Yes Sir, having you around has given the men new spirit. Your reputation precedes you, Sir."

"The good Lord has seen fit to bless me. He has put me here for a purpose and I will follow His will even if it leads to Whitehall, New York." They both laughed. "So what do we have to work with?"

"Not much, Sir," said Smith. "Other than the two gunboats you see here, each with a 12-pounder, we have the 9-gun *Growler* and the 7-gun *Eagle*, both sloops of war. All of the ships are in need of repair, especially the gunboats. We just raised one of them a couple of months ago. The caulking in the walls is so bad you can stick your hand through in places."

"What about the crews?" asked Macdonough, knowing the unfortunate answer before his subordinate announced it.

"Not good, Sir. We're undermanned in all quarters. General Bloomfield has ordered the new sloop *Hunter* to be manned by his own troops, the 11th infantry, and commandeered it for the army's use, if you can believe it, Sir."

Macdonough momentarily lost his usual composure.

"Not only has he seen fit to man my ships with incompetent land-lubbers who know nothing about sailing, now he's commandeered the biggest ship on the lake for the army. How ridiculous. What's he going to do, tow it over the road to Canada with oxen?"

His second in command, Smith, laughed at the witticism. "That's not the worst part, Sir. They refuse to consult us in the upcoming invasion plans."

Macdonough stopped laughing. "That's ludicrous. How do they expect to invade Canada without the navy, without command of the lake?"

"I warned you about him. He'll expect us to toe the line and come to his rescue."

"What, over the frozen lake? We will be iced in by the time they invade."

"Maybe so, Sir, but don't expect any cooperation from the army. Sometimes it's as if they're on the other side. They say General Dearborn is coming to command the invasion forces. You'd think the President himself was coming with all the commotion."

"Has he ever commanded in battle before?" asked Macdonough.

"I don't know," said Smith. "But they have a force of at least 3000 regulars and 4000 militia in Plattsburgh. They're camped all along the Saranac and are moving in supplies. The scouts say the English are building up their own forces at St John's and Isle aux Noix. They're building ships there as well."

"How are the building efforts here going?" asked the new commander. "Do we have enough workers?"

"We've got some new volunteers from up north who have just come in. We're hoping with the new men we'll make good progress, Sir."

"That's good news," said Macdonough, relieved at the information. "That means we can take the fleet up to Vergennes and arm them as soon as spring comes and the ice melts. Well, Mister Smith, we have a lot to do and not much time. We should get moving. I want to inspect the ships first thing in the morning."

"Yes, Sir, but I was hoping to invite you to dinner at one of the local grandee's houses. He's a ship builder."

"Ah, Mister Smith, I believe you and I are going to get along just fine. A ship builder you say?"

"Yes, Sir, he's very anxious to meet you and I thought you'd have a lot to talk about."

"Then lead on, Mister Smith. Let us meet this ship builder, shall we. I could do with a good meal."

They both laughed and left to get ready for the evening.

Chapter 5

Western Mountains, District of Champlain, NY, November 1812

Jesse followed the tracks in the newly fallen snow. It was the first snowfall of what promised to be a long winter and it was just what Jesse had been waiting for. So he had skipped school and borrowed his father's hunting rifle.

Even though it was only a few inches deep, the snow made it easy to follow the tracks of his prey, which appeared to be a good sized buck. Jesse had his gun primed and set to fire. He was quiet as a cat as he moved through the woods. He heard the rustling of something in the trees off to his left and crouched, listening with his musket ready

He waited a moment, and when he heard the sound again, moved off cautiously in that direction. He was a patient shooter and always made sure he could clearly see what he was shooting at. He didn't want to be responsible for shooting some farm boy by accident. So he waited until he saw the source of the rustling noise. When he saw what it was, he smiled and put his gun down.

"What's she doing out here?" he wondered out loud, as he gazed upon a good-sized beef cow. It probably belonged to one of the farmers who bordered the woods and had gotten out of its pen. He was about to turn around and head deeper into the woods when he had a thought.

His father had told him recently how there were thousands of soldiers in the village, but a shortage of food. Perhaps he could help the situation and even make some money for the family. After all, no one would miss one measly cow, especially if they weren't aware it had gotten out.

He looked around furtively, raised his gun, took aim and squeezed the trigger. The lead ball exploded from the barrel of his musket hitting the animal, which was facing him, right between the eyes. Its front legs collapsed like broken twigs and it fell immediately to the ground without making a sound.

Jesse spent the rest of the morning building a travois and butchering the cow, which he packed on top of the travois and dragged out of the woods. He then borrowed his father's horse and wagon and rode into the village to sell the beef to the soldiers, who were sure to pay top dollar. He would be a hero.

However, things didn't quite turn out as Jesse had envisioned. When he was asked where he got the meat, a question he for some reason hadn't anticipated, he was suddenly tongue-tied. He tried to evade the question but it persisted like a pesky fly and he was soon found out and arrested.

A quick search of the area surrounding the woods soon uncovered the offended party, an old farmer who hadn't even known the cow was missing. He had left the gate open once again, which he often did, much to the chagrin of his neighbors who were always finding his cows in their corn fields.

Jesse's father had to go into town and take custody of the wayward youth, after paying a fine and making arrangements with the forgetful farmer for the restitution of his butchered cow. Jesse and his father rode home in silence, with Mike's horse tied behind the buckboard. He had a good mind to backhand his son and knock him off the wagon, but the memory of what had happened the last time he struck the boy prevented him from doing so. Instead of having the effect like the words of the bible said it would, of tempering his son and teaching him discipline, it made him sullen and even more unruly. Mike didn't like the way his boy was now afraid of him. He was determined to make up for his burst of anger, so he held his hand and his tongue, but he was sorely tempted. He wondered what he was going to do with his son, his oldest and his pride and joy. If only he didn't have such a wild streak.

When they got home, Mike calmly told him how much his antics had cost his family and how he was going to pay it back.

"I've made a deal with Mister Barnwell, the farmer. He said you could pay off the cost of the cow by helping him out at his farm, keep an eye on his cows for him, do some hunting for him. He loves turkey but can't see good enough to shoot them anymore. You are never to touch my gun again. If anything happens to that gun I won't be able to hunt. Then where would we be? I don't know what I'm going to do with you, boy. I want you to grow up and be a man. You won't be any good to anyone, including yourself, the way you're going. You better straighten up. When you're done with school and homework, you will work for Mister Barnwell to pay off your debt. You will work every day until six in the evening, including weekends. Then you will come directly home for supper, do chores and go right to bed."

"I was doing it for you Pa, I was trying to help the soldiers and make money for you," pleaded Jesse, stating his case.

"You were wrong to shoot that cow, Jesse. How do you think it makes me look, having a cow thief for a son? You have to be taught right from wrong. For doing right you get rewarded. For doing wrong, for whatever reason, you got to get punished. You're going to school tomorrow and the next day and the day after that, until you finish the eighth grade. Do you understand? I hope so, for your sake, because next time I won't be so understanding."

Jesse was mortified and crushed by the whole affair. How could something done with such good intentions end up so wrong? He would have preferred a beating to a future of the drudgery of school and tending Mister Barnwell's cows. The man was half-deaf and half-blind and needed a full time nursemaid. He had more cows then he knew what to do with and probably never would have known the thing was missing if they hadn't gone and told him.

The next day in school he didn't hear a word the teacher said and got scolded for daydreaming, though he was only thinking of the trouble he was in. After school the boys in the school house crowded around him eager to hear his story, but he had to tell them he couldn't talk for he had to go take care of Mister Barnwell's cows.

It only took a few days of this drudgery for Jesse to make up his mind and attempt his escape. Running away to the village, he attempted to join the army. He might have succeeded despite his young age had the lieutenant in charge of recruitment not recognized the young would-be soldier his sergeant had just signed up and informed the boy's father. Mike Lebow showed up a few hours later in a buggy to pick him up.

"Come back in a couple of years," the lieutenant yelled to the boy as he reluctantly got on the wagon.

"It'll be a lot longer than that," replied his father. He was beyond angry at this point and had all but given up on his son, but he kept his temper in front of the lieutenant. "The boy's only fourteen. He won't be old enough to join the army for another three or four more years yet. He's still got to finish school. He's in the eighth grade."

"Well, now," said the lieutenant. "You must have put on a good show for my sergeant to sign you up. We take them young but not that young, though I must say, your boy is maturing fast."

"Well, he's got a long way to go before he's a man, and if he pulls any more stunts like this he may not make it." Mike Lebow glowered at his son.

"Don't be too hard on him, Mike. His heart is in the right place. As a matter of fact, I've been thinking. I hear they still got a couple of openings in the first class at the Academy here in town. Perhaps he could go there. They have a very good program. They even have military drills and parades to get the boys ready for the army if they should so chose. It might be just the place for him."

"Naw, I can't afford to send him to school in the village, and it's too far to walk every day. He's got chores to do for his ma. It just wouldn't work."

"I know a family here in town that could put him up. All you'd have to do his pay a small fee for his upkeep and room, about what it would cost you to have him stay home."

Despite Mike Lebow's bad temper and rough demeanor, he, like every other good father, wanted his son to succeed in life, and to him that meant a tough kind of love like his father had shown him. Most of all he wanted his son to have a good education because he was convinced that was how a man got ahead in the world. He had served in the war like Sam's father and was as brave as any man, but he hadn't advanced like some others who had little of his strength and skill. What they did have was an education. They could read and write. Mike Lebow could barely write his name, and had almost killed the well-meaning school-man who tried to teach him. Still, it was one of the things he was most proud of. He practiced it every day when no one was looking, or when he was alone in the tavern in the mornings. Even with practice though, it was something he found difficult and demanding. When asked to sign his name, he'd take the pen with a flourish and then, with his eyes focused and his face grimacing in concentration, he'd sweat out his name letter by letter, sounding them out as he laboriously wrote them, smiling proudly when he finished.

The fact that his son would soon graduate from the 8th grade was also a source of pride. That is if he ever finished. Jesse was the only one in the family to even go to school let alone attain that academic level. That was one of the reasons Mike was so upset at Jesse for running away and trying to join the Army.

He knew he was going to have trouble with the boy for the next couple of years, with the war on and Jesse intent on taking part in it. Maybe the Lieutenant was right. In Plattsburgh he would be in the middle of things with little incentive to run away. There was no place more exciting and event-filled as far as his son was concerned than the village, especially now with all the soldiers parading about. Perhaps the drilling and uniforms at the academy would satisfy his son's military urges for the time being. On further consideration he realized it was an offer that would be difficult to refuse.

"I don't know, Mister Curtis, I'll have to think about it," said Jesse's father. "In the meantime, Jesse here's got a lot of explaining to do to his mother."

He eyed the tall officer, the head of recruiting for the area, with a questioning look. He had done some hunting with him the previous year, bagging a nice black bear together up on Lyon Mountain. The Lieutenant had gotten him a couple more hunting expeditions since then, but he wondered why the sudden interest in his boy.

"Why you so interested in my boy, Lieutenant?" he asked suddenly. "I don't mean to be rude, but you know me. I'm pretty plain speaking. Why do you want to help the boy like this?"

"I like his spirit, Mike," said David Curtis. "He showed a lot of initiative coming here and getting himself signed up. He's a bright boy and we need all of them we can get. With a little education, no telling where a young man like your Jesse here might end up, and if he wants to join the army, well so much the better. Might as well get a good start. Anyway, I know you'll pass the word around down at the tavern that there are a lot worse things for a man to do than join the army."

"Ah," laughed Mike Lebow good naturedly. "I knew there was a catch, but I'll oblige you and tell everyone I see to come to the village and talk to Lieutenant David Curtis. He'll set them straight."

Curtis laughed in turn. "Good day to you then, Mister Lebow, and to you Jesse. I hope to see you back here in a few days to continue your education. Don't think it will be easy. Plattsburgh Academy has a very strict regimen. It will be just like the army, except you'll be learning something. By the time you leave there, if you make it all the way to the 12th grade, you might even become an officer. We look there for good men, men who will become leaders."

"Hear that, boy?" said Jesse's father, starting to like the idea. "The Lieutenant here is offering you a chance to go to school and become an officer. What do you say to that?"

Jesse wasn't sure, but he didn't have to think long before he made up his mind. It wasn't the army, and he wouldn't be fighting redcoats, but it was a chance to get out of that dismal old schoolhouse he'd been going to since he could walk, and away from his tedious chores and overbearing father. Best of all, he'd be in the village where everything was happening.

"All right," said Jesse, not sounding overly enthused. He knew he'd get a good whipping when he got home, but it would be worth it to be in the village. Who knows, an opportunity might yet present itself to fight redcoats.

Chapter 6

Western Mountains, District of Champlain, NY, November 1812

It wasn't winter yet and it had already snowed. Now it was raining, a cold, hard late autumn downpour. General Dearborn in Albany had started building up his forces in the Lake Champlain arena, marching over 2500 regulars to Plattsburgh to train and help prevent smuggling and fraternization along the border. The real reason for the build up, however, was a possible invasion of Canada and the taking of Montreal.

Even more important to Sam's world, his cousin Jesse was going to school in the village, at some sort of academy. Sam had vague notions of a military type establishment where the kids wore uniforms and marched but he wasn't sure if that was what it was really like. He hadn't talked to his cousin since he left a few days earlier with hardly a word, except to say that he had tried to join the army and this was his punishment. They were going to make him go to school until he would be too old to join the army. He looked sad, but Sam envied him all the same. Jesse would be in the middle of things and only minutes away from the gunboats and soldiers.

"Did you hear about Jesse," he said that evening at dinner. "He tried to join the army and now they're making him go to school in the village, and they're not going to let him out. He has to go right on to the 9th and 10th grades, right up to the 12th."

"Jesse has been offered a wonderful opportunity," said his father. "I hope he makes the best of it and doesn't squander this chance. I was thinking we might do the same thing with you. Mike sold one of his horses to help pay Jesse's expenses. He said the Lieutenant mentioned a couple of openings. How would you like to go on to the upper grades, perhaps become a doctor like Mister Fisher?"

"No way," said Sam vehemently. He still thought Jesse was being punished. "I don't want to go to school anymore. I'm sick of school. I want to help fight the war and defend my country."

"I don't want any more talk about the war at my table," said his mother, upset at the fact that her sister's boy had run away and tried to join the army. "It's bad enough Augusta married that Frenchman, now his boy is turning out just like his father. Imagine, shooting one of Mister Barnwell's cows and running off to try and join the army."

"That's no affair of ours," said Sam's father. "That's between Jesse and his parents."

"I want to join. I'll be old enough next year," said Sam, who had recently turned seventeen.

"What, you want to sleep in a tent?" said his father sarcastically. "Winter's coming. But by all means, be my guest. Before you do let me tell you something. There's nothing worth more in life than a good education. Your mother and I didn't think sending you to school in the village, to the academy, was possible, but your cousin's good fortune has shown us it just might be after all. Think about it before you run off to join the army. Don't throw your life away."

"I don't want to join the army," said his son. "I want to help them build ships to win the war, like Colonel Fisher said. They're the key to winning the war, he said so. Anyway, Uncle Bill can't teach me how to build ships."

"And how do you propose to learn?" asked his father. "You'll only be in the way."

"I'll learn, I'll do whatever I have too. I can do simple carpentry. You taught me that. I'll learn as I go, like you told me you did, little by little. You didn't know anything about farming when you started."

"Your Uncle and my buddies helped me," countered his father, finding his son's arguments hard to argue against.

"I'll get someone to help me like you did."

Ben Turner was silent, considering his son's words.

"I want to go to Buffalo and help them build ships on Lake Erie," said Sam.

"Buffalo? Your hero is right here on Lake Champlain. You don't have to go all the way out to Buffalo to build ships for the navy. Mister Fisher told us he was coming."

"You mean Macdonough!" said Sam suddenly remembering the Colonel mentioning one of "Preble's Boys" was coming to take command of the fleet on the lake.

"Yes," laughed his father, finding his son's sudden reaction humorous. "He's in Whitehall. That's where the fleet is being wintered."

Sam could hardly believe it. One of the most famous and renowned of the navy's commanders was only a hundred miles away. Now his dream became all the more real and his desire more burning. He would do anything to serve with the great Lieutenant Thomas Macdonough, a person he had heard about and read about since he was a child. It was an opportunity of a lifetime.

"Then I want to go there to help them build ships like Mister Fisher said. Macdonough needs to win command of the lake."

"Then what?" asked his father. "What will you do when all the boats are built? They can't go on building them forever, you know. Remember what Mister Fisher said about paying for the ships."

Sam hesitated, not sure how to answer. "I don't know," he replied finally. "Then I want to be on the ships when they fight the British. I want to join the Navy."

"What? You must be out of your mind!" his father shouted, much louder than he intended.

"Benjamin, please don't shout at the table," pleaded his wife, Catherine. "You and Sam can discuss this after dinner."

"There will be no discussion," said his father, ending the conversation then and there. He knew there was nothing he could do if his son decided to go. Still, he tried to reason with him. "It's winter time, Sam. Wait until the spring. Nothing's going to happen until then. The lake will be frozen up before you even get to Whitehall. What's the darned hurry?"

"I'm afraid I'll miss the whole thing."

"You won't miss anything," said his dad. "Everyone thought the last one would end quickly and they'd miss all the fighting." He laughed. "You should have seen 'em after the fighting went on for eight years. There's no hurry I tell you."

"You went off to war when you were my age."

"War came to me. I didn't have a choice. You do. Besides, I didn't have an opportunity like you do. I wasn't as lucky as you could be. I never got a chance to go back to school after the war and finish my education. I had to raise my family. Let me see about getting you into Plattsburgh Academy like Jesse."

"I'm too old for school now," said Sam in dismay. "Maybe if I was younger like Jesse, but I'm almost old enough to join and you can't stop me. You said I need to learn a trade, what's wrong with the navy?"

"Why do you always insist on doing things the hard way?" he asked his son, though he already knew the answer. It was the same reason he hadn't listened to his father's advice when he was young and thought he knew it all. Everyone has to learn the lessons of life on their own.

"You don't know everything," objected Sam, getting up from the table without asking permission.

"Excuse yourself, young man," demanded his father indignantly.

"Oh, let him be Benjamin," said his wife. "He's just confused. This war's got everybody crazy. The Carlyles are leaving. They say it's not safe. The English are stirring up the Indians along the border."

"That's nonsense," replied her husband, aware of most of the activities in the area. "There's a detachment of light infantry working with the Indians to cause some commotion, but that's mostly at the western end of the state. They've got over 2500 regulars and over 1000 state militia in the village and vicinity. Some say they're invading Canada, and I wouldn't be surprised. No, I don't think we've got anything to worry about. I'd say it was the other way around."

"Then why won't you let me go and help?" pleaded Sam, who had sat back down after his father's admonishment.

"Working on the ships is one thing," conceded his father. "You're right when you say it's the single most important thing that we can do right now to defend our country against invasion. Anyway, it makes more sense than joining the navy. We can talk

46

about that later, though I don't know why you'd want to sleep in a tent in Whitehall this winter when you can be comfortable here at home until spring."

"Where's Whitehall?" asked Sam, only having heard the name a few times.

"Down at the other end of the lake. That's where I hear they're working on the fleet."

"Do you know where it is?" asked Sam, tentatively.

"Sure I do," said his father. "I fought down in Saratoga, if you remember. It's not far from there."

"Your father's been to Philadelphia," interjected his mother, "when it was the capital."

"I know Ma, I've heard the stories a hundred times."

"And now you want your own stories, is that it?" said his father.

Sam didn't know how to answer and sat mute until excused from the table. The next day Benjamin confronted his son as he left to work with his Uncle, not sure he would see him in the evening.

"If you're really that intent on going…" he said.

"I am," interrupted his son.

"Then I guess I can help you. You're right in some ways. You could learn a lot, and it would help the country immensely. But your timing is wrong. If you'd just wait a little…"

"I'm going, and there's nothing you can do about it."

"I'm not trying to stop you. I said I'll help you. I'll take you down to Whitehall and see you settled. You can work on the ships. Boat building's a good skill to know, and you have all the basic knowledge. It will be good for you. But promise me you won't join the navy until we've talked again."

"That depends on what's happening with the war. What if they need me?"

"Ok, we can talk about that when the time comes, when you turn eighteen. For now, I'll help you get to Whitehall. We'll take the wagon. We can leave tomorrow before the bad weather sets in."

"Thanks Dad. You're the greatest. I'll never forget this."

"I hope I don't live to regret it," said his father, not sure what had just happened.

The next morning, after a day spent packing and getting ready, and a night of half-sleep as Sam contemplated his new life, he and his father took the wagon the twenty miles east to the village of Plattsburgh. From there they drove down the lakeside road south, over the spectacular chasm at Ausable and through the tiny hamlet at Keeseville. They stopped for the night in a place called Elizabethtown, where they stayed in a stable with the horses and wagon. The next day they drove through cow country and wooded wilderness. It was some of the wildest country Sam had ever seen, as they wove their way south between the steep sides of the Adirondack Mountains and the Lake Champlain.

The second night they stopped at a little lakeside hamlet called Port Henry, where they stayed in an inn, both sleeping together on a single bed. As they lay in the dark waiting for sleep, his father told him old Fort Ticonderoga was near by, but they wouldn't be able to see it. Even though his father had been there and knew the way, they bypassed it the next day so they could reach Whitehall early enough to get Sam situated.

It was a good thing they did leave early, because the road from Port Henry to Whitehall was atrocious, no more than a furrowed, rock-strewn, narrow pathway. It snaked through the forbidding mountains and forest in a tortuous route, with cut-backs and fallen trees that made passage all but impossible except for Sam's strong back and his father's skill with a team and wagon.

They got to the vicinity of Whitehall around noon, after leaving Port Henry at six that morning. They walked down a wide dirt lane through country crowded with trees of all types clothed in what was left of the late autumn leaves. Small farms were scattered on the rocky hillsides. As they approached the hamlet they could hear hammering and the sounds of men working. Following the sounds, they drove down the road toward a steep, wooded mountainside with a stone cliff at its base.

They passed the main street of the village, which ran to the right. There were saloons and shops along both sides of the dirt street, with a few horses and wagons tied up at hitching posts.

They followed the road to the left, as it ran along the mountainside's stony base, until they could see men working in a large field. A short distance beyond that was the narrow end of the lake. There were flat bottomed boats pulled up on the shore, half-complete, and a schooner anchored in the bay. It stirred Sam's heart to know they belonged to Macdonough's fleet and that he would soon be part of it.

"What do you want?" said a sentry, standing on the road, before the gate. He was dressed in a dirty uniform, and carried a musket, and he didn't seem at all friendly.

"My boy here's wants to volunteer," said Sam's father.

"Is that so?" said the sentry, unimpressed and in no mood for civilians.

"Yes, that is so," said his father. "I wouldn't have stated it if it wasn't so."

"Well, our volunteers usually come in groups, and I'm usually informed they're coming. No one's informed me about you."

"That may be Sergeant…"

"Corporal, Corporal Sargent, Sir,"

"What?" said Sam's father.

"Corporal Henry Sargent. My last name's Sargent, Sir." He spelled his name.

"Oh, well that could be confusing," replied Benjamin smiling politely.

Unfortunately, Sam, who loved a joke, just caught the pun about Mister Sargent's last name. "Corporal Sargent!" he said, bursting out laughing.

"Sam!" said his father embarrassed.

"Oh, that's all right, Sir," replied the sentry, looking at Sam and smiling. "He's not the first one to laugh at the irony of it, and he won't be the last. I just wonder what will happen when I make sergeant."

"Well, I hope that happens soon, Corporal," answered Sam's father. "In the meantime, is there a place we can stay for the night? My boy's a fine carpenter and learns quickly. He's a hard worker and figures to help his country in the war effort."

"Well, if that's the case," said the corporal, "follow me. I'll get him signed up with Sergeant Ames. And remember, greenhorn," he looked at Sam. "You're in the real army now, so next time you laugh you may get your teeth knocked down your throat."

"Got that?" said his father, looking sternly at his son.

"Yes, Sir," replied Sam, sorry he had laughed like that in front of the corporal. He resolved not to let it happen again. Too bad his resolve wasn't stronger than his sense of humor.

"Thank you, Corporal," said Sam's father. "But I think you misunderstood. We're not here to sign up for the army. My son has come to volunteer to help build ships."

"I understood perfectly, Sir," replied the corporal. "But the only volunteers signing up here are with the army, unless you to want to talk to Lieutenant Smith and join the Navy."

"Is Commander Macdonough here?" asked Sam, despite his father's stern glare.

"No, the Commander has gone north. I doubt he will be back here until spring. They say he's getting married. No, if you want to volunteer to work on the boat crews building the ships, you'll have to talk to Mister John Nichols. He lives in the big house on the hill. You can't miss it. Maybe he'll give the boy here a job or let him apprentice."

"Yes, thank you Corporal," replied Sam's father, turning and leading his son away. "John Nichols is just the man we came to see."

Village of Plattsburgh, NY, November 1812

Things weren't going well with the 6th Infantry. The army was overmanned and undertrained, not to mention under-supplied and ill-equipped. No adequate barracks or quarters had yet been constructed, thus the men slept in tents on the cold hard ground. Many of them were sick and it wasn't even technically winter yet.

Part of their job was manning small patrols around the countryside interdicting smugglers, not so much criminals as poor, hard-scrapped farmers who had been trading across the border for decades. They didn't see any reason to stop now just because their countries happened to be at war with each other. Unbeknownst to all of them, however, things were about to become much more interesting.

Ordered to assemble at the debarkation point in Champlain a few miles north of the village with six days rations and what he could carry on his backs, Corporal Nate Peters was told they were going to invade Canada and not stop until they reached Montreal. He had joined the army back in 1811, almost a year before the war, after hearing of the Indian attack at Tippecanoe. He had languished in the small outpost here at Plattsburgh since that time, but the war had changed all that. Being one of the more experienced men at the fort, he had quickly earned his corporal's stripes. Now he was finally getting a chance to fight. If all went well, he thought, he'd have his sergeant's stripes in no time.

At the staging ground, in a huge range of broad, flat fields interspersed with stone fences and lines of trees, was the largest number of troops so far gathered by the US. Thousands of them were scattered as far as the eye could see, 8,000 by all counts, regulars and militia from two states, infantry and cavalry, even massed artillery, all mixed together.

The American forces were confident, informed by spies that the Canadians, mostly French speaking citizenry along the border, had been forced into service and would not put up much resistance. There were only a few thousand British regulars reported on the other side, and the Indian forces were offset by their own native rangers, both groups of which had been killing each other long before the white man came.

Then for some reason, after less than an hour of marching, everything came to a halt. They stood in formation for another hour, each man wondering what the delay was, before they were told to stand down and bivouac for lunch.

As they waited by their camp fires, boiling water for coffee and eating hard biscuits and whatever else they had, rumors started to circulate that the reason for the halt was that the militiamen from New York and Vermont had refused to cross the border into Canada. It was against the law of their states for them to do so, and both state governors had refused to sanction any such relaxing of the statutes.

"Where'd they think they were going?" asked Nate to no one in particular, when he heard the scuttlebutt. "Everyone knew we were invading Canada. Why did they come along in the first place if they weren't going to cross the border?"

No one had a good answer. To add credence to the rumor, a short time later, while they were being ordered back into formation to continue their march northward, they met long lines of militiamen in their gay and colorful uniforms marching in the opposite direction, their officers riding in the lead as proud and arrogant as ever. It boiled Nate's blood. However, all that mattered to him was that he was marching north again, toward the enemy and glory.

The thought that more than half their army was retreating back to Plattsburgh and their force of 7000 was now not more then half that number, never entered Nate's mind. If it did, it didn't matter. After all, the ones deserting were green militia. What could they do? He was getting a chance to invade Canada and fight the English, teach them a lesson, earn some respect. What could be better? He was going to be part of history, like his father and his father's father before him.

With the approach of darkness, which came early this time of year, they camped for the evening. Some of the men were without so much as a jacket or thin blanket to protect them from the cold snowy night, which descended like a breath of Arctic air as soon as the sun went down. All fires were forbidden because of the proximity to the enemy.

The next few days were disheartening and humiliating, leaving a sour taste in Nate's mouth. Everything was in confusion. Everyone seemed to be in charge, but no one knew what to do. The army floundered like a half-dead fish washed up on the shore. First they marched forward to attack. Then they retreated to regroup. The few times they actually encountered the enemy and met the least resistance, they retreated like a wary fox without really testing the opponent's strength. "Fall back" seemed to be the order of the day, even as they approached the gates of Montreal.

Every half-hearted attempt to attack the enemy's defenses ended in the same humiliating withdrawal, with hardly a shot being fired. It seemed their generals were more intent on bringing everyone back alive than in winning a battle, and that suited many of the men just fine. The only deaths occurred by friendly fire when an American party fired on a company of Colonel Zebulon Pike's men near LaColle in Quebec. After several more days of fruitless attacks, all driven back without the least effort, the defeated army, cold, damp and short of rations, pulled their forces back to Plattsburgh where they would stay for the winter.

Nate was in such a sour mood on the way home that he hardly noticed the cold and discomfort, arriving back at the cantonment late at night on the last day of the month. To his irritation there were still contingents of militia strutting about town in their clean new uniforms, while those of the regulars, Nate's included, were filthy and torn from days of sleeping outdoors in the rough and marching through brambles and thickets. They had hardly had a chance to fire their guns, and then only at vague targets in the distance, so far away the flash of their muskets could be seen before the sound was heard. The men never really saw what they were shooting at, but aimed at the puffs of smoke.

It was shortly after this, in the first week in December, when the final tallies came in that declared Madison the official winner in the recent presidential elections. He was still president, which meant another year or two at least of war, time enough for the U.S. Army and Nate Peters to redeem themselves.

Chapter 7

Village of Plattsburgh, NY, December 1812

Jesse's father wasn't sure he had made the right decision concerning his son. True, there was one less mouth to feed, and the boy was getting an opportunity for an education he otherwise might have never had, but it left his mother without an extra hand to do the chores. Worse, he was afraid his son would run away anyway and squander his big opportunity. He had sold the horse he would have given the boy on his sixteenth birthday. Part of the money went to pay off old man Barnwell. The rest went for tuition and room and board for the next year. It was a modest sum compared to what most paid, but a large amount for Jesse's father. As far as Mike Lebow was concerned, his son was on his own now. That was the end of it. If he messed up he better not try coming back home.

Jesse was making the best of his situation, even though he wasn't exactly happy to be going to school, but Plattsburgh had its advantages. He was finally out from under his father's thumb and making a reputation among the kids in his class as someone the older boys couldn't bully, though a few had tried. Jesse had sent them home crying. Because of this and his abilities in the various athletic games they played - racing and wrestling, shooting and riding, ball games the Indians taught them – he had become something of a leader in his eighth grade class. At the academy, each grade was taught by itself, although outside the classroom it was a free for all with every boy for himself. That's where Jesse excelled.

The Lieutenant hadn't lied, for besides a good academic program with geography, history, English and math, there were military exercises and parades. Of course, Jesse and his friends often went shooting after school and during the weekends. Just about every boy in every hamlet in every state of the new country had and shot a gun. Some, like Jesse and his cousin Sam, were shooting before they could even walk, but even among these fellows' standards, Jesse was an exceptional shot.

Most of the boys at the Academy were from the village of Plattsburgh itself, with a few from the outlying districts, who mostly kept to themselves. Jesse however, because of his skill with his fists and a gun, soon became one of the most popular kids in school, unusual for a lower classman and one so young.

The Gordons, with whom Jesse lived, were nice enough. About the same age as his parents, their own child had died a few years before. They were happy to have a young person around again, although Jesse was a little uncouth for their tastes. They did their best to curb his worst habits – like spitting on the floor - and made him feel at home, though they had some peculiar ideas about things. They were almost like Quakers as far as Jesse could tell. Other than that and a rather plain tasting diet, the Gordons weren't so bad. After school until supper time, Jesse was on his own, usually traipsing through the woods and countryside with his trusty gun and a few good friends.

One of his closest friends at school was a young classmate named Daniel Dobbs, a precocious 12-year old who was one of the best drummers Jesse had ever heard. His clean, strong drumbeats stirred Jesse's heart, which was also moved by Daniel's incredible good looks. His blond hair and bright blue eyes attracted admiring stares everywhere he went. Jesse was instantly attracted to the youth and protected him from the older boys in the class.

On that early Sunday November day when the army had marched north to attack Canada, the school had been alive with excitement. The boys, too preoccupied to attend to their lectures, were dismissed early. Most of them went down to the newspaper office at the Plattsburgh Republican, where a crowd was forming about the entrance, eager for information.

The whole town was in an uproar. False rumors and sensational accounts were rampant. Some said the Canadians along the border had rallied to the American side and Montreal had surrendered. Others, that Indians from out west had been shipped in by the British and had surprised and massacred the army, and were now on their way to the village. Few believed the more outlandish stories, but people were on edge nevertheless. No one knew what to think, not even Thomas Macdonough the commander of the fleet himself, who was now in Middleton, Connecticut getting married.

Then when the militia started returning alone without the regulars, the rumors grew even wilder. Unfortunately, none of the returning militia units were local. Thomas Miller's Clinton County Boys had remained with the main army, being one of the few not to turn back at the border, so firsthand knowledge was difficult to come by. Everyone waited for news from the front, which, when it came, spoke of casualties and friendly fire, lack of supplies and low morale.

Militiamen crowded the village streets and thoroughfares, making a nuisance of themselves, causing trouble and acting like they owned the place. It got so bad that a young woman couldn't walk down the street without being whistled at or insulted.

One day, shortly before the army's return, Jesse and his friend Daniel were crossing the new bridge over the Saranac on their way to school after meeting at Danny's house in the better part of town. A group of militiamen in their gaudy, red-scarlet uniforms barred their way, laughing.

"This here's a toll bridge," said the biggest and meanest looking of the group, a corporal with a rifle slung over his shoulder, a long, steel bayonet making it look even larger. "It's going to cost you a quarter to cross."

The other men laughed. Some had bottles, which they drank from every now and then.

"This isn't a toll bridge," said Daniel. "We cross here all the time."

"Just ignore them Danny," said Jesse. "They just think they're big shots 'cause they got uniforms.

He started walking around the man, who stepped in his way.

"Hey, you!" shouted the militiaman in his best parade ground voice. "Don't give me any of your crap, boy." He stood in front of Jesse looking down at him with his arms folded and his feet apart. "You can pay or you can swim. Take your pick."

"Then we'll swim across. Come on, Danny," said Jesse. "There are other bridges." They started walking back.

"Hey!" yelled one of the men, leaning on a post next to the bridge. "Little Danny here look's like a girl with his long golden locks. Are you a boy or a girl?"

The men laughed some more. The corporal followed Jesse and his friend as they moved away, taunting them.

"Hey, boy! Answer the man. Is your friend a boy or a girl?"

Jesse turned on him with his hands at his sides balled into fists. He was riled now.

"First you tell me if you are really soldiers or a bunch of sissies, all dressed up in red. You're the ones that look like girls. You look like a bunch of redcoats. You better be careful or some real soldiers might think you're redcoats and shoot you."

"Watch your mouth, you little scamp," said the corporal turning red and taking a step toward Jesse, his arms extended as if to grab him. He stood close to Jesse glaring down threateningly at him. Jesse stood his ground and seemed to grow an inch taller as he thrust his head at the man. He was only getting started.

"Why are you fellows back here causing trouble, anyway?" he said. "Why ain't you out fighting with the army? Why'd you all come running back to Plattsburgh while the real army's out fighting the redcoats? What's wrong with you, are you afraid? Is that why you all came running back?"

Jesse had spilled his spleen. Unfortunately, these weren't school yard bullies. These were weary, frustrated and humiliated men, some with whiskers, all outweighing him by sixty pounds and carrying rifles with bayonets. Several of them got up from their seats on the bridge or straightened up as if slapped.

The corporal, too mad for words, reached for Jesse and grabbed him by the collar. "Why you little..." he sputtered. He was big and strong and had Jesse in a vice-like grip. Jesse was sorry he hadn't been running when he said those words instead of standing right in front of the man at arm's length. Then he realized it probably didn't matter where he insulted the man from because the fellow had a gun.

Just as Jesse thought he was about to get murdered or at least thrown off the bridge into the river 20 feet below, someone yelled, "Halt! Hold it there Corporal!" He looked over to see a tall man in an officer's uniform, but unlike the others', his was blue with red embellishments. He had a long sword at his side and a pistol in his hand.

"What do you think you're doing, Corporal?" he said, striding up to the man. "Unhand that boy! You know there's to be no trouble with the locals."

"But, Sir," stammered the surprised corporal. "He called us, he…"

"I don't care what he said," replied the officer. "If you men have nothing better to do with your liberty than stand around and cause trouble, you will be confined to quarters. Now get back to your camps!"

"But Lieutenant, he said we were cowards," objected the militia corporal.

Lieutenant Vetter was in no mood for arguments. The political fallout resulting from their refusal to cross the border would be bad enough without his men alienating the local inhabitants.

"That's an order, Corporal," he yelled. "Now move!"

Even Jesse began to move at the command.

"You all right, son?" the lieutenant asked, as the men sheepishly moved to obey his orders.

"Yes, Sir," answered Jesse. "They wanted us to pay to cross the bridge. I told them they looked like redcoats."

The lieutenant laughed. "I don't blame you for being mad. They'll all be going home tomorrow. But you're right. They do look pretty ridiculous in those gaudy dragoon uniforms."

"Are you in the army?" Jesse asked, not recognizing the uniform, which looked clean and new. He had never seen such an impressive looking man before, with a broad chest full of gold buttons and a thick black beard. He stood tall and straight, with gleaming buckles and sword. He still held the pistol in his hand.

"No, son. I'm in the state militia like them. They're dragoons. That's why they're all dressed up so pretty like, real dandies. Think they're the cream of the crop, they do."

"Cream of the crop?" asked Daniel.

"Yeah, you know, the best of the best, just because they ride a horse all day."

"Do you have a horse?" asked Daniel.

"Sure he does, dummy," replied Jesse, not wanting to appear stupid himself in front of their savior. "He's an officer, ain't he. Officers ride horses too."

"That's right, boy," answered the lieutenant smiling. "I've got me a really nice horse called Honey. She's a golden tan color just like honey from a bee."

The boys gaped in awe.

A few days later the army came home.

Word arrived at the school that Saturday in late November that the army was encamped at Champlain and on its way back to Plattsburgh. Jesse and a group of boys from the Academy made their way in the cold, damp, clear morning air out to Dead Creek, at the north end of town, to greet them at the old plank bridge.

As soon at the first troops came into sight along the north lake road, Jesse and the boys let out a cheer, and kept cheering and clapping as the men walked by. Instead of happy victorious troops, however, they saw nothing by disheartened, defeated men, not so much defeated by the enemy as by the timidity and incompetence of their leaders. Line after line of demoralized, humiliated troops marched by. The boys soon stopped cheering as it was eliciting hostile stares from the soldiers. They sat in numb silence as the army traipsed by. Jesse had never been so depressed in his life.

Things only got worse later that day when he got back to the Gordon house. He had been anticipating the Christmas holiday when most of the boys went home to their families. He was looking forward to going home himself. He missed his mother's rich cooking and despite himself, he missed his younger brother and sisters. Then just before the Academy closed up for the season, the Gordons told him how happy they were that he'd be spending Christmas with them. Unbeknownst to Jesse, and against his mother's objections, his father had agreed to let him stay with his hosts through the holiday. As a matter of fact, Jesse got the distinct impression that he would never be going home again.

Whitehall, NY, December 1812

While Jesse toiled the day away in school, Sam was still in Whitehall building ships, though most of the work had been finished. He had indeed been hired by Mister John Nichols, the shipbuilder, who needed men and knew a good worker when he saw one. Sam was hired on the spot.

So far they had built two new gunboats and three sloop troop carriers, not to mention refurbishing and finishing the 8-gun *President*, which had been recently purchased and refitted for military purposes. The fleet had been moved to Whitehall for the winter, but Macdonough was now in Burlington with his new wife and would stay there until spring when the new ships would go north to be armed. It had taken a prodigious effort, but they had accomplished their task, no small thanks to Sam, who had turned out to be an exceptionally good carpenter and fast learner. He took to ship building like a well-dampened sail takes to the wind.

So it hurt him all the more that he wasn't allowed to join the navy now that the main work was done, but had to stay a civilian, working for the ship builder Nichols. Now that winter had set in and most of the work was done, things around the small hamlet of Whitehall had become downright boring. He had half a mind to send for his father through the post and have him come get him. There was still the vague hope, however, that if he stayed around something might happen to get him on a ship.

Of course, Macdonough needed sailors and gunners even more than he needed ships to carry them, but Sam was still too young and had no nautical skills to speak of, just a thirst for adventure and a love of the stories about the great naval duels of the past.

Being a good carpenter, it had been easy for Sam to build a cabin for himself and one of his mates. Others did the same. There was soon a small street of huts and cabins in the field at the end of the lake where only a few weeks before there had been the hulls of gunboats and sloops. The smoke of their wood stoves and fires curled up from the makeshift stovepipes and chimneys in the cold, clear early December air.

Sam was probably the most loved and at the same time most hated man in the camp. If you liked a joke and didn't mind one being played on you, he was the life of the party, a laugh a minute. But if you lacked that sense of humor that allowed you to laugh at yourself while others laughed at you - which is a rare gift indeed - he became enemy number one. He was always playing practical jokes, putting pitch or tar on the outhouse seat, dropping water or worse on peoples' heads as they walked by in the street beneath him. Sometimes, if the person earned his special ire, he'd move their privy in the night and cover the hole with branches so the unwary owner would miss the john and plunge into the hole. There were several incidents where Sam would be pinned to the floor of some tavern with an irate heavyweight trying to bash his brains in. Like the time with the apple farmer, however, Sam generally managed not to get hurt. If his sense of humor didn't necessarily make him popular, his tendency for helping people won him many friends.

The weather turned out to be severely cold that winter. An early storm had frozen the lake solid. The mountainside by the road to the encampment was a massive sheet of ice, which every now and then broke off and crashed to the ground, to the eternal detriment of anyone beneath. If it wasn't for the friends he had made in the village during his short stay, Sam probably would have starved. Game was scarce and supplies even scarcer.

Sam had grown close to the Nichols family over the past few months. Mister Nichols had made his fortune in the Revolution building gunships for the rebels. It didn't hurt that he was also smuggling timber to the British, but he escaped detection and became the hamlet's wealthiest citizen. He was now contracting with the new American navy on the lake to build ships and supply timber. He was the one that made everything happen. Mister John Nichols also had a daughter named Sarah, who Sam liked. They gradually got to know each other and the feeling became mutual. That's why this evening he was sitting in their warm, friendly dining room having a turkey dinner with the family.

"I say it's going to take more than a few gunboats and galleys to keep the British out of the lake," said Mister Nichols.

"We've got the *President*, and *Growler* and *Eagle*," said Sam proudly. "That will be enough."

"Not by a long shot," said the ship-building entrepreneur. "The British have much more firepower than a few 12-pounders and 6-pound army guns."

"But surely we'll build more ships in the spring," said Sam, echoing what he'd heard among the men.

"So will the British. It's a race, Sammy, and victory goes to the swiftest."

"Well, we've been pretty swift. There's been a lot done since November."

"That's the truth, Sam, and you've been a big part of it. We couldn't have done it without you. I've never had a harder worker. You seem to pick things up like you've seen it all before. You sure you Father isn't a shipbuilder?"

"Yes, I'm sure. I guess I love ships. I want to serve on one in the lake."

"I don't know about that, but we'll need lads like you if we're to stay ahead of the British. They have a lot more resources than we do."

"What do you mean?" asked Sam, not sure he knew what Mister Nichols was talking about and wondering if maybe he should have gone back to school like Jesse.

"I mean they have more money to build ships with and pay sailors with. We've got nothing. We get the scraps left over from the dwindling custom duties after everyone else gets their piece. Well, you can't build a navy on scraps."

Mister Nichols had decided opinions on things and didn't mind sharing them with a young man, especially if that young man happened to be interested in his daughter, and that interest was reciprocated. Any man who married his Sarah would have to have the right attitude toward things, and he believed in instilling that attitude early.

"Now, I'm no lover of the war," he continued. "But since it's happened, I intend to make the best of it. I'm no lover of taxes either. I'm the last one to give over my hard earned money to some banker in New York or bureaucrat in Washington. Nevertheless, you can't fight a war without money. If we're serious about winning this war, and I think we are, we need to start levying taxes on internal goods and products and use that money to build ships and cannons and pay soldiers and sailors."

"My father and Mister Fisher from Boston said the same thing," said Sam, starting to get the message. "But it's all so complicated. A lot of people don't like taxes."

"I know, Sammy. It's the same old story. Love and taxes."

"What?" said Sam, perplexed.

"Oh, don't worry," laughed Mister Nichols. "You'll know what I'm talking about soon enough. Why don't you and Sarah go into the sitting room and have some hot chocolate. There's a big fire going. I'll be in shortly."

He watched his daughter and her young suitor depart for the next room, and wondered what the future and the war would bring to them.

The next day Sam was in camp thinking of the night before and Sarah Nichols. Despite his agreeable thoughts, darker feelings soon crowded out the pleasant memories. He had been passed over, left behind. It made him burn with anger and humiliation. He was so agitated he could hardly lie in bed. If it wasn't for the cold, he would have jumped up and paced the room. As it was, his foot rustled back and forth against his coarse wool blanket with agitation.

All the ships had been built. The fleet's crews had gone north without him. All that was left behind were the sick, the malcontents and him. He hadn't left his nice cozy family home to come down to this forsaken place to build cabins. He missed his father and mother. Maybe it was time to go home.

He had lingered in his bunk longer than usual. His bunkmates had already left for breakfast. Sam turned around one more time and closed his eyes. Trying to change his frame of mind, he imagined Sarah lying in bed next to him. A rapid knock at the door interrupted his revelries. A moment later, Corporal Sargent burst into the one room cabin.

"What are you doing still in bed?" he demanded. "You're not sick are you? Cause if you're sick that's too bad. We ain't got no doctor here and I ain't going to become one."

"Calm you self, Sir," said Sam. "There are no sick people here."

"Well, then get out of that bed Mister! Now, if you want to eat."

"I'm not hungry. I had dinner last night at Mister Nichols house. It was fantastic. There was turkey and fresh carrots and peas, and potatoes mashed up real soft, and butter, and biscuits and pie." Sam stopped short, realizing his error by the look on the corporal's face. The army man's mood turned sour.

"I guess you had quite a banquet last night. I'm happy for you Mister Turner. How nice you got to eat like a king while your poor messmates are starving in their cabins. I had cold beans last night, with a biscuit hard enough to knock a man's teeth out, with not so much as a pinch of butter. Sour coffee and no sugar. That's my fare, Mister Turner, and I had it better than most of the men. Now, get out of bed! Everyone's waiting for you."

"First of all Corporal, I don't take orders from you. I work for Mister Nichols. I'm not in the army, remember?"

Sam couldn't quite believe the words coming out of his mouth, but even thoughts of Sarah Nichols couldn't dispel his simmering anger at being left behind. The corporal turned beet red. Sam was actually afraid the man's head would explode.

"Why you little… How dare you… you little… As long as you're in my camp you'll do as I say," the Corporal finally sputtered. "You volunteered, you yellow-eared, green-bellied piece of dung. As far as I'm concerned you're under my command. You know what they do to deserters and shirkers in the army? They shoot 'em!"

"There's no deserters here," replied Sam, indignantly, getting up and pulling on his drawers. He wasn't going to argue with Sargent in his underwear. "I volunteered to build ships. Now the work is done the navy doesn't want me anymore. I begged to go with them."

"You're too young to join the navy, boy," said Corporal Sargent, liking the boy's spirit and calming down a bit. "Anyway, they don't need carpenters where they're going."

The corporal's anger came more from fear that his best worker had become sick like the others than the fact that Sam had slept late. Things were slow, most of the work was done, but now he had to deal with the sickness. There was a regular epidemic of dysentery and pneumonia taking place in his little camp.

"They'll sign you up when they need you. You got a while yet. The fleet will hole up here until the ice thaws anyway. I need you until then. There's still a lot of work to do. We need to finish getting the cabins built for the winter. There's a lot of sick men. I can't have you lying in bed all morning. Are you sure you're all right?" He took a hard look at Sam.

"Yes, Sir, I feel fine. It's just that, well, I, um, like you said, all the work's been done. They don't need me anymore. I'm, eh, I'm going to go home."

Sargent looked at the greenhorn with contempt. Finally, he spoke.

"What, things too tough for you? The first time you don't get what you want, you want to run away?"

Ever since the fleet had left without him, Sam had begun to doubt himself. Despite the encouraging words of his Mentor, Mister Nichols, and the admiring glances of his daughter, Sam felt small, a nobody from nowhere, a speck from a place so small it wasn't even a dot on a map. Who would want him? He might as well go where everyone knows him, where it's safe and warm. Might as well go where I'm appreciated, he thought.

"They took everyone but me," Sam said, almost in tears.

"I'm here, ain't I?" replied Sargent, hotly. "What am I and your messmates, a bucket of mush? We're doing our duties. I thought you wanted to work to defend your country? That's what you said? Now you want to run away home?"

"I want to work on the ships. If I can't work on them, I want to serve on one."

"Well, what can you do? Can you sail a ship? Can you fire a cannon?"

"No, but I can shoot a gun fairly good, and I can learn the rest. They need carpenters."

"You'd just be in the way. You've got a lot to learn, boy, and you won't be learning any of it if you run away home. Maybe if you get up a little earlier and ate out less at the mansion, and didn't miss morning mess, they would take you. I'll talk to the lieutenant, tell him my best workman wants to join the navy. I doubt they'll take a little underage jokester like you. You can't play pranks on people like you do on a ship you know. They'd throw you overboard with an anchor tied to your leg. No, you're too much of a troublemaker."

"I only do that 'cause I'm bored. I don't mean any harm. I'm just trying to have fun, but if it means getting on a ship in the navy, I'll never pull a joke on someone again. I swear. Anyway, what can I learn here? I already know how to build a stupid cabin."

"I need you here. You're my best man."

The corporal was loath to admit it to the headstrong youth, but if it kept him from leaving, he'd have said anything. In any case, it was true.

"How are you planning on getting back home anyway?" he continued, "winters coming on."

"I'll send for my pa."

"What? And make your old man traipse down here through those mountains in the middle of winter. You really are a selfish kid."

"I'll go myself then."

"You'd freeze to death the first day out, you little snot-nosed tenderfoot. Look Sam, you won't get what you want by running away," said the Corporal, in a more conciliatory tone. "You've got to stay and stick it out, see things through to the end. Who knows how things may turn out, but if you don't stay and see, you'll never know what that end could have been. Stick it out. Make yourself needed. I'll put in a good word for you, but you've got to show me what you're made of. At least here you have a chance of being noticed. Besides, you have it made, dining with the richest man in the village, courting his daughter. You could have it a lot worse. What, are you daft? You want to throw all that away?"

Corporal Sargent looked at Sam as if he had already made up the lad's mind for him.

"Come on, sailor, I'll buy you some hard biscuits and sour coffee for breakfast."

Sam looked at the grizzled old Corporal and suddenly felt a stab of affection. The man probably had as much chance of making Sergeant as Sam had of getting on a ship, but his words were filled with wisdom. It was to Sam's credit that despite his bitter disappointment, he listened to what his corporal said and heeded his advice.

"What are you so danged anxious to get in the navy for?" Sargent asked, as they walked out of the cabin together to the mess. "What's wrong with the army?"

"Nothing," answered Sam. "It's just that all the famous battles I read about in the books are naval battles, stories about Lawrence and the 'Constitution'. I'd give my right arm to serve under someone like that."

The corporal laughed. "Yeah, you'd be a regular little one-armed Nelson, I'm sure," he replied. "Good enough, then, we'll see. In the meantime, get going on finishing those cabins. It look's like it's going to be a nice day today but it promises to snow hard in the next day or so. I can feel it in my bones."

"Yes, Sir. Sorry for being tardy, Mister Sargent. It won't happen again."

True to his word, Corporal Sargent mentioned Sam to Macdonough's second in command on the lake, Lieutenant Sidney Smith, when he arrived from Albany on his way to Burlington a few days later. He told him of the lad's boat building skills and enthusiasm. He also told him of the rising toll of sickness and disease. Smith stopped a few days in Whitehall to observe the situation firsthand before continuing on to report to Macdonough. While there he had a chance to observe young Mister Turner and some of the other men up close.

The first thing he noticed was how fast Sam worked and how he led the other men, some of them much more seasoned than he was, in putting up the cabins. His work was excellent, the buildings sturdy and warm. The next thing that attracted his notice was the way Sam cared for the sick men in the camp. He seemed to have a natural empathy toward those who were ill and knew how to best treat their needs, whether it was cold compresses or warm wraps. He put their needs first and never once showed the slightest fear or concern for his own safety. Smith was suitably impressed. He had resolved earlier to recommend moving the whole encampment north, even though they had just built shelters for the winter. He further resolved to recommend Sam Turner for ship duty as an assistant carpenter when he came of age, and an apprenticeship in the meantime.

Village of Plattsburgh, NY, December 1812

Things were going just about as bad as things could go for army in Plattsburgh. The troops were in pitiful shape, demoralized and decimated with sickness, the same combination of diseases afflicting those down in Whitehall, but more so due to the number of men.

It was one of the worst winters the old-timers could remember in a north country filled with fierce snow storms and blizzards. Because there were so many sick and dying and so few to care for them, the bodies were piling up outside the forts. They would bury over 200 before the winter was over, two to five a day, nature accomplishing what the enemy with all their guns and swords had failed to do

"It's just like Valley Forge," said one of the old-timers from Colonel Pike's corps, sitting around a table at the pub.

"What is?" asked Nate Peters who was sitting at the bar, remembering something about that from his history books. He had been busted for brawling with a big-mouthed militia corporal soon after his return to camp, and was now a private again. "You mean Valley Forge where George Washington was?"

"The very same, lad. It's worse here than it was back then," said the sergeant who must have been as old as the oldest Exempt any of them had ever seen. "I should know. I was there."

"Oh, here we go again," said one of his tablemates. He laughed and nudged the man beside him.

"Laugh all you want," said the old sergeant. "But I was there that winter on the banks of that damned half-frozen river. It was hell. The fighting was a relief from the cold, and we didn't have so much as a jacket to keep us warm, not like you spoiled babies with your thick coats and blankets. And we was hungry too, no crops or game for miles. We ate anything we could get, even rats and dogs."

The men laughed again. "You always did have a fondness for dog stew," joked the same man, causing an uproar.

"Well, it ain't nothing to laugh about," replied the old sergeant, making his point. "The way things are going, it'll soon be just as bad here."

"We got huts," said one of the men.

"That ain't going to keep the sickness away," answered the old man. "And it ain't going to feed you when the supplies are gone. We're already on half rations."

"There's plenty of farms around with food for the army," volunteered Nate from the bar, who had been living well with supplies from his family. Many of the other men didn't have it so good, however.

"Yeah, and who's going to pay for all this food?" asked the sergeant. "The army ain't got no money. We haven't been paid in over three months. Men are deserting in droves on the way here. No one wants to serve in this godforsaken place."

Even though they had retreated in defeat, being part of a fighting unit that worked together like a precision machine had given Nate pride and a purpose. If only he survived the winter.

Chapter 8

Village of Plattsburgh, NY, May 1813

Macdonough had recently arrived in the village, passing over from Burlington in his new flag ship the *President*, sailing across at Cumberland Head to enter the bay between the 'Head' and Crab Island further to the south. He surveyed the entrance to the wide harbor with a studied eye, as well as the small island about a mile and a half to the southwest, which protected the bay from a southern approach. The area had good defensive prospects, he noted.

He was greeted at the dock by his second in command, Lt. Sidney Smith, who had just arrived from Whitehall himself.

"Hello, Sir. How was your sail over?"

"Good, Mister Smith. A glorious day," said the commander.

"How is married life treating you, Sir?" asked the Lieutenant.

"Very good, Sidney, thank you." Some superiors might have taken offense at the familiar tone of his subordinate's remark, but Smith had attended his wedding in Middleton and knew his wife's family, so he thought the Lieutenant's question perfectly normal. "If I'd of known marriage was so good I would have gotten married sooner."

They both laughed.

"So this is Plattsburgh," began Macdonough looking up at the shore where buildings were clustered along the lake. Church steeples were visible on the ridge beyond.

"This is the main village on this side of the lake, where most of the business and commerce is done. It's a key strategic point along the north-south corridor between New York and New England, as I'm sure you are aware, Sir. The actual District of Champlain itself covers quite a few miles, up to Chazy in the north and the mountains to the west."

"Yes, I've seen the maps. I've been doing more than sampling the delights of married life this past winter."

"I'm sure you have, Sir. Captain Lawrence has had some success I hear."

"He is a good man," said Macdonough. "The British will have their hands full with that one, I'm sure." They both laughed again, picturing the indomitable captain and his little ship the *Hornet*, bristling with guns. "His promotion was much deserved. I wish we had him here."

"Yes, that would be nice, Sir," said Smith. "But then he would be the ranking officer, Sir. I'm not sure there's enough glory on this lake for the both of you."

This time Smith had gone too far with his familiarity. Despite his good nature, Macdonough found himself offended by his friend's remark.

"There's plenty of glory to go around, Mister Smith. I'm sure we will all get our share of it before this war is through."

"Yes, Sir. Sorry, Sir, I didn't mean…"

"That's all right, Mister Smith. I knew exactly what you meant. We, all of us, go where our superiors order us to."

"Speaking of that, Sir, what do you think of the new Secretary?"

"Well, he certainly has strong credentials. Anything would be better than Mister Hamilton. The man didn't know a frigate from a gunboat. Mister Jones knows his business. He'll be an improvement, I'm sure. It's the new Secretary of war that's got me worried."

"Oh, who's that?" asked Smith. "I hadn't heard Madison was appointing a new one."

"Yes, an old intriguer from Aaron Burr days, General John Armstrong."

"Like you say, Sir, ours is not to reason why but to simply obey."

"It's the navy way, Mister Smith." They both laughed again.

"Some say now that Napoleon's army's been defeated, that the British will send all their men here," offered Smith, voicing something that was being said more often of late.

"I doubt they're through with Mister Napoleon yet," answered the commander. "And even if they were, they'll have enough on their hands sorting things out over there to keep them busy for awhile. I'm sure Mister Madison knows what he's doing."

"I wish I could be as sure as you are, Sir."

"Have faith in the Lord, Mister Smith. He will see us through in our time of trouble."

"Yes, Sir," replied Smith, not quite convinced. "You'll find things pretty quiet here for the most part."

"Yes, I'm sure," observed Macdonough, looking out at the quiet harbor. "I expect the most action we'll see here is ship building. This is a race, Mister Smith, and may God give us the speed and determination to be the winners. Speaking of winners, have you heard any word of Porter and the *Essex* in your travels?"

"No, Sir. No one has heard from them. I hope they have not been lost at sea."

"I doubt that, Mister Smith. Captain Porter is not a man to be caught by a storm. No, more than likely he is cruising the oceans, having too much fun harassing the British to return to port."

"Let us hope so, Sir," said Smith.

"So, Mister Smith, how does the fleet stand?"

"Very well, Sir. We have the sloop, the *President* and its six guns, and the *Growler* and *Eagle* with four guns each, along with the two gunboats. All their alterations are completed and the armaments mounted. The fleet is still undermanned, Sir, and many of those crews we have are landlubbers from the army. I am still looking for a surgeon's mate as well."

"So, it is about as I thought. We have a lot of work to do."

"Oh, Sir, have you heard the news from out west?"

"Yes, the offensive against York was quite successful."

"Yes, Sir, but did you not hear that Colonel Pike was killed during the assault?"

"Why, no," said Macdonough momentarily stunned. He did not know the man personally, but like many others had heard much about him.

"Yes, a great loss. He was quite popular around here."

"Yes, he is known far and wide for his discoveries and leadership in battle," said Macdonough, sincerely regretful at the news. "I am sorry to hear of it. It only makes our task that much more difficult. I'm afraid a lot more good men will die before this conflict is over. There seems no reason for it. It's as if those making the decisions don't know that men are dying for such trivial reasons."

"They didn't seem so trivial a year ago, at least not to Mister Madison," said Smith.

"True, but congress still refuses to pass any tax provisions or re-charter the National Bank to help pay for the war. The country would have run out of money if it wasn't for that loan from John Jacob Aster. What would we have done then?"

"I don't know, Sir. My question is, now that we have the money, what are we going to do with it?"

"That, Mister Smith, is a very good question."

Whitehall, NY, May 1813

Much had happened since mid-March, much of it not good for the fledgling nation in the grip of its first war. There were some stunning victories far away at sea where Americans held their own in single-ship combat with the British. But in mid-March, Admiral Warren arrived at Chesapeake Bay with his squadron and his 74-gun flagship. Since then he had been raiding the Chesapeake and Baltimore areas at will, burning vessels and towns and pillaging the countryside. At the turn of the year the Americans had made a successful surprise attack on Elizabethtown, just across the St. Lawrence from a recaptured Ogdensburg. That small victory had been offset, however, by the fiasco out west where the British retook Frenchtown on the River Raisin and captured General Winchester and 500 men, 40 of whom were massacred by the Indians. "Remember the Raisin" became a battle cry even in far off Whitehall.

While the world was changing quickly for some, for good or bad as luck would have it, it seemed to change not at all for Sam Turner. The lake had long since thawed and the fleet had sailed to Vergennes to be armed and fitted, but Sam had not gone. He was told that he was needed where he was, but from where he stood, staring out at a narrow empty bay, there didn't seem to be much need for him here. There was still plenty of work to do, but that was taking place fifty miles up the lake. Being stuck in Whitehall was the worst fate Sam could have imagined.

Even Jesse, who was still in school, was in a better position, thought Sam. At least his cousin was in Plattsburgh were Macdonough was and the fleet was headed. Even Corporal Sargent had gone north with one of the troop transports, ferrying men and equipment to the village. The only thing that saved Sam was the occasional visits to the Nichols house, where his infatuation with the shipbuilder's daughter had turned into a full-fledged romance.

Instead of resenting the young man's attention toward his daughter, Mister Nichols seemed to approve. More than approve, he seemed to encourage it, and was partly responsible for Sam's continued presence in Whitehall. After all, when the man in charge of ship building in the village said he needed a person, the navy listened to him. There weren't many eligible young men in the hamlet, and certainly none with Sam's personality and ship building skills. More than that, Sarah's father saw something in the lad that made him think Sam was destined for great things. He didn't want to see the young man waste his life needlessly as a swab on some gunboat, and he certainly didn't want an eligible potential son-in-law to get away now that Sarah was marrying age. He had met Sam's father the month before when Ben had made a short visit to see his son, and thought very highly of him. The man's war record spoke for itself.

While Sam was discouraged at his lack of progress toward serving with the fleet, he was encouraged by news from out west where the Americans had recently attacked and burned York. What really sustained him through the long slow thaw of spring, though, was the news from the Atlantic, where the small American fleet was more than holding its own. A new Secretary of Navy had been appointed, a little 52 year old man named William Jones. Soon after that a stunning series of one-on-one victories occurred. The story of the little 20-gun brig *Hornet* especially fired Sam's imagination. He daydreamed that he was

74

on it as she captured her first prize, the British brig *Resolution* with $23,000 in gold on board. A prize like that could make a man rich for life, he thought. He imagined himself on the bridge as the intrepid little ship dueled with the 18-gun brig *Peacock*. These small naval victories buoyed Sam through the disheartening news of the tightening British blockade of Atlantic ports and the amphibious attacks in the Chesapeake Bay area. It all seemed so far away from Whitehall, NY, which to Sam seemed like the middle of nowhere, where he could only dream of fame and glory.

"Have you talked to the Lieutenant about me yet?" Sam asked Nichols for the tenth time that week.

"No, Sam. I have more important things to discuss with the Lieutenant than you," answered Mister Nichols. "The fleet was fitted with their armaments in Vergennes and is now in Plattsburgh. The carronades and long-guns have all been mounted."

"Can I go up with the gunboat?" Sam asked, pointing to the lone gunboat tied to the loading dock.

"You know I don't have any say in that, son. You'll have to ask the Lieutenant that yourself."

"But Mister Nichols, you promised that when spring came you'd help me get an assignment on one of the ships. You said yourself they need men."

"If you play your cards right, son, we might get you a commission. Why be a common sailor, grunting under a heavy load all day when you can be an officer. You can be the one giving the orders."

"I'd have to go back to school."

"Just for a little while, down in Albany."

"I don't have time for that. The war will be over by then."

"I wish you were right, but I have a feeling this war will be with us for awhile, just like the last one. Six months won't make much of a difference, but being an officer will. Anyway, Sarah graduates from school in a few weeks. You want to be around for that, don't you? They'll be parties and dancing and all the cider you can drink."

"Yeah, I guess so, but I feel the whole war is passing me by. I have a lot to learn, and I'm wasting time here."

75

"Well, we can fix that. I know a few fellows who have done some sailing in their time and not just on this lake, although that's enough. Maybe we can get them to show you the ropes. How would that be? By this time next year, you could be a midshipman on his way to commanding your own vessel."

Sam doubted that, and wasn't sure it was what he wanted. He just wanted to be a crew member on one of Macdonough's ships. It didn't matter if it was as a lowly sailor or on a gun crew, or just as a ship's carpenter. He'd learn what he could and would become the best darned seaman to sail the lake.

"Look Sam, I've been wanting to talk to you about something else," said Nichols looking at him seriously. "You have other options you know, that is if you don't want to go back to school."

"What do you mean, Sir?" asked Sam, not quite sure that he liked the way his employer was looking at him.

"Well for one thing, there may be more work coming our way. The government just got a loan from that fur trader fellow, John Astor, that will keep them solvent 'til the end of the year. They may vote another ship or two for the lake to keep up with the British. I'm hoping to get the contract, and if I do, I'll need a good foreman to lead the work crews. I was wondering if I could count on you. The pay would be good."

"Foreman? Me? Gee, Mister Nichols, I appreciate it, but I don't think I know enough. I've only been building boats a little while."

"You've been working for me almost six months now, and you're the best man I've got. You're perfect for the job. You know what you're doing and you work hard. The men respect you even if you do get them mad at you once in awhile with your practical jokes, though you seem to have grown out of that. I'm offering you a great opportunity."

"Yes, Sir. Thank you, Sir," said Sam.

"There's something else I have been meaning to discuss with you," Nichols said, appearing to struggle for words. Sam remained silent.

"Sarah will be out of school soon. She's awful fond of you, you know. And well, I, ah, we, um, I discussed it with my wife and she thinks you two would be a splendid couple, and I agree. What are your intentions toward my daughter, Sir?"

Sam was momentarily taken aback. He didn't know exactly what to say, so he took his time before answering.

"We've talked about maybe getting married after the war," Sam confessed finally.

"There's a good living in the shipbuilding business. I haven't done so badly," said Mister Nichols.

"I could only hope to succeed as well as you have, Sir," replied Sam. "But there's still so much I want to do."

"And well you should, my boy. Well you should," said the older man, sizing the younger one up. "I agree, you should both wait. Sarah's still too young, but when the time does come my boy, you have to be ready, and to be ready, you have to start now."

"Yes, Sir. That's why I want to get on a ship as soon as I can. Time is passing me by and it's killing me."

"Oh, I'm sure you'll live, Sammy," said Nichols. "And we aim to make sure you do."

Chapter 9

Burlington, Vermont, Late July 1813

Thomas Macdonough was back in Burlington in support of the new commander of the northern army, General Wade Hampton. He was less than happy with the duty. It had been during his meetings with Eleazer Williams in mid-May when he held a council of war with his officers that he learned of the British troop movements toward Oswego and Sackets Harbor. He had relayed this intelligence to headquarters. That information had been at least partly responsible for the successful though costly defense of the American stronghold. However, Plattsburgh had been depleted of troops in the process. Since then there had been one disaster after another.

One of his gunboats overturned in the lake during a fierce spring storm, the heavy winds churning up the lake like an ocean tempest. He had warned the men about this lake, how the waves can go from dead calm to ten-foot swells in the blink of the eye. The lake was deceptively deadly that way. A small craft was especially vulnerable, but even a large flat bottom craft like a gunboat, if not handled properly by men who knew the water, could be swamped. It took them the better part of two days to get it upright and afloat again. It was a miracle no one was lost. He said a silent prayer and thanked his Maker for His aid.

He had been concerned about the lack of discipline among the mixed and inexperienced crews and the cavalier attitude, especially from his friend Sidney Smith. His First Lieutenant seemed to forget sometimes that he was no longer in command. That would matter little now, however, since Smith and two of his ships with all their crew had been captured by the English. The thought still stung him to tears of shame, not to mention anger at the sheer stupidity of it.

It wouldn't have been so bad if he had never mentioned it to his Lieutenant, but they had talked about just this very thing many times. Don't get lured into the narrows near Isle aux Noix where the British had their base at the northern end of the lake.

There would be no room to maneuver once in the narrow channel between the island and the rocky western shore, especially if the southerly wind gave out. Smith had taken not one, but two of their best ships straight into the narrows chasing some gunboats. They were trapped and tried to fight their way out. One man killed, nineteen wounded was the result. The English had already renamed the two captured sloops, one of them, the 'Shannon', in honor of one of the ships captured by the Americans in the Atlantic. His ears burned with the humiliation of it. Worse than that, they had been rearmed with 11 guns each. After all their hard work, the English now had superiority on the lake.

He felt bad that his friend was now imprisoned in some rat-infested Quebec hell-hole with his crew, but he would have punished him severely had he been able to do so. The man just did not listen. Now that Macdonough had finally been promoted to Master Commandant maybe things would be different, but that wouldn't be much help to Sidney Smith and his men.

Macdonough tried to shake off the doldrums by vigorously shaking of his head. He surveyed the square in front of the house in which the new army commander was staying. It belonged to a Judge Woods and was right in the center of town. The judge, who knew the general from his days in New Orleans, had loaned it to Hampton for his headquarters while he was in Boston for the summer. Macdonough's own house, where his wife and he had stayed all winter, was not far away, a few blocks down the road toward the lake. Their time together had been the highpoint of his life. Now he was being pulled by strings in ways he wasn't sure he liked.

"That's very unfortunate about your man Smith," said Wade Hampton, the new commanding general, once Macdonough was announced and in his presence. "Something like that would never have happened under my command."

Macdonough held his tongue. "My fleet is ready to support your offensive, Sir. I've already requested replacements for the lost ships. We'll need at least a 20-gun sloop with 18-pound longs and three experienced lieutenants."

"Oh, is that all?" said Hampton sarcastically. The southerner seemed more English than most of the British officers

Macdonough had encountered, his attitude haughty and disdainful.

"No, Sir," continued Macdonough. "I'll need at least six good middies and as many gunners. Twenty or so ordinary seaman will also be needed to man the new ships."

"That's your concern, Lieutenant. The army's not responsible for manning your ships. As a matter of fact, I may need some of your marines if I'm to carry out this offensive."

"Sir, you have almost 4000 men here. What do you need a few dozen marines for? Most of them are in Plattsburgh anyway." He wouldn't have normally spoken this way to a commanding officer, even an army general, but the man's attitude and disregard of common courtesy had raised his hackles. He was still being treated like a mere lieutenant.

"Don't presume to tell me how many men I need or what I should do with them, Mister. I'll have none of your navy insubordination here, Sir. Is that understood?"

"Yes, Sir. Sorry, Sir," said Macdonough. "It's just that Williams and his scouts have been saying for weeks that the British are building up their forces on the border and are liable to attack Plattsburgh at any time. At least let my fleet help shore up the defenses there."

"That is not possible," answered Hampton. "I need you and the fleet to support the army and the army is staying in Burlington. This is a coordinated affair involving thousands of troops spread over hundreds of miles, not some single-ship duel. Everyone needs to follow orders and stick to the plan. Anyway, you don't believe a few resentful Indians do you? That's just what the Indians and the British want us to think. No, the main threat will be in the west. My attack is to be a flanking move, and well timed. There is much to do. I shall not be dissuaded or diverted from my plans by the vague rumors of a few untrustworthy savages. By the way Mister Macdonough, what's this I hear about a British force invading Cumberland Head undetected recently. How could this happen, Sir?"

"There's nothing to explain General. It was not an invasion, but a small boat under a flag of truce that wanted to parley. They were probably spies sent to probe our defenses, but they saw nothing of import. They just slipped through our lines with all the disruption from the capture of our ships."

"Not a very impressive record is it, Mister Macdonough?"

Macdonough gave up any further attempt at convincing the general to see reason. He held his breath and his tongue until he was peremptorily dismissed a short while later.

"Why that dumb, arrogant wind-bag wouldn't know his elbow from a forecastle," Macdonough said to Eleazer Williams, who he happened to meet in the square outside the General's house.

"What did he say about the reports from my rangers?" asked the Indian scout and one time minister.

"He doesn't believe it, and even if he did, he doesn't want to hear anything that would interfere with his plans. He'd walk his men off a cliff if it said to in the plans."

They both laughed.

"He is truly an enemy to his species," said Williams.

Macdonough agreed and they laughed again, something the new Master Commandant and his comrades did often.

"I don't see how he can deny the reports of my men after what happened in Sackets Harbor."

"We were lucky we had somebody in charge then that listened to reason," said Macdonough. "I'm afraid those days are over."

"What are you going to do?"

"There's nothing I can do. Technically I'm under the General's overall command, and he's going to demand the fleet support his offensive."

"By the time he gets ready to move, there will be snow on the ground and the lake will be frozen. He has a reputation for procrastination and blaming others for his mistakes."

"So I've heard, but those things have a way of catching up with a man."

"Well, let's hope they don't catch up to him while he's leading our men into battle."

"Let us hope and pray."

"Oh, by the way, Master Commandant, congratulations on your promotion. It couldn't be more deserved. You have done much good on this lake, Sir, if I may be permitted to say. It is too bad what happened to Sidney Smith."

"I told him many times not to get trapped in the narrows."

"As did I, but he craved glory and disregarded the risks."

"I'm afraid there's a lot of that going around these days, or even worse, those that disregard any glory at the smallest risk. I wonder what kind of general our Mister Hampton is."

"I don't know, but I think I prefer the former, no matter how bad, to Mister Hampton any day," said Williams.

"So do I, Mister Williams," agreed Macdonough. "So do I."

Village of Plattsburgh, NY, Late July 1813

Jesse was out of school for the summer but less than happy. He had spent a lonely Christmas and New Year with the Gordons, who, although they tried to make him feel at home, could not alleviate his homesickness. His second semester at the Academy had been dismal, his grades bad and his behavior even worse. Besides his depressed state, there were just too many distractions in the village for a boy with Jesse's attention span. All they talked about at school was the war.

He thought he'd be able to go home in the spring when school got out, but his father came down to his graduation and told him he had rented out his room to one of his mother's relatives. Jesse would have to stay with the Gordons. He had made the arrangements and they were more than happy to have him, for despite his uncouth ways and bad habits, he was a good boy and they enjoyed his company. He always had a lively story to relate. They were even beginning to see some improvement in his studies. The last thing Jesse wanted to do however was to go back to school in the fall, where he would be in the 9th grade.

There was a lot going on that spring, with Macdonough in the village and his fleet anchored in the Bay. Jesse and his friends had sat and watched them from the boatyard. They even saw the Commander come ashore in one of his ship's boats rowed by six sailors. Jesse was impressed by how fast they rowed and how quiet they were, not a word spoken except a quiet command now and again. Then everything changed at once. One minute, all sorts of activity and hustle and bustle, the next nothing. Militia and regular army units alike seemed to disappear from the village like mist in the sunlight.

"Where'd everybody go?" asked Daniel, the drummer boy. "The army camps are empty and the militia have gone."

"I don't know," replied Jesse. "But good riddance."

"Even the navy boats are gone."

"Must be something going on, but whatever it is, it's not around here."

"Let's see what's going on down at the barbershop," suggested Daniel.

"I don't know. Mister Finley might not be too happy to see me after what Sam and I used to do."

"Who's Sam?" asked Daniel, who had heard the name mentioned before but couldn't put it together with a face.

"He's my cousin. He was my best friend before I came here and met you. He's down in Whitehall someplace building ships for the fleet. He built those ships that were sitting in the Bay last month."

"I hear they got captured," asserted Daniel remembering something his father said.

"What, our ships? No way," insisted Jesse. "They didn't capture any of our ships. Who said so?"

"My dad," responded Daniel, whose father was a successful merchant in the village.

"Well, I don't know where he got his information, but he's full of cow turd."

"He is not," answered Daniel. He didn't like it when Jesse talked badly about his father, but then Jesse talked badly about everybody, so it probably didn't matter.

"Well, they haven't captured any of our ships. That's ridiculous," insisted Jesse emphatically.

They walked down to the east end of town, down the hill to the mouth of the river. There were no militiamen blocking their passage today.

"Where is everyone?" asked Jesse, as they walked to the barbershop overlooking the river and the lake beyond. "The place is deserted."

"So is Mister Finley's shop," observed Daniel.

"What do you boys want?" inquired the barber when Jesse and Daniel walked in. "I'm in no mood for your shenanigans today."

"We're not here to cause trouble," said Jesse. "My friend Danny here needs a haircut. He's got a nickel."

"Didn't I just cut your hair last week?" asked the barber, looking at the son of one of his best customers. He turned to Jesse. "If you ask me, you're the one that needs the haircut."

"Naw," said Jesse, motioning his reluctant friend toward the chair. "Missus Gordon cuts my hair. She won't like it if I go somewhere else. No, Danny here's our drummer boy and he has to look his best on parade. Isn't that right Danny?"

"I guess so," responded Daniel, getting into the barber's chair. He wasn't thrilled about having another haircut, but if it meant hearing the latest gossip from the mouth of the town barber himself, it was worth it.

"You're a drummer boy, eh?" probed the barber, putting a cloth around the boy's shoulders.

"He sure is," interjected Jesse, sitting in the nearest chair by the wall. "He's got the fastest beats you ever heard. Isn't that right Danny?"

"I guess so," answered Danny. "I sure practice a lot."

"Ain't that the truth," agreed Jesse.

"So what are you boys still doing around town?" asked the barber. "Most folks who haven't left yet are getting ready to."

"Why, what's happening?" Jesse inquired.

"Haven't you heard? The British are coming."

"What?" they both said in unison.

"That's what they say," continued Mister Finley. "They're moving along the whole border, from here all the way out west to Detroit. They could attack Plattsburgh any time."

"Where's the army?" asked Jesse.

"Where's the fleet?" echoed Daniel.

"Gone," answered the barber snipping at his young customer's long curly blond hair. "The fleet's across the lake in

84

Burlington with some of the army. A lot of them have gone out west to Sackets Harbor."

"Where's that?" inquired Jesse.

"Out Buffalo way, on Lake Ontario. Say, how much did you say you wanted cut?"

"Just give him a trim," answered Jesse before Daniel, who would have said none, could reply. "Leave it long in the back there."

"Why did all the soldiers leave if the British are coming?" asked Daniel.

"Good question," replied the barber. "I guess they don't care what happens to us."

Daniel looked at Jesse like he couldn't wait to jump out of that chair and run home to his mother. Before he did, Jesse wanted to settle their argument.

"Daniel here says the British captured some of our ships."

"Oh?" said the barber. "Where did he hear that?"

"My father told me," said Daniel, finally speaking up for himself. "He said they chased some English gunboats and got trapped. A man was even killed. They were all taken prisoner."

"You boys shouldn't be going around talking about such things. You don't know if it's true or not. That's for grown-ups to discuss."

"Why?" asked Jesse, still not believing his younger friend was right.

"Cause there's a war on and who knows who's listening, or who knows what." Maybe that's just what the English want folks to think. Anyway, if your parents are smart, they'll have their horses hitched and wagons packed ready to go at a moment's notice."

"Thanks, Mister Finley. Here's your nickel," said Daniel, jumping out of the chair at the first opportunity and flipping the money in the barber's general direction.

"Wait, I haven't finished," yelled the perplexed barber, bending and picking up one of the few nickels he had made that day. "Darned kids," he muttered as they ran off.

"What are you going to do?" asked Daniel, as they made their way back up the hill to his home.

"Nothing, why? What's the big deal?" replied Jesse.

"Didn't you hear him? The British are coming. They've captured all our ships and the army is gone. We'd better tell our parents."

"First of all, my parents are twenty miles from here and the people I live with are probably on the English side. They don't seem to care much either way. I'm not afraid of those stupid redcoats anyway. If they come here I'll shoot their eyes out."

His younger friend wasn't so confident.

"I'm going home to tell my parents. We should be ready."

"What, to run? I ain't running."

Jesse hoped the British really were coming, maybe then he wouldn't have to go back to school.

There was still a lot of day left, a late July scorcher, the hottest so far of a hot humid summer.

"I got an idea," said Jesse. "I got some extra powder, why don't we melt down some of your lead soldiers and make some balls and go shooting. I'll let you shoot my gun."

Daniel had been after Jesse all summer to show him how to shoot. Unlike most of the other kids, Daniel didn't have his own gun. As a matter of fact, he had never even fired one. That's why he decided to be a drummer boy. You could be in the army and not have to shoot a gun, not that he wouldn't have liked to. He'd just never had the chance. Now he was not only being offered an opportunity to go shooting, but with the school's best shot.

"Really?" he exclaimed, grasping at the opportunity.

"Yeah. Get your soldiers. We'll get old Henry at the forge to melt them down for us. I've got a mould to make balls."

An hour later they were leaving the forge with a leather pouch full of half-inch lead musket balls, heading north out of town to the old plank bridge across Dead Creek.

It felt good to have his rifle in his hand. It was only an old bird gun, nothing fancy, but Jesse kept it well-oiled and clean, and it shot true. To him it was the best thing in the world. It was light with a long barrel and a trusty flint-lock. He could down a bird in the air moving away from him at 40 yards. Today however, they were after other game.

"We'll go up to the creek and shoot some snakes," said Jesse. "If you can hit a snake swimming in the water you can hit just about anything."

"Snakes?" said Daniel with a shudder.

"Or maybe we'll shoot some rats," suggested Jesse, pointing to a seagull infested area next to a neck of land a quarter of a mile ahead that formed the northwestern shore of Plattsburgh Bay where Macdonough's fleet had recently stood.

"Rats!" echoed Daniel, even more disturbed.

They reached the bridge, a rickety plank structure that spanned a few gurgling feet of water known as Dead Creek, which connected the lake to a wide swampy area.

"Follow me," ordered Jesse, leaving the dirt road leading north and going under the bridge to follow the creek, which ran from the end of the bay to a swampy expanse of half-submerged trees and marshland known to the locals as the "crick".

"I come here all the time," confided Jesse. "Mostly by myself, you know, to shoot. See, there's one. See that snake swimming along there?" He pointed to a black dot, darting in a zigzagging course through the swampy water, hardly visible.

"Yes, I see it," replied Daniel, finally spotting it and staring in awe. He'd never seen a swimming snake before, let alone shot at one. There was no way you could hit it with a ball. It was too far away and too small.

"Watch," whispered Jesse, wanting to show off before he gave a lesson. He lay down on the grassy bank of the creek and aimed his gun carefully. Calming his breathing, he focused his eye on the tip of the barrel, where he had chiseled a small notch. Slowly putting pressure on the trigger, he followed the snake's movements, anticipating its pattern until he had it centered. He squeezed the trigger with a quick fluid snap that left the barrel of the rifle perfectly still. The snake's head popped off in a red-misty puff, like it had been exploded from inside. Danny yelled with joy.

"Wow!" he cried. "Bull's eye!"

"Aw, that was nothing," muttered Jesse. "I've shot them even further away than that."

After another exhibition of his marksmanship, blowing the heads off a few more snakes at ever further distances and popping a few frogs and turtles just for good measure, Jesse finally relented and let Daniel shoot his gun. It was only after the drummer boy reminded him it was his lead soldiers they had used to make the balls and he should at least get to use a few, that Jesse finally gave in and handed him the gun. Daniel didn't do too badly, considering Jesse had to show him everything from how to hold the musket to how to aim and pull the trigger. They used up seven of their last nine balls, shooting at a large tree limb, which Daniel finally hit with the last shot but one. He yelped for joy.

"That was pretty good, Danny," complemented Jesse. "You're a natural. You just gotta practice."

"I wish I could, but my Pa doesn't want me shooting a gun without him, and he's too busy most of the time. That was real fun. Can I go again, one more time, please?"

"I don't know, Danny," said Jesse, looking in the pouch and seeing the single ball. "We might need this on the way home. What if a nice turkey or a deer shows up?"

Jesse didn't like being without at least one round in case game or a stray redcoat appeared. After all, there was a war on. Shouldering the rifle as if on parade, he and Daniel started marching down the road, Jesse in the lead, the little drummer boy following, humming out a beat on his imaginary drum.

Village of Plattsburgh, NY, Late July 1813

Private Nate Peters was one of the few regular troops left in the village of Plattsburgh. Maybe if he had kept his corporal's stripes they would have taken him, but he had lost them brawling. So when the call went out for the troops to assemble at their various disembarkation places for points east and west, Nate was left behind. Part of him didn't care. He kind of liked the resulting peace and quiet, but a greater part of him resented being passed over. It was like a slap in the face. The smiles on the faces of his friends as they marched by offended him, as if the joke was on him.

The new general was in Burlington across the lake with the bulk of the army. They would be taking part in the great offensive planned for later in the fall. Others had already participated in the defense of Sackets Harbor. Nate spent his time cleaning barracks and latrines, and drinking in the local pub.

The town folks were in a panic and looked at him with hostile stares, especially the women, as if it were somehow his fault that the army had deserted them, as if the few soldiers left here wouldn't die to defend them. Many of the town's people had left, many more were leaving. Nate and the few hundred remaining regulars didn't have that option.

It seemed that no one knew what was going on. Those who knew stayed silent and those who didn't were spreading every kind of wild rumor. Nate's own superiors were even less helpful. His new sergeant was just as ignorant as he was or even more so, not being from the area and knowing no one. His lieutenant, a political animal with big ambitions and his own agenda, only told them what he wanted his men to know, and that for his own ends. Private Nate Peters rued the day he had joined the army.

"I don't care what you say," said Nate's mate, a tall, lanky, dirty-haired private from Maine who sat across from him in a dark shack that reeked of urine. The men sometimes went there to drink after buying a bottle from a local sutler. It was the middle of a hot humid day, the last day of July. "I'm high-tailing from this pig-hole first chance I get. I'm not going to be left here to die like some sheep for the slaughterhouse."

"You better be careful Tom. They shoot deserters in the army," warned Nate.

"I don't care," answered Tom. "Half the men they send up here desert on the way here. They haven't shot any of them."

"There's always a first time, and with your luck, it's liable to be you."

"It's better than staying here and getting bayoneted by some British grenadier," replied Tom.

Nate was just about to counter his friend's argument, when an army corporal burst into the shack.

"Everybody to your posts, quickly!" he shouted. "The British are here!"

Nate ran out of the impromptu pub with the others, following the corporal. He was a bit disoriented, and not a little inebriated, and when the bright midday sun hit him he was almost blinded. He would have stumbled to the ground if his companion hadn't held him up.

"I guess it's too late to desert now," Nate said, half in jest.

"This is what I get for listening to you," responded his friend.

They looked around. Militiamen and regulars were frantically running in all directions. Nate and his friend from Maine did the same, rushing to their posts near a sharp bend in the river. They didn't make it far, the oppressive humidity and heat of the day, not to mention their own condition, catching up to them.

"I shouldn't have had that last bottle," complained Nate, holding his stomach and sweating profusely.

"What I wouldn't give for my canteen and a nice cold drink of water right now," said his drinking companion.

"What are you men doing? Get moving!" ordered a sharp voice. They both looked up to see a militia officer on a rearing horse staring down at them. "To your posts, men! The British are coming!"

He yelled it again as he rode off on his charger. Nate and Tom moved off at a more leisurely pace and eventually made it to the edge of town. As they approached a small cluster of red brick buildings and two-story wooden houses - just under a mile from their starting point - they could hear scattered musket fire, some near, some further off. To their right was the lake, to their left the river and the hills beyond. There were several ships in the bay and from the bright red and blue flags they were flying, the Union Jack, it was obvious they weren't Americans. The bay was crowded with what seemed to be a hundred smaller boats and galleys ferrying men in red uniforms toward the shore. It was a full-fledged invasion!

Nate never thought of running, even when he saw the overwhelming odds he and his men were up against. He urged his comrades on and ran to the south bank of the river, as close as he could to the landing point of the enemy on the north bank. There were already boats ashore and British regulars forming on the bank. A few militiamen stood on the opposite bank firing at them. Nate joined them. The sound of gunfire increased as the

British, who stood in straight lines in the open, began to fire back.

As he stopped to reload his rifle, Nate noticed a boy standing on the wooden bridge that spanned the river near its mouth. He saw the boy raise his musket and aim it at a gaudily dressed officer who was leading his men ashore with his sword raised, obviously someone of high rank. A shot rang out and the tall conspicuous man fell to the ground like he was made of lead, not to move again, killed, it appeared, instantly.

All activity ceased on the opposite shore as the fallen leader's men crowded around him. Then a cry rang out and it seemed every British gun was shooting at the boy on the bridge. Nate could see the wood splintering even from where he stood further down the bank toward the lake. He wondered who it was and if anyone could have survived that deadly volley.

Unknown to Nate, the unfortunate leader of the landing force, a young Major, was the son-in-law of the commander of the invasion, Colonel John Murray. He was an up and coming officer and popular with the men, and his loss was felt by all, not to mention the Commander's favorite daughter.

With that, the invasion by Murray's 800 man amphibious force began in earnest, as more and more British arrived on the shore and began firing at the small defending force on the opposite side of the river. Nate soon realized that if the enemy got to the bridge or forded the river beyond they could easily flank the defenders and get to their rear to cut them off. The distraction on the bridge had given the Americans the initiative, if only they could act on it before the British recovered.

"Come with me!" Nate shouted, getting up and grabbing a few of those around him, militia and regulars alike. "To the bridge! We've got to hold it until the Major and the reinforcements arrive!"

Much to his relief, the men around him joined him in the mad race to the bridge. He could see groups of the enemy begin to move in the same direction. Nate and his men got there first and made a stand, hiding behind trees and rocks, fences and posts, firing at the enemy as they arrived. Soon they were overwhelmed by the English, however, who outnumbered them four to one. The whole north bank seemed to be covered with red coats, every street and common, and more were pouring out of the ships like ants.

Nate knew it was only a matter of time before they were outflanked. Then he saw them moving up cannons, which they had somehow managed to bring ashore. He glanced around and saw British regulars running further up the river to ford it, reach their rear and cut them off. Soon the enemy would force a landing on the lake behind him. It didn't look like the Major was coming with reinforcements, and any militia there were had run off with the first determined volley from the British. He and the small force of regulars were alone and about to be overwhelmed.

Just when Nate was about to give up hope, there was the roar of a cannon, followed by another. A wide swath had been cut in the mass of red coats rushing at them up the river bank. Nate turned to see two of their own guns mounted on the south shore, at its closest proximity to the British landing site, manned by a group of Veteran Exempts. Nate almost saluted the hardy old veterans of the last war, but he was too busy fighting off those who were still coming.

He could hear the pops of their muskets and see puffs of smoke as they fired, all of them seeming aimed at him. The sound of wood and stone splitting and splintering filled the air, along with the all too frequent sound like a buzzing insect as a musket ball whizzed by his ear. It was time to move, but there were no officers in sight. His sergeant was behind a building praying out loud. His lieutenant, who was not with them when they ran back to defend the village, was nowhere to be seen.

Nate looked around him. Fifty yards behind his small force was a square, two-story brick house with a stout four foot stone wall around it. It sat on a slight rise, and overlooked a flat field between it and the bridge. It would make a good defensive position if they could get to it in one piece.

His lanky friend from Maine, despite his vow to desert first chance he had, was still by Nate's side.

"Tom, take those men with you and station them at the stone wall," ordered Nate, pointing to a group of ten regulars and then behind him at the brick house. "Give me a covering fire when you get there, will you?"

While his friend led the men back to the house, Nate gathered the rest, including militiamen and the sergeant, who were all standing about with frightened faces. It looked as if they were ready to stampede to the rear, which would have been suicidal.

"You men," he shouted. "Fall back with me when I tell you." His eyes fell on those who seemed about ready to flee, his rifle pointed in their direction. "Wait! Keep down." His voice boomed. Everyone did as he commanded.

At that moment a covering fire rang out from behind the stone wall.

"Now!" he yelled, and led the men back as the covering fire continued. As he ran, he saw one of his men throw up his arms and fall. The man lay still with his arms straight over his head. Nate bent to help him, but the man was already dead, a bullet in the back of his head. Nate put his ear to the man's mouth. He was not breathing. He gulped and kept moving, making sure the rest of the men made it back alive. He was the last to leap over the wall as bullets pinged off the stone. Soon the British were swarming across the bridge.

Nate managed to stage an orderly retreat that kept most of the men alive and the British at bay, until they were quite a bit south of the city near the Salmon River, where they were met by more militia and the Major. He, instead of coming to their rescue, had taken the rest of his 120 man force and retreated the seven miles back to the settlement. The British, who had stopped pursuing them at nightfall, now had complete control of the village, which they had begun to burn, as well as any ships they found anchored in the bay. Nate and his comrades could see the reflection of the fire from the lake several miles away.

It was a sad day for America, but especially for Private Nate Peters. He had not only watched many of his comrades and friends die, but had seen men fall dead at the end of his own musket, men he had killed in the prime of their lives, far from their homes and loved ones. He wondered if the four or five men he had shot still lay dead in the field or under some bloodied blanket. He especially remembered the expression on one man's face he had killed at close range just across the bridge from him, as he looked Nate in the eyes and died … the anger and surprise

… the hurt and despair. The thoughts and images of war haunted him long into the night and made sleep impossible.

Chapter 10

Village of Plattsburgh, NY, Early October 1813

That hot day in late July on the bridge had changed Jesse's life in ways he could hardly imagine. It's funny how a simple decision to take his friend shooting could result in such far reaching consequences, consequences Jesse was only now beginning to deal with. One had to be careful for what one wished, for Jesse had gotten his wish to shoot a redcoat.

It had all happened so easily, as if it had been ordained and Jesse was just playing the part written out for him. He couldn't get the events of that day out of his mind. They played repeatedly in slow-motion detail.

They had left the crick and headed back to the village along the lake road to the north bank of the Saranac River, where Daniel noticed a squadron of ships in the bay as they were crossing the bridge.

"Hey, look," he said, pointing eastward toward the bay, into which the river emptied a short distance away. "Look at all the ships. The fleet must be back."

Jesse followed his friend's gaze and saw several large ships anchored in the bay, along with gunboats and dozens of large rowboats with sails that the French called bateaux. The scene just didn't look right. Something was out of place, especially the Canadian galleys. Then he noticed there were no American flags. Instead, another flag was waving over the ships, different, but somehow recognizable. Jesse's mind refused to accept the obvious.

Exactly as everyone had been predicting for weeks, the British had finally landed. Jesse watched in disbelief from the middle of the bridge, as men started lowering boats from the ships. Soon after that, men in red coats began swarming down rope ladders into the boats like baby spiders out of a hole. Jesse and his friend stared in disbelief.

"They're our men, aren't they?" asked Daniel, as the redcoats began to row toward the shore.

"I don't think so," replied Jesse. "That's the Union Jack those ships are flying. They're British."

They stood there mesmerized as the ships' boats, thirty marines in each one, followed by larger boats and bateaux, started ferrying hundreds of men to shore.

"We better go tell someone," suggested Daniel. "We better get out of here."

Jesse said nothing but watched the scene unfold like a dream before him. Soon the lead boat reached the shore followed by a dozen others. Their occupants jumped out and started forming up on a small circular beach at the mouth of the river, only fifty yards from the bridge where Jesse and his friend Daniel were standing.

Jesse had been rooted to the spot in shock. He couldn't have left that bridge if it had been on fire. He couldn't run away when his town was being invaded by redcoats, no matter how scared he was. He hardly heard his friend shouting for him to come away, although the day was as quiet as the grave and Danny was standing right next to him. Even though it was the reasonable thing to do, Jesse couldn't run. His outrage overcame his fear.

He noticed a tall man in a brilliant red uniform with gleaming brass buckles and spotless white trousers, who appeared to be giving commands. His sword was raised above his head as he led his men up and along the river bank. It was obvious he was the leader. Jesse's heart began to beat rapidly. He had one ball left. This was an opportunity that he had dreamed of since he first heard war had been declared. He had a chance to actually shoot a redcoat! He could vaguely hear his friend's entreaties to leave the bridge, which seemed eminently reasonable, but something clicked in his brain and he steeled himself for the act.

"Come on, Jesse. What are you doing?" yelled Daniel in alarm. Jesse, still as if in a trance, took the lone ball out of his pouch and loaded his musket, ramming in some powder as well. Then he slowly raised his rifle and aimed it in the direction of the assembling soldiers.

"Just like shooting snakes," observed Jesse, pointing the barrel of the gun at his target. He had no thought of the consequences of his act. The chance to shoot a redcoat was just too much for him to resist, that and the rage at seeing these foreign invaders strutting about on his turf. What were they doing here anyway? Who did they think they were? Who did they think they were dealing with, a bunch of yellow possums? Did they think we Americans would just roll over and die, or bow and kiss their boots? Someone was going to pay, come hell or high water. Come what may, someone was going to learn a lesson. That he might be the one to learn the lesson never occurred to Jesse. The "come what may", should have given him some pause, made him think about the wisdom of his actions. But what could be wiser than to shoot the leader of the redcoat invaders? It might make them think twice before they invaded another man's country.

No one seemed to notice him, the British below too intent on the few American defenders who were beginning to show up on the southern bank of the river. Sporadic musket fire could be heard from both banks. The officer was leading a detachment up the embankment to the top of the hill overlooking the river and just downstream from where Jesse and Daniel were standing on the bridge. Daniel was silent, his mouth open in mid-sentence as he stood looking at his friend in horror. He wanted to run, but his legs had turned to stone. He was riveted to Jesse's fate, like a lamb at a stake.

A lone shot rang out and the magnificent looking man in red with gleaming gold braid and a tall black hat crumpled to the ground. The boys stood transfixed at the sight as his men rushed to the fallen officer's side. Jesse stood stiff as a statue, his gun still raised and pointed where the fallen man had stood.

"Up there! Look, on the bridge!" someone yelled, as others pointed in Jesse's direction.

"The shot came from up there on the bridge," said another. "Look, there's the culprit now."

A shot rang out and then another, splintering the bridge near where Jesse stood. Soon the mini-balls where tearing into the wooden structure all around them as they ran for cover. Daniel ducked screaming and ran for the opposite end of the bridge as the bullets tore up the wood planking just inches behind him.

Jesse dove for cover behind a fencepost, rolling on his shoulder to break his fall, a move he had developed playing Indians with his cousin. It stood him in good stead this day, for the part of the bridge where he had just been standing was so riddled with bullets the railing fell off. He laid flat on his stomach, hugging the ground. Peeking up over the rise he was laying on, he peered in the direction of the British. He expected them to be rushing up to the bridge to finish the job, but they were preoccupied with a group of about forty or fifty regulars and as many militia, who had arrived on the other side of the river. It was just the opportunity Jesse needed.

"Danny, are you all right?" he whispered loudly toward the other end of the bridge. "Danny, can you hear me?" There was no reply, only the increasing pops of musket fire a short way further down the river as the two forces confronted each other.

Jesse crawled across the bridge on his hands and knees, his empty musket all but forgotten. He couldn't believe the damage the bridge had sustained, splintered and bullet-ridden, railings shot off and posts chewed like beaver logs. He felt a tremendous sense of concern for his friend. He called out his name again, louder, but nothing came back but the popping of the musket fire.

"Danny! Danny! Are you all right?" he yelled, standing up and running the rest of the way to the other end of the bullet-splintered structure. His friend was nowhere to be seen. Jesse was shocked at the pitiful lack of cover at this end of the bridge, which seemed to be even more shot up than the opposite end. He looked around frantically for his friend. Then he glanced down the embankment at the far side of the road, where the land formed a small gully before rising back up a hill. There at the bottom of the grass-covered ditch lay his friend, looking for all the world like a small broken doll. Jesse tried to call his name, but all that came out was a choking sob. He tumbled down the slope and fell on his knees at his friend's side.

Jesse's life had been a living hell ever since that fateful day.

There was nothing he could do for his poor friend, whose small body was riddled with bullets. Soon a fierce battle was raging all about him as both sides fought for the bridge. Jesse did the only thing he could think of to protect his friend, and covered Daniel with his body to shield him from any further harm. Luckily, they went unnoticed in the confusion and smoke of battle. When the British finally drove off the small American force contesting the bridge and started to reconnoiter the area, they discovered Jesse and his dead friend.

Danny had paid the ultimate price for Jesse's folly. Jesse tried to play dead, lying atop his fallen friend, but when one of the British soldiers poked him with his bayonet, Jesse yelled and jumped up, more afraid they would stab Danny, who could feel no more pain, than for himself.

"Leave us alone!" he yelled, clinging to Daniel. "Can't you see he's hurt?"

"He's not hurt," said another soldier, after prying Jesse from the corpse and examining the body. "He's dead."

At first the soldiers seemed to be sorry for Jesse, at the obvious distress he showed for his friend, but after awhile one of the officers started asking questions.

"Are you one of the boys who were up here shooting at us?"

"Yeah, that's him," said another. "He's the one that shot the Major."

At that point the soldiers turned hostile. Jesse was taken at bayonet point to the landing commander's Headquarters on a promontory overlooking the bay on the north head of the river. Jesse recognized the house, a long, white two-story structure with green shutters, although he had seldom ventured down to this part of the village. It had a well-tended front garden and a white picket fence. There were rooms in the back for lodging and an unpainted stable in the rear, with a large field of short grass on the left where some soldiers were picketed. One of his classmates had said it was owned by one of the Delords, a rich and influential family in the village.

Jesse waited under guard in the large yard at the side of the house. It was crowded with bivouacking soldiers. Some were pitching small tents. Some were roasting various items over open fires. Some leaned against their weapons eyeing him with amusement or anger as the case may be. Many already knew who he was and what he had done and were not happy to see him. Finally, he was ushered in before the commander.

Colonel John Murray did not like Americans to begin with and had relished his assignment to take an 800 man amphibious force and strike some terror into the hearts of the local inhabitants

99

just across the border. It was more than time to make the Americans pay for their unprovoked and dastardly invasion attempt. The risk was minimal, since their new American general was safely ensconced across the Lake in Burlington with no navy in sight. Murray's fleet captain, Pring, had sole control of the lake with his two recently captured brigs now under an English flag.

He was devastated at the news of the death of his young son-in-law, and was in the act of writing a letter to the young man's soon to be grieving parents. He dreaded what the news would mean to his own daughter, who he did not intend to inform. He had just finished his letter when news of the capture of the suspected murderer was brought to him.

"Are you sure he's the one?" he had asked, as Jesse was escorted into the room. One piece of information had followed so closely on the heels of the other that the British Colonel did not believe his good fortune. These Americans were going to pay for their insolence and their treachery. His son-in-law was not the only one killed that day, although the English quickly won the battle and scattered the small force of regulars and militia defending the village.

"Yes, Sir," said Jesse's escort, an officer who was in the fallen young Major's regiment. "Several of the men identified him, Sir, including myself. He and his friend were standing on the bridge. He still had his rifle pointed in our direction when we spotted him."

"Are you the one who killed my son-in-law?" asked Murray, glaring at Jesse.

"I don't know what you're talking about. Your men killed my friend. He never hurt anyone."

"You and your friend are murderers. You killed a very brave and promising young officer."

"I didn't kill nobody," lied Jesse, falling back on his number one defense.

"I have eyewitnesses who say you did."

"Well, they're lying. Our men were shooting at you fellows from across the river. Anyone could have shot him. You're invading our village. What do you expect?"

Murray's eyes flashed. He whipped his sword out of its scabbard with a sharp ring, and brought the flat side of it across

Jesse's face so fast that he had no time to react. The force of the blow snapped his head back, making him lose his balance and fall backward against a chair. He was both hurt and humiliated as he slowly got back to his feet holding his bleeding cheek. The wound would soon heal but he'd carry a small scar to remind him of the incident. It would be just big enough to be noticeable and make him look distinguished, not to mention tougher. Jesse burned with indignation as he rubbed his cheek.

"I'll have none of your insolence, you little gutter-snipe," the British Colonel had said to him. "The man you so wantonly killed is worth a hundred of you."

"We should put him before a firing squad if you ask me, Sir," said the escorting officer, "for what he's done."

"How would you like that, boy?" said the Colonel, standing over Jesse with his sword still drawn. Jesse feared for his life but refused to cower. "Where are the military stores?" asked Murray, continuing his interrogation. He had already found the boy guilty of murdering his son-in-law, now he was going to find out what he knew. "Where's the arsenal?"

Jesse answered in a low voice, "I don't know."

"We'll find out anyway," said the colonel. "It will make things go easier for you if you tell me."

"I'll never help you," said Jesse.

"Oh, yes you will, one way or another," said Murray. In spite of himself, the colonel admired the boy's courage, as well as his marksmanship. From what he had been told it was quite a remarkable feat. Still, he had a mission to accomplish and he would use whatever means necessary to achieve it.

"You think you're brave, don't you?" said Murray. "Shooting a man like that from a distance, with no warning. Do you want to see what a great thing you've done with your irresponsible actions?"

Jesse didn't know what he meant, but it sounded like in school when he was about to get into trouble, only worse. Murray didn't wait for an answer.

"Come with me," he said to the lieutenant, who with a guard and their prisoner followed the Colonel out the side of the building to a long gray stable in the rear. The stable door was open and Jesse could see a line of bodies covered with sheets lying on the hay-covered floor. He froze in alarm, but was prodded forward by his guard's bayonet.

"See what you did with your treacherous act," said the Colonel, his voice choking with emotion as he threw back one of the sheets to uncover his dead son-in-law, a small round hole where his right eye should have been. "You've cut down my poor daughter's dear husband in the prime of his life." He stopped, overcome with emotion.

The bullet had entered the dead man's brain, killing him instantly. He didn't look so big or impressive to Jesse now. In fact, he felt kind of sorry for the man, like when he had shot his first prize buck. But he had cut off the deer's head anyway and hung it on his bedroom wall. He felt just as much pride that he had caused the enemy so much trouble, but he was certain they were going to execute him any minute, especially the way the colonel was carrying on.

"You'll pay for what you did," Murray said finally. "You better tell me what I want to know. Or do you want to see more of the results of your handiwork?"

The colonel walked over to another sheet, smaller than the rest, and pulled it back suddenly. Jesse's heart stopped beating. He could no longer breathe. He wanted to close his eyes but couldn't. He could only stare at the pitiful figure lying there. It was Daniel. He was covered with blood and shot a dozen times. Yet his face had the peaceful look of an angel. His blue eyes were closed as if asleep. His long blond hair was curled along his forehead.

"Daniel!" cried Jesse, and then collapsed.

That had been two months ago but the memory of it brought him back to that moment faster than the speed of light. Then it was happening all over again, and he couldn't breathe or speak. He was getting better at snapping out of it and avoiding the thoughts, but not entirely.

The British had threatened to shoot him in front of a firing squad. In the end however, they were more interested in information than killing another local youth. One dead boy was enough as far as Murray was concerned, for he was more intent on plunder than murder. When Jesse recovered from his fainting spell he found himself back in the main house on a small divan. He was ordered to take them to his parent's house. When he explained he lived twenty-miles away and was staying with a family in town, he was ordered to take them there.

Jesse waited outside as the Colonel and several other officers went into the house and confronted the Gordons. He didn't know what they said, but when it was all over the Gordons had agreed to help the British in exchange for Jesse's safe return, obviously threatened not only with his execution but with others as well. Shortly after that one of Mister Gordon's friends arrived, a Mister Ackley, and went into the house with the British.

Jesse had waited outside the whole time, wondering what was happening. He didn't like the fact that they were all in there together talking. A short while later, a number of soldiers were sent running off in different directions, as if a whole batch of orders were being carried out based on what was being said in the house. It made Jesse very uneasy. He burned with curiosity but there was nothing he could do.

Much later that evening, after not eating since early that day, Jesse was finally released to the Gordons' custody, though the British posted a guard outside the house to make sure he stayed, just in case the Colonel changed his mind or found out the intelligence he had gained that night was untrue. The information he obtained, however, was well worth the life of one little gutter-snipe.

That evening as he tried to sleep, Jesse could hear the sound of explosions, as powder and ball were shot off like fire-crackers. The British had found the critical military stores and arsenals, and had set them and other military buildings on fire, after carrying off everything they could. It was a big haul. The British had Jesse's guardians and their friend to thank.

They finally left, after sacking and burning the town – even though Murray had promised they would do no such thing. His army continued to pillage and burn all the way back to Canada, from Cumberland Head and Point Au Roche, to Chazy and Swanton in Vermont, causing thousands of dollars worth of damage. The militia and regulars had been chased all the way south to the Salmon River and beyond. Wade Hampton, the General of the northern army only sixty miles away in Burlington and aware of the attack, lifted not a finger to help the besieged town.

Jesse had gone back to his home in the mountains west of the village as soon as he could, taking off one night soon after the British left. By then a letter had been discovered that could only have fallen out of Murray's pocket, describing how the invading forces had found and destroyed the enemy's stores and arsenals, and mentioning who had helped them. One of the names listed was a Mister Ackley. Jesse's host Mister Gordon was implicated as well. They had both been arrested and brought down to Albany for trial in September, but were all found not guilty for lack of evidence. No one would come forward to testify against them, and the letter alone was not enough to incriminate them. The only real witness, Jesse, was in places unknown.

Jesse's homecoming was less than auspicious. He thought his father would be proud of what he did, but he was horrified when Jesse told him the story. Jesse didn't mention his best friend had been killed or his suspicions about the Gordons, although he insisted he wasn't going back no matter how hard his father whipped him. The thing that got Mike Lebow the most upset was that he had paid up next year's tuition in advance. If Jesse wasn't going back to school Mike would just as soon have the British take him. He wasn't going to have him loafing about his place all winter, especially now that the school term had started.

Then one day the lieutenant who had helped Jesse get into the Academy in the first place came for an unexpected visit.

"What can I do for you, Mister Curtis?" said Mike Lebow, greeting the Lieutenant at the door. "I wasn't expecting to see you."

"No, Mister Lebow. I hope I'm not disturbing you. I just heard what happened and wanted to come here personally to commend your son for his bravery under fire at the bridge. His action in killing the commander of the invasion helped give the defenders time to form up and rally, and put up a stout resistance. One boy was killed and it was only a miracle that saved your own son's life."

"He didn't tell me no boy got killed," said his father looking balefully at his son.

"Your son's a hero, Mister Lebow. He's just the type of young man we need in this country's new army, although he's still a couple years too young. I'd like to see that he finishes his education and perhaps becomes an officer."

"I'm not going back with the Gordons!" shouted Jesse. "I hate them."

"That's understandable, Jesse," replied the Lieutenant. "They've gone to live in Canada with Mister Ackley. You can stay with my wife Jane and me if you like. Or I can find you another family to live with. After word of what you did got out there are plenty of people who want to take you in. What do you say Mister Lebow? Jesse?"

His father agreed immediately, for that's what he wanted to see, Jesse back in school and out of his hair. Jesse wasn't so sure. He didn't want to go back to school, but he really didn't have many options open to him. His best friend was dead. He felt empty and old, crying every day for the loss, unable to tell anyone of his feelings. Sam was far away somewhere. Jesse didn't even know where he was. He had no job, nowhere to go. Only his mother and siblings were glad to see him. To everyone else he was a burden and a bother. Even his Plattsburgh hosts had turned out to be collaborators and traitors who had had to leave the country. He felt totally alone and unloved. Perhaps school wasn't so bad after all, especially if he got to stay with Lieutenant Curtis.

"I guess so," said Jesse slowly, "if I can stay with you and Missus Curtis."

"Then it's settled," said the lieutenant, another future officer all but recruited.

Chapter 11

Plattsburgh Bay, NY, Early October 1813

Unknown to Jesse, his cousin was only a few miles away. He had finally gotten his wish and was on one of Macdonough's ships, but it had been a circuitous and painfully slow route. Until a few months earlier, he had still been festering in Whitehall, refitting a few of the new ships Macdonough had managed to purchase and for which his employer, Mister John Nichols, had been contracted.

Sam had worked through the summer perfecting his craft, laying keels and setting masts. He had accepted his employer's offer and was a crew boss with twenty or thirty men working under him on any given day. With his increased authority came the opportunity to help man the ships on their test cruises. There he learned the basic seamanship skills one would need to make one useful on a sailing ship. His arms, already strong from twelve hour days of hammering and lifting, grew even stronger. His hands were calloused from pulling on ropes and hawsers. He was earning himself a reputation as a leader, especially for someone so young.

They had heard about the invasion of Plattsburgh. He was in Burlington at the time, still not with the navy but at least out of Whitehall and on a ship. He was on the new 20-gun sloop they had just fitted with armaments in Vergennes. Because it required additional carpentry work before it was ready, Sam was taken along on the voyage to Burlington where Macdonough and the fleet were waiting to complete the work.

He was with them when the British attacked soon after their invasion of the village across the lake. Pring's fleet appeared to the north one morning on the open lake and swept into the harbor, cannons blazing. Two of the invasion fleet were the 11-gun sloops captured by the British earlier that summer. Sam was standing on the new ship, hammer in hand, staring out at the enemy in the harbor, three sloops and as many gunboats and galleys. It was like a scene from out of one of his picture books.

"You better get down from there," said a sailor who was showing him the ropes. "You're a nice big target standing up there."

Sam ignored him until a cannon ball landed in the lake not ten feet in front of him, skipping across the waves and showering him with water. He ducked for cover. It grew hot and heavy after that and Sam, although doing nothing but keeping his head down and undercover, was right in the middle of it.

Macdonough and his fleet although outgunned, were not unprepared for the encounter, having received intelligence from Williams' scouts that the British squadron had headed their way, while the retreating British army marched north wreaking havoc as they went. The Royal Navy was intent on doing a little of their own destruction, but they'd have to get by Macdonough's defenses first.

He not only had his own ships' guns, including the new 20-gun brig Sam was on, but he also had several batteries of Wade Hampton's artillery.

A fierce artillery duel ensued, as Pring's ships pounded the harbor defenses and more and more of Hampton's artillery began to join the fray. Soon there was heavy fire from a nearby hilltop that turned the tide of battle. Eventually the British were driven off, but not before they delivered some punishment of their own.

The ship Sam was on held its own, even though only partly crewed, and that by men inexperienced with the new ship and each other. Sam helped the best he could, following the orders bellowed at him by the Boson's mate. He did this through the whole battle ignoring the chaos and mayhem around him, but it was after the battle that Sam really distinguished himself.

When the battle was over and the British ships headed north to make their way unmolested back to their base in Canada's Isle aux Noix, Sam looked around. As the smoke cleared what he saw appalled him. Men were lying on the deck all around him, their blood and body parts everywhere. He was half deaf from the sound of the loud cannonading, but wished he had been blinded instead, for what his eyes beheld would haunt him the rest of his life. Truly this is what hell must be like. Instead of fleeing from the horror, however, Sam was drawn to those in the midst of it to see if he could somehow alleviate their suffering and pain.

He immediately went to the closest injured sailor and tried to staunch the flow of blood. He could see the man was going to die. There was nothing he could do. So he made him as comfortable as possible and went to the next, a gunner with a large jagged splinter of wood close to an artery in his thigh. Sam calmed the man and carefully removed the knifelike object, cleaning and binding up the wound as best as possible. As he moved among the injured tending their wounds, he corralled those recovering from the shock of battle and got them to help carry the wounded to safety. At one point he was working next to the ship's surgeon.

"Who is that lad?" the surgeon asked one of the crewmen.

"I don't know, Sir," said the mate, a middy newly assigned in Vergennes. "He came with the ship when it sailed up from Whitehall. He's a carpenter, I think. He stayed on in Vergennes to finish some work on the way up. They call him Sam, if I remember right. He works for the shipbuilder."

"Good lad," commented the surgeon, making note of the young carpenter.

That had been several months ago. Now Sam and the fleet were in Plattsburgh, still in support of General Wade Hampton's offensive, which many in the navy, including Macdonough, doubted would ever leave the village. Even though Sam was technically still too young to join the Navy - he would be eighteen in November - he was being sponsored by the chief surgeon himself and was now a ship's carpenter with the possibility of becoming an assistant ship's surgeon in the future. His dream had come true, but it had come at a terrible price.

He wondered what had become of Jesse. When Sam had first arrived back in the village, in early August, over a year now after he and Jesse's last escapade, he had looked his cousin up at Plattsburgh Academy, and was told Jesse had gone home. When Sam asked his father about his cousin during his last visit to town a little while later, he replied that Jesse had gone home for a spell, but he was no longer there.

Sam had little time to worry about his cousin, however, who unbeknownst to him had recently returned to the Academy and was enjoying his new life with the Curtis's.

Plattsburgh, which had been all but deserted in August, now seemed to be the hub of the universe, with men and supplies arriving by the ship and wagonload every day, as Hampton, with Plattsburgh now as his base, built up his invasion force.

Everyone wondered when he would finally move. It had to be soon, for the well-respected General Izard had recently arrived in town and everyone knew he meant business. Izard had been ordered to the area to oversee operations by the new Secretary of War, General John Armstrong. Maybe he could sort out the difficulties caused by the animosity between Hampton and his counterpart in the western theater, Major General James Wilkinson. They were supposed to coordinate their actions, but this was proving difficult, considering how much each man hated the other. None of this was Sam's concern, however.

"How are my galleys coming, young Sam?" asked the Master Commandant. Sam was still not used to having the commander himself address him thus and found it difficult to answer.

"Good, good, Sir," he stammered. "They should be ready in time for the General's invasion."

"Oh, I'm sure of that," answered Macdonough. "They could be completed in December and still be ready in time, the way the General proceeds. Do you know he's having his men build a road all the way to the enemy?"

"I've heard it said, Sir, but that's been finished, Sir."

"Then let us hope the General will move soon. Oh, by the way, I have some news of your cousin, young Mister Lebow."

"What, Jesse? You've heard something about Jesse?"

"Yes, he's quite a local hero by the sound of it. Singlehandedly shot the commander of the invasion force, with a single shot from fifty yards."

"That's my cousin," said Sam proudly.

"Well, he's lucky to still be alive. A young boy who was with him was killed and your cousin was captured. They were going to put him in front of a firing squad. I guess the man he killed, some Major, was the commanding general's son-in-law."

"That figures," said Sam, expelling his breath loudly.

"I guess he escaped somehow, although no one seems to know precisely how."

"My cousin is a very ingenious, clever little rascal. He can be downright dangerous when he gets riled."

109

"I guess so young, Sammy. That runs in your family, eh?"

"Yes, Sir. I reckon so," said Sam.

"Well, don't worry. I hear he's back in school and doing well."

"Thank you, Sir," replied Sam, relieved that everything was okay with Jesse. He made a mental note to visit him first chance he got.

Just then one of Macdonough's officers ran up with a dispatch.

"Sir, this just came in for you," he said, handing Macdonough a small sealed envelope.

"What's this, orders?" conjectured the commander, opening and reading the message. "Ah, no such luck. The British are raiding the Champlain area." He turned to Sam and looked at the almost completed galleys. "Get these boats finished, Mister Turner. If the British come again I want to be ready for them."

"Yes, Sir," said Sam saluting and jumping back onto the nearest galley to urge his men on. "We'll be ready, Sir."

Chapter 12

Chateaugay, NY, Late October 1813

General Wade Hampton, despite most of the good money against him, had finally started his offensive and moved his 4000 man force along his new road north to Chateaugay, nestled in the northern foothills of the Adirondacks next to the river of the same name. They had passed through the western mountains on the way to the river, unbeknownst to Nate Peters only a short distance from Sam Turner's home.

Nate had been promoted to corporal along with his friend Tom, who still talked of deserting, but now with more urgency. Nate's fast thinking and leadership at the bridge and during his orderly, fighting retreat had been noticed, even if it had been downplayed by the Major in charge at the time. Still, Hampton hardly took the time to sign the promotion papers and would hear nothing of medals, not for retreating, no matter what the odds and circumstances. Regardless, Nate was proud of what he had done and knew that if given the chance he would rise even higher in this man's army. Now he was helping his sergeant lead a platoon across the border from Chateaugay into Canada.

Nate felt emboldened by the size of their force and the number of large guns they had, more than he had seen in any one place and on the move before. From the intelligence they had from their Indian scouts they faced no more than thirteen hundred French Canadian and English militia, and a few dozen Indians. This time things would be different.

Nate was looking forward to settling the score with the British for what they had done at Plattsburgh. The extensive damage was still being repaired. The burnt houses and barns were being rebuilt. The lost livestock and property had been replenished. People were beginning to return to their homes, but the scars of war were still fresh, as was the humiliation felt at fleeing before the enemy, no matter how outnumbered.

It was late in the day. They had formed a skirmish line and were probing through a pine wood in advance of the main army.

Shortly, the sound of muskets erupted further down the line. First a single pop followed by another, then more in increasing succession, until a steady volley moved up the line toward Nate, getting louder as it came. He yelled for his men to hit the ground just as the balls started tearing through the pine needles all around him. They had found the enemy. They were directly in front of them.

Soon the blood-curdling yelp of an Indian could be heard, far too close for Nate's comfort, making his hair stand on end. This was probably as close to fighting Indians as he would ever get, and he wasn't so sure he liked it. He cocked his gun and listened, looking around the large pine tree he was standing behind for any sign of the enemy. There was none. Then suddenly, a gleam of brass in the waning light, followed by another war cry, then a rush of color and gunfire as the enemy rushed his detachment through the trees. Militia, regulars and Indians all mixed together, all of them it seemed intent on killing Nate and his men.

"Fire!" he yelled, leveling his musket at the first attacker he saw in range, a Canadian militiaman with his rifle aimed in his direction. Nate's musket fired an instant before the other man's ball whizzed by his head. Nate's ball hit the man dead center at the same time, knocking him over backward so hard his feet came straight up in the air when he fell. Nate had always been taught to aim at the largest part of the target, not the head. Still, the musket ball whizzing by his head gave him pause. He didn't have long to linger.

He saw a flash and a streak of white out of the corner of his eye and raised his rifle instinctively just in time to ward off the blow of a long saber wielded by an officer on horseback. The officer slashed at him again, and once more Nate warded off the blow with the barrel of his gun, jabbing his long bayonet at the man and horse in turn, to hold them at bay. His opponent attacked again with added fury but was shot off his horse by one of Nate's men, giving him time to duck behind a boulder to reload his musket.

The attack was ebbing. He shot a few more of the enemy, who were pulling back and forming their own line behind the trees in front of him. Nate and his men had made a successful stand against a determined attack. Now it was their turn. With their obvious superior force the outcome was already determined, or so thought Nate and his men.

The tide of battle was turning. Nate and his company, still in the front line, had been steadily pushing back the enemy, even though it had long since grown dark. There was a full moon, and more of Hampton's army kept arriving on the scene and were shuttled to the front. Nate had already organized a flanking movement along the river to cut the Canadians off or force them to retreat against the overwhelming numbers. Despite his low rank, he was one of the few on the field who had any experience in actual combat, Hampton keeping most of the more experienced officers close to him in the rear.

"What are you doing?" asked a young lieutenant riding up on horseback. "Where are you taking these men? Who told you to organize this party?"

"Sorry, Sir, but there was no one else around, and I, well, I was, we were going to try and use the river road here to flank the enemy and come up on their rear, Sir. There's a ford a short way down this bank here."

"Who are you with, Corporal?"

"Simond's regiment, the 6th, Sir, but..."

"I have orders from the general himself to pull these men back. That includes you Corporal. Now fall back."

"But, Sir, there can't be more than one or two hundred of them in our front. Our information tells us there are not more than a thousand of them total, many of them disgruntled Frenchmen."

"Is that so, Corporal? And where did you get this information?"

"From the Indian scouts, Sir. I heard Mister Williams say so himself when he talked to the Major."

"Well, I'd just as soon believe a mule as some thieving Indian," said the lieutenant, looking down at Nate from his horse. "We have different information Corporal, and our information comes from reliable sources. They say this is just a diversion to lead us forward into a trap. The general is smarter than that. Now follow orders and pull back."

Nate was dumbfounded. "But..."

"Pull back, Corporal, and that's an order!" yelled the lieutenant riding off to repeat the order further down the line.

"That's ridiculous," muttered Nate to no one in particular.

"I told you what you were up against, Nate," observed his friend Tom. "You can't win. That fellow would just as soon spit on you as look at you."

"So what do you want me to do, desert?" asked Nate. "Is that your answer to everything?"

"Why not?" replied his lanky friend from Maine. "More and more of them are doing it. I heard out of that last group of 200, 24 deserted on the way here. They don't even wait 'til they get here before running off."

"Ah, Tom, you're just making things worse. We actually have a chance to win here. We're pushing them back. Our scouts tell us we outnumber them. All we need is a general with a little nerve and we can finally win for a change. Take some of their land, see how they like it. Instead, they've got us retreating."

"Ours is not to reason why. Ours is but to obey, that is if you want to stay here. I've got other ideas, and now's the perfect time." Tom looked around. "No one would miss us if we just slipped off and disappeared, just another wartime statistic."

Nate didn't answer but watched the men sullenly begin to move to the rear. Most of the firing had stopped along with their offensive.

"What are you waiting for?" inquired his friend, "More humiliating defeats? Or maybe a stray musket ball with your name on it?"

Nate wasn't sure if he could take another cowardly retreat, but he wasn't about to desert either. "Do what you want, but as long as I'm breathing I'll do my duty to my country."

"It's a job, Nate. Twenty bucks a month, not some romantic notion for God and country. You're naive if you think anyone cares about that."

"That's what you think, but you're wrong. I care. As long as there's people out there that want to take what's ours, deprive us of our liberty, invade our sovereign soil, people like me will care and fight and die to defend it. You can run if you want, and who knows, maybe you can hide where they won't find you, but don't think they won't hunt for you. And if and when they find do you they'll put you in front of a firing squad."

"Oh yeah, what about the hundreds who are deserting every day, you don't hear about them being shot."

"I wouldn't worry about them if I were you. I'd worry with your luck you'd be the first one. It's not worth it Tom. This is just a momentary set back. The General's just regrouping before the big push. We'll be in Montreal by tomorrow."

By the end of the following day, however, Hampton's army along with Nate and his platoon had retreated 20 miles back to Four-Corners at Olmstead, Quebec on the border. There was virtually no force of equal size opposing them, yet they were returning to Plattsburgh defeated. Nate was not the only one disappointed.

Later the following day, after their humiliating return to Plattsburgh, Nate was sitting in the 'Ark' with his sergeant and another man who was introduced to him as the Indian agent Eleazer Williams. Nate recognized the man from around town and knew he was somehow connected with the army. His friend Tom had never returned to camp and was presumed missing.

"If Hampton had listened to you all this could have been avoided," said Nate's sergeant to their guest. "We could all be in Montreal now. That man just doesn't listen."

"I do not know what his problem is," said Eleazer Williams. "He would not listen to a thing I said. I have never known one so stubborn and pig-headed. I don't know how many times I told him there was not more than thirteen hundred or so militia with a few regulars in front of him. He insisted on believing there were several times that many and that the whole Indian nation had risen up before him. Why does he not listen?"

"Because he is pig-headed, like you said," said the sergeant, eliciting a laugh from Nate who was a bit giddy sitting in such esteemed company. "He insisted on listening to the advice of a few old cronies from his New Orleans days, who know nothing of the situation here or the local Indians. Their information is so contrary to good sound intelligence you'd think they were working for the enemy."

"Well, they could not be more effective if they were," said Williams. "Hampton was completely unnerved by what they were telling him. He kept insisting the attack on Montreal had been called off even though Izard's messages said it was not and my

115

scouts told him the way was only lightly defended. That there were not near the forces he was estimating and not nearly as formidable."

"Even worse," said the sergeant. "I was with them when he got General Wilkinson's order to join him out west. Wilkinson was counting on him to either create a strong diversion here or join up with him there, but Hampton did neither. He ran back to Plattsburgh. Now Wilkinson will have to try and take Montreal by himself."

"'Tis a pity," said Williams.

Nate listened to the conversation and wondered how they knew so much. Sitting close to Williams he could plainly see by his broad features and dark coloring that he was a full-blooded Indian, but his speech and clothing belied that. Nate couldn't put the fact that he was an Indian together with his appearance. Could this well-dressed, well-spoken man have grown up in a longhouse, wearing deerskins and feathers, eating Indian food and speaking a foreign tongue? No wonder Nate was confused.

Eleazer Williams was also confused at times, straddling two worlds as he did – the ancient world of his fathers and the new world of the whites, which he had adopted whole-heartedly. He had learned their language and customs, along with their religion as his father had told him to do. He had even learned to read their "book of books", the bible. He taught it to others, both of his race and outside, for he was a fully ordained Congregational minister. He had done these things because he was told to do them, because there was strength and power in the white man's religion and especially in this book. For the Bible taught his people how to walk with their God, the Great Spirit, He That Is Above All Things, and with that God came the white man's power. So his fathers had said, and so Eleazer believed.

The God of these greedy Americans must be powerful to subdue the great Iroquois nation of his forefathers, and the English they had sided with in the previous war. He had seen what happened to his parents and relatives, neighbors and friends, all dispersed or dead, the few remaining disenfranchised and deprived. He did all he could for his people, but there was still so much left to do. This war did not help things.

Like most of the Native Americans on both sides of the border, Eleazer was ambiguous about the war at best. Most of all he wanted peace, a lasting peace his children and grandchildren could rely on, and he would work along with his Indian and white brothers to make that happen. It was the very ambiguity of the Indians' situation that made Hampton and others like him distrust their information. That same ambiguity, however, made it possible for them to gather that intelligence in the first place. They were the unseen minority, a once proud and mighty people subjugated and poor to the point of no longer being visible to most. So they could obtain critical news of troop arrivals and movements, ordnance and strength, right under the nose of the enemy. That the Indians might also be spying on the Americans had unfortunately also occurred to more than a few, thus Hampton's reluctance to take his scouts' information at face value.

The conversation turned to the state of the army, Wilkinson's offensive, and what was going to happen to Wade Hampton, who had returned home in disgrace.

"Is there not any general in this army who knows how to fight," asked Nate, voicing all their thoughts.

No one answered.

Chapter 13

Western Mountains, District of Champlain, NY, December 1813

Sam and Jesse had finally been reunited. Sam surprised his cousin at the Academy one day after school. To make an added impression Sam had worn his uniform, a blue jacket with striped pants and a wide-brimmed hat.

"Sam!" Jesse exclaimed on seeing his cousin for the first time in over a year. "You've gotten tall. How you been?"

"Fine, Jesse, and you?" said Sam, noticing the scar on his cousin's cheek but saying nothing. "I've heard great things about you. You've gotten quite a reputation as a hero around here."

"Aw, that's nothing," replied Jesse, not wanting to talk about it. "Just people talking, that's all."

"Well, it sounds like you made quite a name for yourself as a marksman and a patriot. They say you killed the commanding general of the invasion force with a single impossible shot."

"It was just a lucky shot, and he was only a Major. No big deal."

"No big deal? They say it singlehandedly almost stopped the attack. They also say a boy was killed and you were captured. Is that where you got the scar?"

Jesse turned red and went deathly still.

"I don't want to talk about it," he said stiffly, putting his head down. "What are you doing here anyway? Where'd you get the uniform? You in the navy or something?"

"Sort of. I'm a carpenter's mate with Macdonough's fleet."

"What?" exclaimed Jesse. "You're in the Navy?"

"Yep. They let me join in November when I turned eighteen."

Jesse should have been excited for his cousin, but he could hardly contain his envy. Here Sam was in the Navy with Macdonough's fleet while he was still in school.

"That's great," muttered Jesse in a subdued voice.

Sam had been struck by the change in his cousin. He seemed so serious and quiet, not like the Jesse of old who would have whooped and howled at his cousin's news, or bragged to high heaven about his exploits. Jesse seemed different, more mature to the point of being almost old for his age. But Sam had also grown during their year apart and had been in battle himself.

"You must be very happy," said Jesse. "It's something you've always wanted. Are you on a ship?"

"No, not yet," said Sam. "The Commander is ordering the building of fifteen new gunboats for the lake. I'll be busy supervising the work down at the docks. I haven't been assigned to a ship yet. It all depends on where they need me."

"You will be, I'm sure," said his younger cousin. "They need good men like you."

Sam asked him about his plans for the Christmas Holiday. Jesse had wanted to spend them with Lieutenant David Curtis and his wife with whom he was now staying while in school, but Curtis's in-laws were visiting for the holidays and there would be no room. Jesse would have also liked to spend Christmas with his family, but his father had rented out his room and told his mother his oldest boy wouldn't be welcomed home for the Holidays. They had enough mouths to feed. Having nowhere else to go, he reluctantly agreed to stay at Sam's after being assured it would be no bother and his aunt and uncle had agreed.

"You can stay in my brother's old room," Sam had said after making plans to pick Jesse up in the wagon the following Tuesday.

It was now Christmas day. They were sitting around a large table at Sam's house with Sam's parents, and his Uncle Bill Carlton and his wife. John Fisher, who was visiting his old comrade in arms from Boston, was also there, as was Sam's other uncle, Captain Ezra Turner. Ezra was his father's younger brother and an officer in the local militia. As usual, despite Sam's mother's objections, they were talking about the war.

"It's a darned shame about General Wilkinson," said Mister Fisher.

"It's all that so called General Wade Hampton's fault," replied Sam's Uncle Ezra. "If he had attacked Montreal as he was

119

ordered or come to James's aid as he was asked, maybe we would have been the victors at Crysler's Farm instead of the losers."

"I hear Hampton has resigned in disgrace to evade arrest," volunteered Sam's father.

"The whole thing is a shame," repeated Benjamin's friend from Boston. "Though I'm not surprised, the two men were rumored to hate each other. Still, it is a black spot upon our nation's reputation. It will only prolong the war and make peace negotiations that much more difficult."

"My advice to you, Sir," said Sam's Uncle Ezra, "is to pay due attention to your arms and ammunition. So they be not far off and fit for hot service at a moment's notice."

"You have to excuse my brother," laughed Benjamin. "He gets carried away sometimes with his duties as a militia Captain. But I'm afraid you and John are both right. Things are going to get more difficult before they get better."

"At least the news from out west is heartening," interjected Sam's Uncle Bill. "What General Harrison and his men did to the British and Indians out at the Thames River will certainly put a damper on their plans out west. The Indians won't be so eager to fight with the English after what we did to their great Indian chief, Tecumseh."

"That was months ago," responded Sam's Uncle Ezra. "Since then things have not gone well. That new General in charge, what's his name, Drummond? The British have re-taken both Ft. George and Niagara. Why just recently they have burned and pillaged several towns on the American side of the border. They massacred people in Lewiston, raping women and killing children."

"Ezra, please," said his wife. "Do you have to talk about such things at the table, and on Christmas Eve of all days?"

"Sorry, Dear," replied her husband. "But these are troubled times and we have to be prepared."

"It was the same in the last war, Dear," Sam's mother said to her husband. "You men can talk after dinner. Let's please not have any more talk of war and killing at my table."

"The turkey is delicious," complemented her sister, Bill's wife, trying to change the subject. "How do you keep it so moist?"

"Ben's mother taught me," answered Catherine. "You roast it in the oven in a big pan and use butter to baste it often. I'll show you sometime."

"I hear you've seen a bit of action, young Sam," noted Mister Fisher. "The British tried to shake things up across the lake, did they?"

"Yes, Sir" replied Sam. "They tried but didn't succeed. We sent them running, although it was touch and go there for a while. They sailed right into the harbor at Burlington and started bombarding us with their 18-pounders. I was on a ship we had just brought up from Vergennes, finishing up some work. A cannonball took a man's head clear off just a few yards from where I was standing. If it wasn't for the heavy army guns up on the hill, we would have had a tough time of it."

"Sammy, please," pleaded his mother in despair.

"Sam pitched right in and helped," replied his father proudly, ignoring his wife's entreaties. This was his house and these were his friends, and if they wanted to talk about the war they darned well would. "He helped them warp the ship back and forth so they could deliver their own broadsides."

"Yet you still wanted to join?" asked the Colonel.

"Yes, Sir. There's nothing like a battle at sea, Sir," said Sam, getting more enthused as he talked. "It was glorious the way they came up with their sails billowing in the wind and their guns blazing, and how they stood toe-to-toe against our defenses firing one broadside after another. What a worthy opponent. To think I stood on the deck of a ship in battle only a few hundred yards from Master Commandant Macdonough himself, one of Preble's boys. It's the stuff of legends, like you read about in books."

"Perhaps they will read about you in a book someday," laughed Mister Fisher with the others.

"We have another hero in our midst," said Sam's father. He had heard it both from Jesse's father and from his younger brother Ezra who was with the handful of defenders that fateful day late last July. "Jesse here is quite the marksman."

Jesse stopped chewing and swallowed hard. He was still trying to digest the news that his favorite bad Indian had been killed out west. It was like his childhood had finally died with the death of the fabled chief Tecumseh. He had dreaded this moment as soon as he saw all the strangers seated at the dinner table, hoping he would stay anonymous in the crowded room. Now he was being asked about the thing he most wanted to avoid discussing.

"Oh?" inquired the Colonel, "And how's that?"

"Do you want to tell them or should I?" asked Sam's father.

"It was no big deal," replied Jesse, helping himself to another serving of potatoes as if they were the most important and interesting thing he had ever seen.

"No big deal!" exclaimed Ben Turner. "800 British regulars landing in Plattsburgh Bay and Jesse, alone, with his musket and a single ball, sitting up on the first bridge shoots the commander of the landing force, a major, as he's leading his men up to the village."

"Shot him right in the eye," said Sam, having heard the story earlier from his friends. "Killed him instantly, didn't it Jesse?"

"Please!" cried Sam's mother looking as if she was about to be ill.

"It's no big deal," repeated Jesse, trying to sink into his seat as far as he could.

"Sounds like quite a shot," replied the Colonel impressed. "We had a few sharpshooters in the regiment back in the Rebellion."

"And I was glad we did," added Benjamin.

"You should think of joining the militia," said Sam's Uncle Ezra.

"Jesse's studying to be an officer," volunteered Sam, not quite understanding his cousin's situation.

"An officer!" said the Colonel, "Good for you lad. Congratulations. Well done."

"It's nothing," replied Jesse. "It was just a lucky shot."

"Lucky my foot," bragged his cousin. "Jesse here can shoot the head off a snake swimming in a choppy lake forty feet off. Hits them every time."

"You must have made the English very angry," said Mister Fisher. "I'm glad to see you came out of it in one piece."

"He almost didn't," said Sam. Jesse wished his cousin would stop talking but Sam was irrepressible when it came to bragging about his famous cousin. "They captured him and were trying to make him talk. They were going to put him in front of a firing squad. That's when the colonel hit him with his sword." He pointed to the scar on Jesse's cheek. Jesse turned beet red with shame and indignation.

"Oh, my," exclaimed Sam's Aunt Lucy, Ezra's wife, who had been listening in rapt attention ever since the boys started talking. She was very interested in what was going on out west, but the war had been brought right to their doorstep in the last few months and these two young boys had been right in the middle of it. "Were they really going to shoot you?" she asked. "You must have been so scared. And your poor little friend killed right next to you."

"Naw, they were just trying to scare me into telling them where all the military supplies were." Jesse tried to ignore the mention of his dead friend, his friend who would have been alive if it wasn't for Jesse. "But I wouldn't tell them anything."

"Some interrogation methods," said Fisher in outrage. "Striking a young boy like that."

"How did you get away?" asked Sam's Aunt Lucy, who hadn't heard that part of the story.

Jesse had practiced his story since the incident last summer, trying different versions of it on various classmates until one of them caught him in a contradiction. He was now more careful and said as little as necessary while trying to change the subject, but he had never tried explaining it to a room full of knowledgeable adults.

"I shimmied out the back of the old barn they were keeping me in. There was a loose board. I kicked it out and squeezed through the opening. There was no one guarding the rear, so I just ducked out and ran home."

"You were lucky, my boy," observed Ezra Turner, the militia captain. "I reckon they really would have shot you. That was the commanding colonel's son-in-law you killed and a very popular officer at that. I would not be surprised if there were not a few of his men who would have shot you themselves if given half the chance. You did a great service to the cause, young man."

"Here, here!" yelled the other men in the room, at which point Jesse grew silent and stared at his plate in embarrassment.

123

Sam's Uncle Ezra picked up on something Jesse had mentioned earlier.

"You may not have told the English what they wanted to know," he said. "But someone surely did. They burned every military building in the village, the arsenals, the commissary, all the cantonment cabins. It was like they had a map drawn out for them."

"Yes," replied Sam's father. "I heard a map fell out of Colonel Murray's hat. It was picked up by my friend, Mister Gilliland, while the British weren't looking. It implicated a Mister Ackley, the one who lives down by the river."

"Yes, I know of him," said his brother-in-law Bill. "He was arrested and brought down to Albany for trial. Unfortunately, they had no witnesses and little evidence so they had to let him go. He just moved his family to Quebec, the scoundrel."

"Good riddance," volunteered Sam's Uncle Ezra. "There have been a few others I hear."

Jesse had stiffened with the mention of Mister Ackley, the Gordons' friend, and watched the conversation come terrifyingly close to disclosing his part in their collaboration with the enemy. He prayed for a way to change the subject but his mind was a blank.

"Yes, but that's all supposition," stated Sam's father. "There's no proof either way."

Sam's father knew that Jesse's hosts in Plattsburgh had been implicated along with Ackley and had to leave town. He also had his suspicions that Jesse may have had something to do with their charge. Perhaps they had made a deal to free his nephew. If so, he heartily approved. What were a few cannons and supplies to the life of a young boy? He looked at his nephew with new found admiration.

"What are you going to do now, young man?" asked the ex-Colonel Fisher.

"I don't know," replied Jesse, glad the conversation had turned.

"Jesse's in the 9th grade, and is going to finish school at the Academy in Plattsburgh," his Uncle Ben answered for him. "I understand his new host, Lieutenant Curtis, is sponsoring him for a commission in the army."

"You going to be an officer in the regulars, Jesse?" asked the Colonel.

"I don't know. The war will probably be over by the time I finish school. I have another year and a half before I'm old enough. A lot can happen by then."

"That's right, my boy," agreed the Colonel. "It's good that you finish school. I wouldn't worry about the war. The way things are going it could last for years."

"I hope so," said Jesse, his tongue loosened by the praise and admiration of these great men. "I want to kill more redcoats."

Jesse was sorry for his outburst even before he finished saying it, but his animosity toward the British had been fueled by pent-up anger at what they had done to his friend Daniel. Even Sam's zealous Uncle Ezra was stunned into momentary silence by the vehemence with which the words were uttered.

Later that evening Sam and Jesse sat in Sam's brother's old room where Jesse was staying and reminisced, bringing each other up to date on things. Each was impressed at how the other had changed. Sam was almost a foot taller and filled out, big-boned and handsome. Jesse hadn't grown much taller, but was strong and wiry like an Indian.

"You think what they said about Tecumseh's true?" asked Jesse.

"I reckon so. If Mister Fisher says it's true, it probably is."

"Gee," said Jesse, genuinely sorry. "It's like the whole world is changing before we've even had a chance to see it."

"Changing for the better, I should say," replied Sam. "The less Injun's fighting with the British, killing innocent women and children and scalping wounded prisoners, the better."

"Maybe so," said Jesse, "But it kind of feels that we've lost something in the bargain."

While they talked, Jesse unpacked his bag. He was putting away a few of his clothes for his stay, when Sam picked up a small object in the bottom of the bag and held it up. It was a small lead soldier.

"Still playing with toy soldiers?" he asked in jest.

"Give me that!" yelled Jesse, grabbing it violently from his hand.

"Whoa. Sorry, cousin. I didn't mean to rile you. I just…"

125

"I'm sorry," replied Jesse, "But I was keeping this to melt down in case I need a ball in a hurry."

"Oh, I'm sorry," said Sam, a little concerned at his cousin's outburst and recent behavior. "The way you reacted, I thought it meant something special to you."

Jesse was silent. He put the only memento of his dead friend in his pocket.

"It does," he said finally, sitting on the edge of the bed and taking the toy soldier reverently out of his pocket.

"It belonged to Daniel," he sobbed, tears seeping from his eyes.

"Daniel, who's that?" asked Sam, in a quiet voice. He knew his cousin was on the verge of something and didn't want to disturb the moment.

"My friend at school, he was a drummer boy in the militia. He was real good too. He could play the fastest, neatest beats you ever heard. He was with me on the bridge when I shot the redcoat Major. They fired back at us when they realized who I was, the whole bunch of them. Boy did they shoot that bridge up. I was lucky and managed to duck under a small mound, but Danny, at the other end of the bridge, he wasn't so lucky. I found him in a ditch. He had been shot up something awful, just awful. It was the worst thing I ever saw, him lying there all full of holes. I tried to help him, but there was nothing I could do. It was just terrible Sam."

Jesse had not shared his grief and sorrow with anyone since it had happened all those months before. Now he was finally unburdening himself to the only friend he had ever really had except Daniel, and he couldn't seem to stop. The dam had burst. Tears sprang from his eyes and sobs burst from his breast. He was unable to stop them after holding them in for so long.

"It was all my fault," he blubbered between sobs. "If it wasn't for me going and shooting that Brit, Daniel would still be alive. It was all my fault."

Sam reached out and hugged his cousin. It was the only thing he could think to do, and as usual with Sam, it was just what Jesse needed. They hugged each other in the middle of the room while Jesse unburdened his soul.

Sam had been in battle and knew what it could do. Though he hadn't actually killed anyone and hoped he never would, he had seen other men killed and the grief and anguish it caused their loved ones and friends. More than ever he hoped the war would be over soon, before many more people suffered the pain his cousin was feeling.

Sam left a short time later, after making sure his cousin was all right. Jesse himself felt much better after his little breakdown, as if relieved of a great burden. The time alone with his cousin had been quite therapeutic, and Sam noticed that he was more his carefree old self again during the remainder of his stay.

Chapter 14

Village of Plattsburgh, NY, May 1814

In May, the first deserters were executed, three soldiers being put to death by firing squad. Despite the new, harsh measures, however, desertions were higher than ever - about 26 deserting on the road to Plattsburgh out of 160 being typical - so something had to be done.

The new commanding General of the Northern Army, James Wilkinson, had arrived in February, direct from his defeat at Crysler's Farm. There had been a number of border skirmishes and bumbling incidents before Wilkinson's arrival, one secret mission resulting in a soldier's death by friendly fire. Then there was the court martial of Lieutenant Gates, who was convicted of cowardice and abandoning his post. And another, a lieutenant who had his sword broken over his head and was cashiered from the army. It seemed that things were deteriorating badly. Until now, however, there had been no executions.

When Wilkinson arrived and set up his headquarters in the comfortable Delord house, there was a buildup of troops and supplies, and high hopes things would be different this time. Those hopes were dashed a month later when Wilkinson and his 4000 man army, with artillery in train, attacked LaColle Mill, a tiny outpost on the Canadian side of the border. What should have been a resounding victory turned into another humiliating retreat.

Things had been touch and go for awhile when a relieving force of 2500 Canadian provincials and British regulars arrived from Isle aux Noix to reinforce the outpost. However, General Macomb arrived on the scene with their own reserves just in time and drove off the British, saving the day. Unfortunately, Wilkinson chose to ignore the advice Eleazer Williams had given him during their council of war before the offensive. It was advice even a lowly non-com would have known enough to heed.

The mill was an old stone structure built strong and sure with reinforced masonry. Heavy guns would be required to breach it, much heavier than the six-pounders and field guns Wilkinson had brought. Williams had also told him to attack early in February before the lake ice began to thaw so the British couldn't bring up their gunboats to support the outpost. Wilkinson chose to wait until late March when he had overwhelming numerical superiority, so his men were bombarded by the heavy ships' guns, while his puny artillery had hardly any effect on the old stone mill. Then despite his overwhelming numerical superiority and Macomb's success in driving off the enemy reinforcements, Wilkinson, apparently unnerved by his heavy losses, recalled his forces and retreated back to Plattsburgh, with 103 dead and 56 wounded, and little to show for their efforts.

To make matters worse, the new General, perhaps in an attempt to make up for his poor performance the month before out west, began a zealous campaign to instill some military discipline in his command. They spent their days building huts and camps south of the river. A number of galling rules and restrictions were instituted. No one could enter the camps without being searched. The men now had to stand on picket duty through the night. They had to man lonely outposts out on the 'Head', looking out for British ships and cavalry. Even gambling and liquor were banned. Why, it was getting so a man couldn't take a leak without breaking the rules. Strict use of assigned latrines had also been instituted.

The only good thing to come out of the whole affair was that Wilkinson had recently been arrested and was awaiting court martial in Albany. He was being replaced by General Izard, who everyone spoke highly of. However, many had been disappointed too many times in the past to be optimistic. Whatever respect the enemy had held for the American army had been squandered by the northern generals. If only this one could earn back some of that respect.

Many, like Nate Peters, wished the fiery little General Macomb was in command, but he was only temporarily in charge until Izard arrived. Although he hadn't lifted any of Wilkinson's onerous restrictions, he had shown a fighting spirit, driving off the enemy and urging his commander to pursue the offensive, and he was much loved by the men. Later, when the British started building up their naval forces in the north and began moving south, Macomb had set up five batteries at the mouth of the Saranac. The fact that he had built furnaces to heat the shot showed that this commander meant business. It gave the men hope that there were still some fighting generals around. Too bad his command was only temporary. Now he'd be under another general's authority, and no one knew what that might bring.

It seemed the man now in command, Izard, meant business also. He made his musicians, whose notes and rhythms would beat out commands during battle, practice seven hours a day, and ordered his men to wear their uniforms under arms at all times. Though not liked by many, these new rules had a direct bearing on their military readiness, not like the arbitrary regulations of his predecessor. All that really mattered to most, however, was how he would act in the face of the enemy, and one could only learn that in the heat of battle itself.

Plattsburgh Bay, NY, End of May 1814

So far 1814 had been a very busy year for Sam Turner. Macdonough, in his bid to gain superiority on the lake, had contracted with Noah Brown of New York City to build and launch a 26-gun ship in sixty days. That was back at the end of February and Sam had been assigned as a liaison to the shipbuilder to oversee the operation for the Navy. They had finished their Herculean task, but just barely, by working overtime and weekends. It had been a hectic, busy two months and Sam was looking forward to some time off, but it never came. As soon as he was done with the brig, he was assigned to work on a 120-foot flat-bottom steamboat that Macdonough had purchased under construction at Vergennes. At least it brought him closer to his girlfriend, Sarah Nichols, in Whitehall.

Even though Mister John Nichols didn't get the contract for the new sloop, Sam had been able to steer some construction work his way. So Nichols didn't mind when Sam managed to make his way to his table for Sunday dinner now and again. He still saw Sam as a likely son-in-law and appreciated his thoughtfulness in sending him work. He was impressed with the young man's progress, while his daughter liked the way Sam looked in his navy uniform.

In April, while Sam was courting and Macdonough was busy constructing his ships, the British were building up their naval forces in the north and began to make their way south, capturing everything in their path. Macdonough, outgunned by Pring's force of the 16-gun *Linnet* and the five sloops - not to mention his dozen or so galleys and a bomb-vessel - stood helpless in Vergennes, trying to get his fleet ready.

Sam had just returned to Vergennes from a lovely weekend with Sarah. He had gone down to Whitehall on the overhauled steamboat to pick up some troops on their way to Plattsburgh. They had been crowded onto the ship with him on the return voyage. He still couldn't quite get used to a ship without sails, but things seemed to be changing faster these days than a person could remember. He still had some work to do on the 26-gun *Saratoga*, the ship he helped build in 40 days - 20 days ahead of schedule. And there were two new gunboats that had to be rigged and armed.

Macdonough, who knew Pring might attack his outgunned fleet at any time, had pulled it further up Otter Creek so it could be covered by shore batteries on the hill. This was a defensive strategy that had worked well in their previous encounter in Burlington Harbor and he hoped it would do so again. Macomb's men from Burlington had set up their batteries overlooking the river. Even the usually stand-offish Vermont State militia lent a hand.

Sam was working on one of the new gunboats at Vergennes when someone yelled out from a mast top that the British were coming. He looked up from his work to see four ships coming up the lake, sails taut against the wind. They had the telltale yellow band on black at the gun-ports of British Men-of-war. They were followed by a dozen armed galleys.

Like the last time, Sam stood in amazement as they came up to the mouth of Otter Creek, guns blazing. Soon cannon balls were falling all around him, splintering wood and throwing up great spumes of water. Although several men were killed, the attack was eventually driven off with little damage to the fleet anchored further up the Creek. Like last time, it was in the aftermath of the battle that Sam distinguished himself, helping and caring for the wounded without orders or direction, saving the lives of many who would have died without his ministrations. The injured were everywhere, and there was Sam, applying tourniquets and tying splints, treating concussions and bandaging wounds, staunching blood and applying compresses. This time he was rewarded for his services and promoted to assistant surgeon aboard the new ship *Saratoga*.

Being on a ship and part of a great commander's fleet was the thrill of Sam's life, even if he found the aftermath of battle appalling. He still hadn't lost his ardent love for sailing ships and the navy, and except for Sarah's hand in marriage, couldn't have asked for anything more than being assigned to the fleet's new flagship. He proposed to her on his first opportunity when he visited Whitehall again a few weeks after the battle, after asking her father for his blessing. Sarah, suitably impressed with his promotion and prospects, accepted. His own father was also pleased to hear the news. He was proud of his son and struck by the fact that his ship was named for that great battle at Saratoga, where he had fought in the last war. It had turned the tide of the war and showed that the British could be defeated on the field of battle. He hoped it would be a good omen for his son.

Shortly after Pring's attack and retreat back north, Macdonough, with his newly completed and armed *Saratoga*, entered the lake. He had now finally gained the upper hand and chased Pring all the way back to Isle aux Noix. The American fleet then made its way to Plattsburgh, were they now lay anchored and ready for action.

Sam looked up his cousin the first chance he got when he was back in town. He found him in a field behind the school drilling with a few of his friends who had formed a sort of school militia. Jesse was the natural leader of the group, barking orders and putting them through their paces when Sam approached.

"Hi Sam," said Jesse, after noticing him standing by the side of the field. "When did you get back in town?"

"A few days ago," answered Sam, noticing Jesse's musket and wondering if it was the same one he had used to kill the British Major with. "I'm with the fleet now, on a real ship and everything."

"Great," said Jesse. Despite his love for his cousin, he was getting tired of hearing of all his good fortune.

"I'm getting married in the fall, too, to Sarah Nichols. I told you about her."

"That's nice," replied Jesse who, despite being sixteen didn't know why anyone would want to get married, especially to a girl.

Jesse still wasn't exactly happy to be going to school. If it hadn't been for Lieutenant Curtis and his offer to let him stay with them, Jesse probably would have bolted long ago. Things had gone well enough when he returned to the Academy after the holidays, and with the Lieutenant's help even his school work was improving. Then, just the previous month, his friend and mentor had been transferred to Albany and Jesse was left with little incentive to stay. The Lieutenant had found another family to take him in, but Jesse was crestfallen that Curtis was leaving. He didn't know how he would continue in school without him. Then he met his new host.

Peter Sailly was a prominent man in town, the federal revenue agent in charge of military procurements. He was knowledgeable of military planning and deeply involved in the day to day operations of the army. He met daily with the various generals and colonels and greatly impressed Jesse when they met, taking him all over town and showing him the various installations and forts. He even took him to the batteries down by the lake. When he complimented Jesse and told him how eager they were to help him get into the army when he turned eighteen, he was instantly won over. Sailly even gave him a brand new musket and encouraged him to practice military drills with his friends at school.

"What are you doing?" asked Sam, "You boys thinking of joining the militia or something?"

"No," replied Jesse, "Just practicing. We formed a little group to practice drills and stuff. No big deal. Nothing like you. You're a real navy man now, I see. What do you do, man one of the guns?"

"Naw, nothing like that. I'm an assistant ship's surgeon, but I'm still doing mostly carpentry work."

"Oh," said Jesse, not particularly impressed. "You always did like playing doctor."

"I wasn't playing last month when the British attacked us," said Sam, remembering the dying and suffering men. "It was pretty bad."

"Yeah, well I'd rather be shooting people than patching them up," replied Jesse.

"These were our own men I was helping," continued Sam, who didn't relish the idea of shooting anyone.

"Well, someone's got to do it, I guess," answered his cousin, who didn't like seeing suffering of any kind, and was more apt to put someone out of his misery than help him.

"Are you still staying with the Lieutenant?" Sam asked, forgetting Curtis's name.

"No," replied Jesse. "He was transferred to Albany last month. I'm staying with the Saillys now."

Sam didn't know the name. Jesse, anxious to show off his new benefactor, got an idea.

"Hey, I know, why don't you come to dinner tonight. Mister Sailly's having some guests over and said I could bring a friend. I don't have any friends since..." He stopped short at the mention of Daniel's name. "Anyway, I'm sure Mister Sailly won't mind."

"I don't know," said Sam, not sure he was ready for Plattsburgh society. "Are you sure it's acceptable?"

"Sure," Jesse assured him. "You're better than a friend, you're my cousin."

Later that evening, Sam knocked on the door of a large, two-story brick house with large bay windows down by the lake near the mouth of the river. Sam, who was intimidated by the size of the house was made even more nervous when Sailly's guests were introduced, two generals, a minister and a judge.

"Jesse, Sam, this is Major General Mooers of the local militia, and General Woolsey of the United States army."

The cousins shook the hands of the military men and said hello with grave voices and serious expressions.

"This is the Reverend Eleazer Williams," continued their host gesturing toward a short, well-dressed man with a large nose and broad forehead. The man looked like an Indian, but was dressed like a minister. "Mister Williams here works with our

Indian scouts gathering information about the enemy. It is his information we are going to discuss tonight."

Jesse stared in awe at the eminent red man in white man's clothing. Sam remembered what his father had told him when he had first seen the Indian agent, and tried not to stare.

"This is Judge Moores," said Sailly introducing the last of his guests.

Jesse introduced his cousin, who everyone seemed happy to meet. Even though Jesse was a bit jealous of Sam for being in the navy while he was still in school, he was proud of his cousin and the fact he was assigned to one of the biggest, newest ships on the lake.

After dinner, which was entertaining and stimulating, the men retired to an adjoining room. Sam and Jesse were invited to join them. Jesse loved the way his host involved him in everything and treated him like an equal instead of a youngster.

They peppered Sam with questions about the fleet and its commander, who Williams knew well and respected, and about the new ship and the recent battle. They were equally interested in meeting the young hero of the bridge who had almost singlehandedly stopped the invasion of last July in its tracks. Although still reluctant to talk about it, Jesse relished the praise and attention, especially from the two generals. With men like these on his side, perhaps he could become an officer some day, maybe even a general like them. They all encouraged him to stay in school, which he resolved to do.

"The border with Canada is sown up as tight as a Scotsman's purse," observed Judge Moores. "It has been so since last fall. Nothing is getting across, north or south, including beef cows. Our efforts are finally having an effect."

"Look at this," he went on, pointing to the newspaper he was holding. "Smugglers Beware. The new trade restrictions across the border are being strengthened and finally enforced. 'Smugglers beware.' How's that for sensationalism?"

"That's good," replied Sailly. "No sense making it easy for our countrymen to feed the enemy. So, Eleazer, what do you think the British are going to do?" he asked, getting to the point of their gathering.

"My scouts say there are many troops arriving from England."

"That makes sense," said the Judge. "The news from Europe is not good. The English have whipped Napoleon for good. Now they'll be free to bring all their troops over here. And these are no mere regulars, but the best, battle-hardened troops in the world."

"I wouldn't go that far," replied General Mooers, a tall man with graying hair and long side-burns, who sat straight in his chair and didn't seem to smile much. He had on a crisp new gray suit of the latest cut. "We have some pretty good men of our own. We can more then hold our own if given the men and arms."

"That's a big if," countered General Woolsey, a younger man with slick black hair and a thin mustache. "We need more men if we are to hold the line here. Washington has got to be made aware of the situation."

"Yes, gentlemen," said Sailly trying to keep the conversation on track, which wasn't easy with two generals and a judge. "Determining what that situation is, is the reason we are here today. Do you know how many troops are arriving?" he continued, glancing at Williams.

"My people say two or three thousand have already arrived," answered the Caughnawaga-born minister, glad to have people who would listen to what he had to say. "They will have five times that many by the fall."

"Where do your men think the British will attack?" asked General Mooers of the militia.

"With that many men, they could attack along the whole border simultaneously," said the judge. "I've read in the papers of reported troop build ups down south as well, along the Chesapeake. There's word of more troops arriving in Bermuda."

Jesse wondered where Bermuda was and resolved to ask his teacher. Sam struggled to keep up with the fast paced, wide ranging conversation.

"My men think this build up is in anticipation of a single large attack," said Williams, "Either west of here along the St. Lawrence, or directly on Plattsburgh. This is no diversion."

"Attacking Plattsburgh would make strategic sense," observed the Judge. "It's the same thing they tried in the last war.

136

March right down the Champlain Valley and the Hudson River and cut New England right out of the action."

"My father said the same thing," Sam blurted out, remembering this same conversation at his family's dinner table, but forgetting his place. "He fought at Saratoga."

"Then he knew what he was talking about," said Mister Sailly, seeing his young guest's embarrassment. "You must be very proud of him."

"It's funny," replied Sam recovering his composure. "I'm serving on a ship named the *Saratoga*."

"That's a good omen," volunteered the judge, raising his glass of wine to both the ship and the famous revolutionary war battle.

"I agree with your assessment, Mister Williams," said Sailly. "I'm convinced they are going to attack here."

"So are we," responded General Woolsey. "That's why we are ordering a build up of our forces. Macomb has been ordered here from Burlington. Our young Mister Turner is here with the fleet for just that same reason. We believe Plattsburgh is the Brits' obvious target. It's the shortest distance from their forces, allows them to use their fleet, and gives them a tremendous strategic advantage if they pull it off."

"Speaking of the fleet, Mister Williams," said the Militia General. "What of the British fleet? Does Macdonough have superiority on the lake or doesn't he?"

"It is hard to say," answered Williams. "The British have very strict security around Isle aux Noix, but my people have many eyes in the forest. They see much but are unseen themselves. The British are building a very large ship, perhaps the biggest ever to be on the lake, with over 30 guns. I would say Commander Macdonough may have a slight advantage in armaments now, but that advantage may not last long. However, any advantage, no matter how slight where the lake is concerned, could make a difference. It is too close to tell, though with the number of men they are likely to attack us with, what happens on the lake may not matter."

"How far along are they with this new ship?" asked the Judge.

"Not far," answered the Indian agent. "They have only begun. They won't be ready for several months."

"October, maybe September is my guess," observed General Woolsey. "We've got to have more men."

"How many do you think you can muster?" asked the Judge.

"Perhaps four or five thousand regulars," replied General Woolsey.

"With another four or five thousand militia," volunteered Mooers.

"That's ten thousand, an equal force," said Sailly, happy the conversation was proving fruitful. "We should be able to hold our own."

"These aren't just any troops we're facing," observed Judge Moores. "The papers say Wellington's troops are being brought over with four of his best generals."

"Let them bring Wellington himself," said General Mooers. "We'll make them wish they were still on the Peninsula fighting the French.

"Viva La French," yelled Sailly, raising his glass in a jovial toast. The others joined in. Even the taciturn General Mooers cracked a smile.

Chapter 15

St. Albans, Vermont, June 1814

Eleazer Williams was sitting in a local tavern on the Vermont side of the lake near St. Albans, Vermont awaiting for transportation across the lake.

"I'll tell you, Mister Williams," said the well-dressed men sitting at the table next to him. "Droves of cattle are constantly passing from northern parts of the state into Canada and to the British. They pass my place almost daily these days."

"I'm sure you exaggerate, Mister Fisk," said the Indian agent. "How can droves of cattle be driven across the state without being noticed? There are patrols everywhere."

"Ah, someone's obviously spying for them. They know where the patrols are and take a different route."

"Are you saying someone on our side is spying for the smugglers?"

"I wouldn't exactly say spying, but they're keeping an eye out for them."

"I will have my people look into it, Mister Fisk, and will tell the general if I find out anything. Thank you."

"Thank you, Sir," said the man, who got up, touched his hat and left.

Williams remained seated for a few moments longer as if in thought. As he was about to leave, a young man in the uniform of a Vermont dragoon introduced himself.

"Good day, good Sir," said the man. "Could I speak with you for a moment?"

"I was just leaving," replied Williams. "I have another engagement."

"I think I have some information you might find interesting," volunteered the dragoon. "Please, let me buy you a drink."

"I do not drink, Sir," said Eleazer Williams, suddenly intrigued. "I'll have a glass of ginger-water and honeyed-vinegar."

The stranger sat down and ordered another glass of ale for himself and a switzel for Williams.

"I couldn't help overhearing your conversation," continued the Vermonter. "Am I to understand correctly that you have the ear of the authorities?"

"You could say that," replied Eleazer Williams cautiously. "I happen to know a few people who you could say are in a position of authority. Why? What information are you talking of?"

The young man wanted to help his country but he didn't want to see his family, who were involved in smuggling beef cattle across the border, get hurt. He had been helping them by thwarting all attempts to interrupt the family business. After all, they had been dealing with their neighbors and relatives across the border for decades. He saw little reason to stop now, even if there was a war on, but he wasn't about to let others smuggle military supplies that could be used in an invasion. He knew the beef was going to the British, but if his family didn't do it someone else would, and it was their only real livelihood. However, others were supplying the material for an enemy fleet and he was going to make sure that didn't happen.

"Sir, I may know something of interest to you. You know that ship the British are building up north? I hear someone's planning on smuggling some spars up for her."

Crab Island, Lake Champlain, NY, Early July 1814

Sam's month in Plattsburgh had been relatively quiet. There was no building going on. Secretary Jones had refused all requests for new ships. There were no war casualties to mend. Macdonough's fleet took no part in recent military maneuvers. Sam had a lot of free time on his hands. To his delight, Sarah Nichols was visiting her Uncle Caleb who lived on Crab Island, just a short distance off shore at the southern entrance to the Bay, near the bluffs not far from Nate Peter's encampment.

He was now sitting with Sarah and her Uncle in his rather large farm house overlooking the Bay of Plattsburgh a mile to the north, having an early dinner of newly-caught lake bass and fresh garden peas, with apple sauce and pastries.

140

"So how do you like the navy and Master Commandant Macdonough?" asked the war department spy, recruited by Secretary of War Armstrong himself to gain firsthand knowledge of the situation on the lake.

"Exceedingly," answered Sam, in his usual enthused manner. "I like them both very much. The Master Commander knows his business and knows this lake. The British won't stand a chance against our new ships. The *Saratoga*, the one I'm on, is one of the finest ships I've ever seen."

"Oh, and how many ships have you seen, my boy?" asked Nichols with a smile.

"Sam built the ship, and several others," offered Sarah, coming to her man's defense. "My father says he's one of the most gifted shipbuilders he's known, and he's been building ships all his life."

"I don't know about that," protested Sam with modesty. "I've only been working on them a short time. I have a lot to learn. Anyway, I'd rather be on one than building one."

"I'm sure you would, my boy, I'm sure you would," said Nichols with a smile. "So tell me about your ship and its crew."

Sam didn't see any reason not to brag about his ship and the fleet. His host could look out his window with an eyeglass anytime and see the ship's armaments for himself. He was an American and Sarah's Uncle, his friend John Nichol's brother, so it had to be all right.

"It has 26 guns, Sir, eight 24-pound longs and six 42-pound carronades, with twelve 32-pound carronades on the quarterdeck."

"Hmm, very impressive, especially the 42-pounders. They will be very effective at close range, but the heavy 24s will be the most important if they fight at a distance. What about the crew then?" asked Sarah's strange uncle.

"We have 250 men, soldiers mostly to man the guns and act as marines, but we just got 20 seamen from out west. Commander Perry sent them."

"Ah, Oliver is making quite a name for himself out on Lake Erie. I just hope Macdonough can match him."

"He can, Sir," said Sam, although Oliver Hazard Perry was a name to be reckoned with.

"What are Macdonough's plans?" asked Nichols.

Sam thought his host asked too many questions. Telling him about the ships, things he could see for himself, was one thing, but divulging the navy's plans on the lake was another matter. Sam was starting to dislike his host. Even though he was Sarah's uncle, he seemed shifty and glib and not altogether trustworthy. Sam was cautious.

"I'm sorry, Sir, but even if I knew I couldn't tell you," said Sam. "That's privileged information."

"Very good, my boy," replied Nichols in a jovial voice, finally relaxing, satisfied this sailor at least knew how to keep his mouth shut, although he was a little annoyed with how quickly Sam had given him his ship's armaments and manpower, especially the fact that Perry's men had arrived, something he did not know. He would have to notify the Secretary. "Did you know the British are building a 32-gun frigate for the lake? It will give them superiority."

"No, I didn't," said Sam. "Commander Macdonough has been requesting permission to build more ships, but Secretary Jones keeps denying him. There's no reason to let them beat us, Sir. We have all the material we need right here."

"I know," agreed Nichols. "And all that the British need as well. They just intercepted a shipment of spars being smuggled into Canada on a couple of large rafts going up the lake. They were meant for their new frigate. The smugglers got away but the contraband was confiscated. The whole interdiction was based on a tip from Mister Williams, the Indian agent, from one of his contacts in Vermont, I believe."

Sam wondered how his host knew so much about what was happening on the lake, sequestered as he was like a hermit on this tiny island just a half mile offshore. But then his ship builder brother in Whitehall seemed to know a lot as well. The siblings must keep up a lively correspondence with each other and the world at large, thought Sam.

"Macdonough and you men are doing a great job," said Caleb Nichols, obviously pleased with Sam's answers. "Perhaps Secretary Jones should be reminded that if the British attack here, like I think they will, navy equality, if not outright superiority, will be critical to stopping them."

142

Sam agreed and decided that he liked Sarah's uncle after all.

"Too bad we couldn't have such men in charge of our army," observed Nichols. "Did you hear about the debacle with Colonel Forsythe?"

Sam and Sarah both said no.

"He was in command of a troop of riflemen. He was supposed to lure the British into an ambush, which would have worked wonderfully except the intrepid Colonel ordered his men to stand and fight. Instead of a victory it was another costly blunder, a prime example of too much courage and too little prudence. Or perhaps rather too much cunning, for they say Forsythe saw it as a trick of his commander to grab all the credit at his expense. In any case, he paid the ultimate price for his folly. The poor follow was killed in the battle. An army that has such internal intrigue and petty in-fighting is hardly an army that will win this war, don't you agree, Mister Turner?"

Sam said he did, although he wasn't sure he understood it all and was partly preoccupied looking at Sarah, who appeared radiant in her light, white summer dress. The conversation shifted to Sarah and the Nichol's family cousins and their many affairs of the heart, and to her own engagement and wedding plans. Sam only half-listened, but thought about the things his host had told him and what they all meant.

That evening, after the end of a long, perfect July day, with the sun poised just above the mountains in the west, Sam sailed Sarah back to the mainland on a small skiff he had borrowed for the occasion. They landed on a tiny sand beach below the bluffs, which overlooked the western shore a mile south of the village boat docks. After pulling the skiff to shore, they sat on a large log and watched the sun blaze in reflection off the eastern mountains as it sank below the gray mountains to the west behind them. They stayed holding hands as the stars came out.

Later that night, they took a carriage back to town where she was staying at an inn with her mother and aunt. He kissed her goodnight underneath the sycamores. That night he fell asleep wondering what married life with Sarah would be like once they had a place of their own.

Later that week, Secretary Jones had an apparent change of heart and finally ordered the building of a new 18-gun brig on the lake. Again, Sam was assigned liaison duties between the firm of Noah Brown and the navy. He went to Vergennes, where the building of the new ship was just getting underway.

When Sam told Noah's brother, Adam, the man on the ground, they needed the brig before the end of August, he said it couldn't be done.

"There's no way," exclaimed Adam, who had himself just arrived from New York. "It will take that long just to get all the material we need shipped up here. That timeframe is just not possible."

"You have everything you need right here," replied Sam. "All you have to do is cut it. There's more white oak in these woods than anywhere in the country." Sam pointed behind them. "It's the best wood in the world for making sailing ships. There's pine for the floors and ceilings, and maple and elm and ash, good hardwood for spars and masts, even chestnut. There's plenty of tar and pitch in those woods, too, and hemp if you need it. I'll have it cut and on the docks in four days. All you have to do is put it together."

So began another Herculean effort by the Americans to gain the advantage on the lake, with Sam Turner leading the way.

Village of Plattsburgh, NY, Late July 1814

The village was full of troops again, many of them green. Border skirmishes had been increasing over the past few weeks. Macomb had moved his 1100 man force north to Chazy Landing to counter them.

Izard was headquartered in an opulent brick building on the north shore of the lake just within the village limits. The house had been leased to him by a rich merchant, who, like many, had left the city for safer havens.

Izard had just finished writing out his dispatches for the day, when his orderly announced the arrival of his guests, three militiamen from Vermont, a major and two junior officers, all dressed in the gaudy, rather dandified uniforms of state dragoons.

He suppressed a smile. What they lacked in fighting ability, he thought, they made up for in panache.

"We hear the English are building up their troop strength at the border," observed the leader of the delegation, a Major Sibley. "We have come to offer the services of the Vermont state militia to do with as you see fit, Sir."

"Thank you, Major," replied the General. "Your help will be greatly appreciated. Prevost has fourteen thousand men, many of them seasoned troops from Wellington's army. But with the forces I have at my disposal and your state's militia, we can more than hold our own. The situation wouldn't be so bad if your people on the other side of the lake weren't feeding them. It's damned unpatriotic."

"New Yorkers are doing it just as much," said the Vermonter defensively. "I mean no disrespect General, but farmers on both sides of the lake have been trading with their Canadian neighbors for generations."

"It's different now, Major," countered Izard. "The beef they're smuggling is feeding those fourteen thousand British soldiers. What do you suppose they're planning on doing with all those soldiers?"

"I don't know," said the Major, although he had a pretty good idea.

"Why even as we speak they're sending out more raiding parties. One of them attacked our pickets in Champlain last night. They're probing our defenses, Major. They're planning on attacking here at Plattsburgh."

"How can you be so certain, Sir?" asked the Major, hoping the general was wrong and they would be spared the brunt of any attack. "How do we know it's not a diversion?"

"I rather doubt that," said Izard. "Not with fourteen thousand of their best troops poised on our doorstep."

"Maybe they will attack further west like they did last year," offered one of the junior officers in the delegation. They had been sent by the Colonel ahead of their militia company, who wanted firsthand knowledge about the situation across the lake.

"I doubt that as well," responded Izard. "There's nothing in it for them. None of those targets would have as great a strategic impact. No gentlemen. It's Plattsburgh they're after. I know it."

The general also mentioned the capture of another raft heading north with more oak wood spars, a thousand feet of planking and 27 barrels of tar.

"We caught the smugglers this time," said Izard. "They will not fare well, I assure you."

"You must have been very lucky to catch them," volunteered one of the young dragoons, the very one who had talked to Eleazer Williams only a few weeks before. "After all, Sir, it's a big lake, especially at night for someone who knows the waters."

"Not luck at all," observed the General, as the Vermonter hoped he would. "We got an anonymous tip from across the lake, one of Eleazer William's informants."

"Ah, then there are some patriotic Vermonters after all," replied the young militia dragoon, with a smile. He felt a little better knowing he was responsible for the capture of these smugglers as well.

"Yes, Lieutenant, thank God for that and you gentlemen," conceded the General.

Just then a currier rushed in carrying an important dispatch.

"An urgent message for you, Sir," he said, saluting and handing Izard a sealed envelope. "From the Secretary of War himself."

The general turned from his guests, tore open the envelope and read the contents, which seemed to stun him. He reread the note several times.

"What is it, Sir?" asked the militia major, unable to suppress his curiosity and forgetting all military protocol. "I hope it is not bad news."

"They want me to take my army and move it to the western part of the state," said the General in a stunned voice. "They want me to abandon the village and everything in it to the enemy. I can't believe it. What's that old intriguer Armstrong up to now? He couldn't do more damage if he were on the side of the British, I swear. Why in God's name would he have me march my men west when every indication and piece of intelligence indicates the English will attack here, at this point?"

146

"Maybe he knows something we don't," offered the major, who knew nothing of the Secretary's history or reputation, but was still impressed by his lofty position in government nonetheless.

"The man knows nothing," fumed the General. "He's a fool. Who in the devil is he listening to? What on earth could he be thinking?"

He looked up at the three militiamen standing in front of him.

"The fate of the nation lies in your hands," he intoned.

"What do you mean, General?" queried the major.

"Promise me you will stand by your word and come to our defense when the British attack, and I assure you they will," said Izard in a strained voice. "You are all that stands in the way of the enemy and certain defeat. For if they take the village there will be nothing to stop them until they get all the way to New York. Promise me you will come."

The three militia men, filled with patriotic fervor at the General's words, stood at attention and swore they would come, even if they had to volunteer on their own and swim across Lake Champlain to do so.

Izard was impressed with their zeal and appreciated their commitment, but was stunned at the news and what his new orders implied. It seemed things were moving fast all around him. He felt like a man standing still in the middle of a buffalo stampede. They were coming right at the village, and he was being ordered to evacuate!

Chapter 16

Village of Plattsburgh, NY, End of August 1814

Jesse Lebow and a few of his friends stood and watched as General Izard and his 4000 man army marched out of the village on their way to Sackets's Harbor, leaving Macomb with 600 effectives and 700 convalescents to defend the town.

General Mooers had called up the militia, a regiment of infantry and a troop of dragoons, but these and the 600 effectives left in the village, even with the promise of more militia, gave Jesse no sense of security. Despite what his benefactor's friends said, he had little confidence in the militia when things got tough. The village citizenry felt the same, for most of them had fled their homes, heading south or east across the lake. The village was virtually empty except for the troops being left behind.

Also in the crowd that day watching the army march out of the village was Jesse's mentor, Mister Peter Sailly. He was not happy about what was happening. Jesse, on the other hand, was thrilled. With the prospect of war coming and the suspension of school in the fall - where he would be starting his 10th year - Jesse was more than pleased. He loved the spectacle of seeing so many men marching in order with their muskets and bayonets gleaming in the sun. He wished he could be part of it, but knew it would only be another year and a half now and he'd be eligible. If he played his cards right, he might even be able to shoot himself another redcoat or two.

"It's a shame," said Peter Sailly, shaking his head. "It's irresponsible, is what it is."

"What is?" asked Jesse.

"They're leaving the village defenseless," replied the revenue agent. "Everyone knows the British are attacking here. The smart ones have all boarded up their houses and left. Even the general knows it's a mistake, but there's nothing he can do about it. Orders are orders and these orders come from the Secretary of War himself, which means President Madison himself must approve of it. I just wonder who is giving them their advice.

Whoever it is doesn't know beans about war. In any case, they should leave these types of decisions to the men in the field. But then don't get me going about politicians directing the war. We had enough of that in the last one."

Jesse didn't know exactly what Mister Sailly was getting at, but liked the way it sounded nonetheless, and it kind of made sense. Why send all the soldiers away when everyone like Mister Sailly knew the British were going to attack here? It sounded like the British had enough men to attack everywhere at once. All of a sudden everything felt very small. Jesse felt small, the army felt small, the village felt small, even New York and the whole country felt small compared to the giant horde of redcoats he imagined just beyond the hill.

That evening there was another council of war in Peter Sailly's house by the lake. This time Jesse got to listen from the back of the room.

"General Mooers?" said Macomb, the general left in charge of the city's defense.

"Yes, General," answered the Militiaman from New York.

"Have you called up your militia?"

"Yes, General. A regiment of infantry and a company of dragoons. They are in place, Sir."

"Good," said Macomb. "I would also like to see if we can call on our neighbors across the lake, those hardy Green Mountain Boys."

"Yes, Sir," replied the militia general. "I'm sure General Strong would be glad to join us. I will see to it as well."

"I'll have Commandant Macdonough detach a ship or two to help ferry them across. The villagers are leaving in droves. There's almost no one left of note, but most of the ones that are still here are ready to fight. Mister Williams, what news have you of our adversary's intentions?"

"It is as I told General Izard. My scouts say the English are building up their forces for an attack on the village," answered the Caughnawaga scout master. "There is every indication the attack to the west is a diversion. It is obvious to everyone they are coming here, everyone that is except the Secretary."

"Whatever his agenda is," said Sailley, "it is not winning the war."

"Perhaps it is another one of his schemes," volunteered Mooers. "It wouldn't be the first time he tried something like that. Look what he and Mister Burr were involved in."

"Now, General," chided Sailly. "That's not quite fair. He was never convicted of any wrong doing."

"That may be, Peter, but it doesn't make him innocent either," said Mooers who had little liking for Madison's Secretary of War, Armstrong.

"I have 600 effectives with another 700 convalescents and sick," observed Macomb, "And 250 prisoners. I have ordered all of them to complete the fortifications before the enemy arrives, which could be any day now."

"Between New York and Vermont, we should be able to gather up at least 800 or more militia," said Mooers. "Maybe a few hundred more volunteers."

"Hardly enough to stop a battle-hardened force of ten thousand regulars," replied Macomb, a wily and crafty fighter. "We will need to use every means at our disposal to deal with them. The troops we have are well-trained and disciplined. General Izard has done a good job. I only hope the militia will be as good."

"They will be," answered General Mooers proudly.

Macomb looked across the table at the master of his Indian scouts.

"Information on the enemy's movements and dispositions will be crucial," he said. "Knowledge of the terrain and the enemy will be one of our major advantages. Eleazer, your braves will be our invisible eyes and ears. Can you do this?"

"The British will not be able to make a move without my people knowing it," responded Williams. "Even now they watch as the English gather at their staging points. I estimate they will attack before the next full moon."

"It is as I feared then," said Macomb with a tight jaw. "I will need intelligence reports every twelve hours. Is that possible?"

"I will give you reports every ten hours, so you will be that many hours ahead of the enemy."

While the generals planned, their men carried out the thankless task of building fortifications. It was a backbreaking job that the troops hated, but they did it nonstop, morning, noon and night. The forts, really nothing more than wood and dirt parapets built atop hillocks, were well located in areas overlooking the river and the bay. The one named Fort Brown sat on a high bank of the Saranac as it snaked its way west from the lake, about a mile from the river's mouth.

Sergeant Nate Peter's uniform was covered with grime from the dirt and sand they were digging and hauling, his face so covered in thick black mud, only the whites of his eyes were visible in the lamplight. He had gone up and down the steep embankment to fetch rocks from the river so many times he almost forgot how to stand on level ground. His lower back felt like someone had tried to bend him around by the hips like a washcloth. Despite his discomfort and fears, he did his best to buoy up his men.

"That's it lads," he said, as the men packed dirt and sand tight around the wooden parapet. "We'll be able to sit up here and pick 'em off as they try to cross the river below. They'll be like turkeys in a pen down there with nowhere to go but up toward our guns."

He helped the men place the cannons so that they could pound the enemy as they approached the river then cover their advance as they crossed, and made sure the rifle fire could be aimed down the steep, long slope leading from the river and up the near bank.

"Corporal Johnson said they've got 14,000 of their best troops just across the border," said one of his equally dirt-covered men. "Come from beating that there Napoleon fellow."

"Good!" said Nate, with a gleam in his eye. He had tasted blood, together with victory and defeat. He had faced overwhelming odds and lived to tell about it. The fighting he had done had steeled his will and tested his nerve.

"That means more of them will die trying to get across that river and up this hill. That means more glory for us, boys," he yelled. "And if it's not glory you want, then you're in the wrong army, because this army will maim you," he yelled.

The men yelled back with a yea.

"Let them come here and see what'll happen to them. We'll give 'em hell, won't we boys," he yelled again.

"Aye! Give 'em hell," they all shouted back as one.

It made his hair stand on end and his eyes glisten.

"Don't tread on us!" he yelled, taking a phrase from the last war. The men repeated it with a roar. Someone yelled out, "The fighting 6th forever!" and they all responded, shouting the regimental number with all their might. Then things grew quiet as they went back to work and their own thoughts. Nate looked at his men with a fondness he found surprising and wished he could only be worthy enough to lead them into battle.

Plains of L'Acadia, Quebec, Beginning September 1814

Sergeant James Fenwick of the 88th Foot gazed over the flat expanse of land south toward the U.S. border and wondered what awaited him beyond the horizon. Most of all he wondered what he was doing here, in the middle of nowhere. He had thought he was going home after ten years of fighting his way through Portugal, Spain and France as part of Major General Frederick Robinson's division of Wellington's victorious army. Instead, he and his men had been sent to Quebec. He looked around him in wonder. There was not a hut or smokestack within miles, a sightline hindered only by a few groups of trees and high mountains in the distance.

As far he could tell there were over 10,000 English, stretching all the way back to Montreal and west to Ogdensburg, with over 1000 carts and at least three dozen cannons. A formidable force, but nothing compared to the numbers used on the continent to fight Napoleon.

The thing that struck Fenwick most of all about this country was the space, the sheer magnitude of the land, forests that went on forever, lakes the size of seas. One province was the size of all England, his home. Oh, if only he could somehow be back in old England instead of stuck in this Godforsaken place. There were at least two dozen Indians in their train, for God's sake. It was truly the end of the earth, a lost world only recently discovered, and as far as Fenwick was concerned, it could just as well be lost again.

He trusted his commander and those who commanded along side of him, although he knew of Prevost, the Governor-General, only by reputation and that was as a diplomat. Everyone agreed that he was no Wellington, but then there could only be one Lord Wellington.

As he looked around his chest swelled with pride. Every uniform was spotless, every musket cleaned and readied. Every bayonet gleamed in the morning light. Every soldier marched straight and in perfect line. It was probably the best trained, most well-disciplined military force in the world, bar none, and it was on a mission to invade a foreign country, a place that by all rights should still be part of the motherland, a colony, like the one he was about to leave. He had no idea of the disposition and number of the enemy, but it could hardly matter, for the force he was part of was overwhelming in firepower and fighting experience. The Americans, whatever their strength, didn't stand a chance.

Fenwick's thoughts were interrupted when he noticed a large group of officers approaching on horseback. One of them carried the Regimental colors along with the Union Jack. The tall gentleman on a white horse looked familiar. General Robinson had come to address his troops.

"I want nothing but the most gentlemanly conduct from everyone," he reminded the men, as they assembled in front of him at the staging area, before their advance across the border. "Although the Americans have committed many atrocities during this war, our victorious armies in the south have taught them a lesson they will not soon forget. We have burned their Capitol without losing a man. Now it is time to show what we can do here, and how magnanimous we can be in victory. Our army is invincible. You have beaten the French and their allies. You have saved the world from a mad tyrant and butcher, and made it safe for all free men. All that is asked of you now is to punish these people who, despite all we have done for them, thought it proper to attack us in our darkest hour. You will be the sword of justice, swift yet merciful. Remember the honor of our King and country rests on your shoulders. Bear it well. Fight bravely and well as you have been trained to do. The Governor-General has issued strict orders. Do not molest any non-combatants. Leave private citizens and their property alone unless they have taken it upon themselves to fire upon us, and then only under strict orders. There are many in America who hate the war and like the English. Many of them have been providing food and supplies to our armies. So let us not bite the hand that feeds us and cause the peaceful citizens any harm. I promise you that any violation of this order will be swiftly and severely punished. Is that understood?"

"Aye," everyone within earshot answered, Fenwick included. He had all the confidence in the world that he would be home soon.

Plattsburgh Bay, NY, September 5, 1814

Sam had been spending a lot of time on the lake aboard the fleet flagship, the *Saratoga*. Mostly he maintained the vessel, keeping it in fighting trim, making repairs and tending sick sailors when the surgeon was busy or off the ship. No one had been doing much sailing recently, however, with the lack of wind the past few days. That hadn't kept Master Commandant Macdonough from maneuvering his fleet up and down the lake.

They were now making their slow, tedious way south from Isle la Motte, just north of Beekmantown, off Chazy, towing the ships by row galleys. Sam was aboard one of these. It was grueling work, pulling the two-man oars against the lake's currents, but Sam didn't mind. It was seamen's work, and he was pulling the new *Eagle*, the ship he had built, so it was all right with him. He encouraged the others, mostly soldiers, who were less eager at the oars.

Although he loved the Navy and his commander, he was less than happy about some of the decisions that were being made. 40 of their best men had been transferred to the *Eagle* to man the guns. That would have been bad enough, leaving the flagship dangerously short of crew, but Sam did not care for Lieutenant Henley, who had come to take over command of the *Eagle* from his friend, Lieutenant Joseph Smith. He wasn't nearly as good a sailor as Mister Smith nor had he been in the Navy as long. Furthermore, Smith, now back on the *Saratoga*, was peeved that he was no longer commanding his own ship. To Sam and many of the crew it seemed Smith had been demoted. Smith felt so as well, and took it out on the men, Sam included. It seemed that Macdonough was favoring Henley by assigning the *Eagle* to him. Adding to the insult, Henley and the *Eagle* were getting some of the fleet's best gun crews.

A stout wind had just blown up from the north and he was on his way back to the *Eagle* as they began to unfurl her sails. Thankfully no more rowing would be needed for the time being. The fleet was returning to Plattsburgh Bay and Sam was hoping he'd get some time ashore so he could visit Sarah, who was still in the village with her mother and Uncle, and perhaps drop in on his cousin as well. With the British coming and the Academy still closed, he wanted to encourage Jesse to go back home and look after their folks.

He was climbing back on board, up one of the *Eagle's* rope ladders, when his friend, Lieutenant Smith, who was commanding the ship until Henley's arrival, stuck his head over the bulwark.

"Ah, Mister Turner. I was just inquiring about you," he said. "You haven't pulled galley duty have you?"

"I'm afraid I have, Sir, but there's a wind coming up so my rowing services will no longer be needed. I was hoping to get a ride back to the bay with you."

"Why, don't you like the *Saratoga* any longer?" asked the *Eagle's* ex-commander.

"No, Sir. It's not that. She's a fine ship," said Sam. "But Lieutenant Henley's with her still, and well, I was, eh, hoping to talk to you. We all wanted to tell you how sorry we are that you will no longer be commanding the *Eagle*, sir. You deserve your own ship."

"Oh, it will come soon enough. Mister Henley is a good man, but for me, I wish I could have commanded her in battle. She's a fine little ship, fast and deadly."

"If you don't mind, Sir, I would just as soon have you second in command of the *Saratoga* if there's to be a battle. And I want to be on her too."

"Ah, Mister Turner, you like serving on the flag do you."

"It has its advantages, Sir."

"Yes, she'll be the first into battle and the most sought after by the enemy, but we'll see if we can keep you on her for a little while longer."

Just as Smith finished speaking there was a shriek followed by the sickening thud of bone and tissue meeting the ship's hard deck. Sam and the Lieutenant ran to the other side of the ship from where the sound had come. As they came to the scene of the accident their view was obstructed by the other men who were gathering around. As assistant surgeon's mate, Sam pushed his way through the crowd.

"Where's Mister Waverly?" he asked of the chief Surgeon.

"He is with the Master Commander and Henley on the *Saratoga*," said Smith. "You'll have to look out for him."

He looked down at the body of the poor mangled seaman lying on the deck, one leg at an impossible angle beneath him, his back twisted in a terrible way. The man's eyes were open and staring, his mouth gasping for air. Sam knew him, a seaman named Willis, about his age. James, if Sam remembered rightly. He was new to the navy and inexperienced aloft. Unsure of himself, he had been sent up to unfurl the main topgallant to catch the rising wind. Hesitating too long before unlatching his rope, he was pulled over when the sail unfurled, hurling him to the deck of the ship.

The man's blue eyes stared up at Sam with a look of desperation and pain, and not a little terror, as if with his mouth unable to speak his eyes had to do all the pleading. It was a pitiful look and one Sam did not soon forget. He knelt by the fallen seaman who was still conscious and starting to go into convulsions. Blood seeped from the back of his head and from his nose and mouth. Sam thought his back might be broken. Perhaps ribs had punctured a lung. It seemed he couldn't breathe. Soon his eyes rolled into the back of his head. His body shuddered as Sam tried to hold him still. The ship started to rock with the waves and pick up speed as the sails, which only moments before young Mister Willis had unfurled, caught the wind with a lurch.

Sam tore off his own white shirt and put it behind Willis's head to try and stop the bleeding. The man's eyes were now closed and he no longer seemed to be breathing. Sam checked for a pulse and could feel none. In his extremity he could think of only one thing to do. Somehow he had to keep Willis breathing until the surgeon could be summoned.

He put his mouth to the unconscious man's and blew in a lung full of air, pinching Willis's nose so it would fill his lungs, which expanded as if he were taking in air on his own. He did this several times, blowing into the unconscious man's mouth, which remained opened. After several breaths, he tore open the seaman's blouse, now stained with blood, and began methodically pumping on his chest, again trying to keep him breathing and his heart beating. No one had taught him how to do this, although he had seen his father miraculously bring a baby colt to life after it had been pulled from its mother's womb with its umbilical cord wrapped around its neck. It had worked for the un-breathing colt. Perhaps it would work for young Mister Willis.

"He's dead, Mister Turner," said the chief surgeon, who had just boarded the ship, putting his hand on Sam's shoulder and bending to examine the body. "He's no longer breathing."

Sam stopped his ministrations and looked at the dead seaman. Most of the people standing around were staring at him, as was Lieutenant Smith.

"You have done all that could be done for him," said Smith.

"His back's been broken, I would guess," observed the Surgeon.

"I was trying to keep him breathing," explained Sam, of his unorthodox methods. "Keep his heart stimulated. Perhaps there's still something we can do."

"You can't keep a man's heart beating if it's stopped," the surgeon assured him. "You can't make him breathe if his lungs don't want to take in the air as is natural. The trauma to his back and system was just too much for his internal organs to bear. I'm sorry lad."

They covered the young Willis with a coat. A short time later the fleet anchored in Plattsburgh Bay. Sam returned to his ship with Lieutenant Smith, who explained the assistant surgeon mate's absence and what had occurred on the *Eagle*, commending Sam for his efforts in trying to save the young seaman.

"He will be a good man to have in a pinch," he told Macdonough, who was reluctant to let Sam off without a reprimand for not returning directly to his ship after leaving the galleys. Sam did not say much, and went below as soon as he was dismissed. He had never wanted to see Sarah so much in his life. He just wanted to hold her with her head buried in his chest until the empty feeling there went away.

Chapter 17

Village of Plattsburgh, NY, September 5, 1814

Jesse was happy. School had been cancelled. He was even more elated that the British were coming. He didn't care about the potential threat they posed. The fact that the army had left the village virtually defenseless did not seem to bother Jesse either, not like it did his Plattsburgh host, Mister Sailly. He was taking his family south to stay with relatives. Jesse had promised he would go home, but he had yet to leave town after hearing the fleet had returned. He rushed to the bay to see for himself.

As he crossed the bridge he could see the fleet anchored in the bay, their masts like leafless trees pointing to the clear blue sky. Closest to shore was the *Saratoga* with her three masts, the brand new *Eagle* next to her, with the 17-gun *Ticonderoga* close by. Further out in the bay was the smaller *Preble*, while Macdonough's six galleys and four gunboats formed a protective perimeter at the mouth of the bay. A fifth ship had been detached to help ferry volunteers who were starting to arrive from Vermont.

The whole town was alive with activity, men in uniform rushing about everywhere as Macomb positioned his forces. He sent Tom Miller's small Clinton County militia north to Chazy, and stationed Lieutenant Fowler with the artillery at the north blockhouse on the point of the Saranac River.

Jesse passed another blockhouse where Captain Smyth, who he knew through his host Peter Sailly, was commanding a group of convalescents sent there to defend it. Some of the men had bandages on their heads, others their arms in slings. Some hopped around on crutches as they moved to their positions around the blockhouse. No one paid Jesse much heed as he hurried onto the bay. There a sentry informed him that the fleet was on high alert. No one was being allowed off or on the ships. When the sentry, who seemed arrogant and put out by Jesse's questions, refused to take a message to Sam for him, Jesse turned away disappointed and retraced his steps back to the Academy. He found a few of his friends there, who, like him, had decided to stay behind when their parents or hosts fled the village. They were getting together to drill.

"The fleet's in town," Jesse informed them, greeting his friends. They all had their bird guns and fowlers, old hand-me-down muskets. "You should see them. One of them, the *Saratoga's*, got 27-guns."

"I heard the new British ship's got 37 or more," said one of the boys, Judd Peters.

"Ah, that's just hearsay," countered Jesse. "Even so, it's not the number of guns but how well they're manned. My cousin says the *Eagle* and *Saratoga* have the best gun crews in the navy."

"You think they'll let us volunteer?" asked another boy, Fred Allen. He was one of the bigger of the students and something of a bully, but not a bad sort if you earned his respect. Like the others, he would shoot anything that moved as long as it was little, furry and lived in the woods. He now lived to shoot a redcoat.

"I don't know," replied Jesse. "Mister Sailly says they're desperate for men. They're even shipping them over from Vermont."

"I heard they called up the whole militia," volunteered another boy, a farm lad from Beekmantown, strong as an ox and about as smart. "They're down at Salmon River, must be 800 of 'em."

"Maybe we can join them," offered Judd Peters.

"Naw," said Jesse, remembering what some of the regular soldiers he knew thought about the militia. "I don't want to be a dumb militiaman, 'First at fun, first to run'."

They all laughed.

"No," he continued. "I want to fight in the regular army."

"Why don't we form our own troop," said Allen. "We're better shots than most of them anyway."

"I don't know about that," replied Jesse, looking at the class bully, who had been completely intimidated by Mike Lebow's boy after their first brief encounter. "They've got some of the best rifle companies in the army. That's why they needed them so bad out west. Anyway, I don't know if they'll let us form our own troop."

You know one of the captains don't you?" asked Judd Peters.

Jesse tried not to get too close to people after what had happened to his friend, Daniel. He thought of himself as a jinx to those he liked, so he shunned any type of closeness. He figured they'd be safer for it and he'd be spared any more terrible pain, but it was a lonely existence. Judd Peters had gone a long way toward overcoming Jesse's isolation.

"Even better," said Jesse, starting off toward the army camps south of town. "I know General Macomb himself."

They marched down the main street, which was usually thronged this time of day with farm carts and carriages all going to their appointed rounds. Today it was practically deserted except for soldiers and dragoons marching to their posts. They crossed the upper bridge and turned south to follow the river to its bend where the forts were being built, then headed for the main fortifications between Fort Brown on the Saranac and Fort Scott overlooking the bay.

"We're here to see the General," Jesse announced at the Fort Moreau sentry post.

"Colonel Smith is busy and not taking visitors," said the sentry, looking over the motley group of 20 or so boys.

"We're not here to see the Colonel," replied Jesse imperiously. "We're here to see General Macomb."

"And who should I tell him is calling?" asked the corporal on duty with a grin. "His majesty, the king of England?"

"We're here to volunteer," answered Jesse. "We want to fight the British."

"Volunteers need to report to the militia," said the sentry.

"Who says?" growled Allen, sizing up the guard.

"I say," replied the sentry, bristling at the large youth's tone and hostile stare.

"General Macomb knows me," said Jesse. "He's supped at my house."

"Is that so," answered the guard, who now thoroughly disliked Jesse and his whole presumptuous crew. "Then why don't you talk to him next time you're having dinner?"

"There's no call to be rude," said Jesse. "You may find you need our help."

"When I do, I'll call you. Now beat it," yelled the guard, finally losing his patience.

Some of the boys, who were all armed, started forward as if to crash the gate and the sentry's head, but Jesse put up his hand and told them to stop.

"What's going on here?" a sharp voice rang out from behind the sentry. They all looked up to see General Macomb striding forward from the fort where he was seeing to last minute defenses. Colonel Melancton Smith, the fort commander was by his side along with a retinue of officers.

"These unruly boys were trying to get into the fort, Sir," replied the sentry.

"That's not true General, Sir," said Jesse stepping forward. "We wanted to see you Sir, to volunteer. We're all good shots and want to fight the British."

Macomb looked at the raggedy group of boys, some dressed in hand-me-downs that were still too big, some in tight-fitting, worn out home-spun garments that had long seen their day, all too young for military service and all carrying weapons of one kind or another. He was loath to take them so young but he needed guns in the worst way.

"Don't I know you?" he asked, peering at Jesse with an amused expression.

"Yes, Sir. I was living with Mister Sailly. You came to the house a few times."

"Ah, yes," said the youngish looking, curly haired commander. "You're the lad from the bridge. If the others shoot like you the British are in trouble."

The others in his entourage smiled and chuckled, but Macomb was serious.

"But you will need to find officers to sponsor you," said the General. "They will be responsible for your conduct."

"I will sponsor them," announced Captain Martin Aiken from the Essex County militia visiting the fort to coordinate his troops with Macomb's regulars.

"I know the lad and some of these boys," volunteered a Lieutenant Flagg, editor of the village newspaper, the Plattsburgh Republican, and a Clinton County militiaman who was also in

Macomb's entourage. "They have been drilling regularly and are all good shots. I will vouch for them as well."

"Ah, very good, Gentlemen," said Macomb. "We will call them Aiken's Rifle Company after the captain here. You boys will report to Captain Aiken and Lieutenant Flagg. Gentlemen, these boys are under your command. You are responsible for them. Use them well."

"Thank you General," stammered Jesse as Macomb and his entourage moved on, still not believing his dream had come true. He was finally in the army. He was going to get a chance to fight redcoats. He and his friends could hardly contain their glee as they followed the militia officers into a nearby field to receive instructions.

"So you boys want to fight?" asked Aiken looking over his new rifle company.

"Yes, Sir," said Jesse. "We want to fight the Brits."

"Oh you do, do you?" laughed the Captain. "Well, you'll get plenty of chance for that if we're lucky."

"This is the boy who shot that English major when the British invaded the village last August," Flagg informed the captain. "Shot him right through the eye, he did. They're all expert shots. Isn't that right boys?"

"Aye," yelled Jesse, joined by the others.

"Well, you're going to have to follow orders and do as we tell you," said Captain Aiken.

"Yes, Sir," they all responded, standing to attention.

"Lieutenant Flagg here says you boys have been training."

"Yes, Sir," answered Jesse stepping forward, the natural leader of the group.

"Well, let's see what you can do."

Without further ado they set up some targets, large pieces of paper painted red with black stripes crisscrossing them, tied onto big bales of hay. Jesse put them through their paces. Lining them up in two lines, one row kneeling, one standing behind them, he yelled out a couple of brisk commands, whereupon they fired in unison, first the row kneeling, then the one standing.

The boys had practiced hard and were natural marksmen. All were quite adept at reloading their muskets, and able to get off two well-aimed shots in under a minute. As the second line fired, the first line loaded their muskets and was ready to discharge them again while the second row reloaded. Tearing the paper end off the cartridge with their teeth … pouring the powder into the pan … stuffing the cartridge down the barrel … ramming the ball onto the powder charge. They pulled back the hammer, aimed and fired in unison, all hitting the target, which was bullet-riddled and shredded by the time they were done with their demonstration.

"Very impressive," observed the Captain. "But the British can do that just as well and there are 10,000 of them."

"We ain't scared," replied Fred Allen, loading his musket again and ramming the ball home. "And we don't intend to stand out in the open like they do, do we boys."

They all grinned and yelled, "Hell, no."

"I'll have no cussing in my ranks, gentlemen," said Aiken, not amused. "Can you boys follow orders?"

"You get us close to the Brits," answered Jesse. "And we'll do whatever you say."

Aiken didn't like anyone obeying his orders with qualifications, but this was just the kind of wild bunch of hooligans that might prove to be a fly in the ointment of the very highly-tuned British military machine. After all, they needed every advantage they could get and every gun they could muster.

"Are you sure you want to do this?" Aiken cautioned, knowing the risks and dangers involved. "It will be highly dangerous. Some of you might get shot, even killed. You will have to kill men. You must be sure."

"We are," Jesse assured him. "They've got no business coming here and trying to take our homes. We want to fight. We want to show them they can't come in here and take what's not theirs. We're not afraid to die, and we're sure not afraid to shoot redcoats."

All the boys yelled their assent with feeling. They were eager to fight and would have done anything to get into battle, although none of them had any inkling of what it would really be like.

A short time later a messenger approached, saluted and handed Captain Aiken an envelope. He opened it and read the contents.

"Well, boys," he said. "The General has decided to send us north. We're going to Chazy, toward the British."

They all cheered and waved their hats.

Chapter 18

Plattsburgh Bay, NY, Evening, September 5, 1814

Earlier in the day Macdonough had ordered his ships to warp into line of battle, hearing that the British were advancing toward the village. Sam had been one of those who pulled on the anchor ropes and hawsers needed to bring the ship's guns to bear on the town.

There had been no word of any movement of the British fleet, now commanded by a Captain Downie, who had been ordered only days before from the Great Lakes to replace the former commander, who had known both the ships and the crews well. The new commander was frantically seeing to the completion and fitting up of the new 37-gun frigate *Confiance*.

Macdonough had had the men confined to quarters since they arrived in the Bay and some of them were beginning to complain. There was one drummer boy Sam had taken under his wing. The boy was only 12 or 13 and although he had volunteered with his family's consent, he was having second thoughts and wanted to go home. Sam felt sorry for him, and as the ship's assistant surgeon, he felt responsible for him as well. Besides that, he remembered Jesse's story about the little drummer boy who had been killed on the bridge and didn't want anything like that to happen on his watch.

Musicians were essential during battle. The drummers beat out commands, while the fifers piped instructions. This was true for the navy no less than the army, and Macdonough made his musicians practice daily for hours so they could play their parts under the most trying and dangerous of conditions, in the midst of battle with cannon balls landing and men dying all around them. Little Charley Rodgers had decided he wanted no part of it.

"You know what they do to deserters, don't you," said Sam, trying to dissuade the boy, who had come to his cabin to confide in him. "I'm sure if we talked to the Commander he would understand. Maybe I can give you a medical dispensation."

"No, they would put me in the brig for sure," replied Charley. "To make an example out of me so no one else decides to quit. But I can't do this, I know it."

"You know no such thing," Sam assured him. "Everyone gets scared and thinks they can't do something until it happens and they find out they could do it all along. You'll see."

"No I won't. I'm leaving."

"How? You'll get caught. Then they'll shoot you."

"I don't care. It's better 'an being blown to bits on this ship."

"You're not going to get blown to bits."

"How do you know? Can you predict the future?

"All right," said Sam finally. Seeing the boy was determined to go, an idea suddenly occurred to him. "If you're so intent on leaving, at least let me help you."

"How?" asked the reluctant drummer boy.

"Come with me."

Sam led him down to the Surgeon's quarters where some of the ship's medicines were kept. The officers were in the mess having dinner.

"Here, take this," he said, handing the youth a small green bottle of liquid. "It will give you cramps for a little while but won't hurt you. Just follow my lead and I'll have you off the ship in no time and on your way home. You're about to have a bout of appendicitis."

"What?" said the boy. "Appendicitis? What's that?"

"Stomach cramps. Now drink that."

A few minutes later Charley was writhing in agony on his hammock, complaining of severe stomach pains, which Sam immediately diagnosed as appendicitis.

"His appendix has burst," he told the seamen he had called to assist him. "We have to get him to shore where they can operate. I'll tell the surgeon. Now hurry!"

The urgency and the authority in his voice convinced the seamen gathered about to carry young Rodgers topside and row him ashore, where Sam borrowed a wagon and conveyed the boy to his family's home. His parents had the carriage hitched with all their worldly possessions ready to go at a moments notice, no doubt waiting until the last minute for their son to return.

Sam was back on the deck of the *Saratoga* before the ten o'clock watch. He felt bad lying to his commanding officer about young Rodgers, but it was better than seeing the boy shot while trying to desert.

"He had all the symptoms of acute appendicitis," he explained. The ship's surgeon and the Master Commandant looked at him dubiously. "He must have gotten into the medicine cabinet and gotten some of this." He handed over the bottle he had given the Rodgers boy to drink. "It would create symptoms similar to an appendix attack, although I'm not sure how he would know of this. He is a clever lad."

"Someone must have told him," observed Macdonough.

"Or helped him," said the surgeon. "Tell me these symptoms again."

Sam reiterated the text book symptoms he had read about in one of the surgeon's medical books.

"When I got him to shore I immediately took him to Doc Arnold's place. He's the only one in town who could do such an operation. I knew if his appendix had burst time would be critical."

"Why didn't you inform me immediately?" questioned the surgeon, still not convinced.

"You were on the *Eagle* having dinner with the Master Commander," answered Sam. "I didn't want to disturb you. I was going to get him ashore where he could be operated on, then come and inform you."

"You should have stayed with the patient at that point," grunted the Surgeon, who in any case would not have wanted to be bothered with such a trivial matter, not when he might be needed for much graver things in a few hours. "You could have seen how the operation was done. You might have to perform such a procedure yourself someday. It's actually quite simple."

"Not long after I dropped him off and returned to the doc's," continued Sam, not particular eager to perform an appendectomy himself. "I was told he had escaped, Sir." Sam looked at his commander sheepishly. "It's all my fault. He completely duped me. It must have been an act all along. As soon as I got him to the doctor's and he was alone, he climbed out a window and flew the coop as they say."

"Another deserter!" thundered Macdonough.

167

"He was only a drummer boy, Sir," said Lieutenant Joseph Smith, second in command of the flag ship. He was also present for Sam's interrogation, and tried to mitigate some of the trouble his friend, Mister Turner, was in. "Anyway, how was Turner here to know. It doesn't appear to be through any fault of his that young Rodgers has run away. After all, he was only a lad of 12."

"He was 13," said Macdonough. "He volunteered. No one coerced him. He was an important part of our crew. It will be much harder to beat commands during battle now with him gone. There better not be any more desertions."

Smith had never seen his commander so angry, but realized the stress and pressure the man must be under, and wondered how he managed.

"I will have the ships double the watch," Smith assured him, saluting and walking out.

"That will be all," said Macdonough dismissing the rest, including Sam Turner who he suspected had some duplicity in the boy's desertion. However, he could understand Sam's feelings and see the fairness of it. What irked him was that they did not trust him enough to come and ask him outright, for he would have granted any such honest request, especially from someone so young who was technically only a volunteer.

Macdonough ran his hands through his thick dark hair and rubbed his eyes. He missed his wife more than ever and wished that no matter what happened she would be safe. Then he closed his eyes and thought of God, praying out loud for the strength and wisdom he would need to endure this test the Lord had given him.

"Oh, Heavenly Father, thank you for all your bounties. Thank you for all you have given me. Let me do Thy Will, oh Lord, that I may be worthy of Thy love. You are the shield of the righteous, the defender of the meek. Let me be a sword in your hands, oh Lord, so that armed with your righteous power I may smite Thy enemies and have victory over those who have come to take our land and homes. I know you are here with us now, Oh Lord, as you have always been, as you were on the mount with Moses in the Holy Land. Let me stand with you Lord, where nothing can stand against you. Give me strength to do Thy will, oh Lord, so the world may know Your glory. Thank you, God Almighty. Amen."

He sat in silent meditation for some minutes, the stress and distractions of the outside world completely dissipated. He felt God was with him at that moment, as he contemplated His greatness and love for His creation. Despite all the hardships and fears, sickness and death, life truly was a gift, and that realization when it fully hit him at that moment overcame him with a joy so great it burst forth in tears of gratitude. After that he felt at peace. A short time later he had an idea.

Dead Creek, Village of Plattsburgh, NY, September 5, 1814 (Evening)

Ordered to report to Colonel Appling at Dead Creek, who was commanding the force defending the north approach to the city, Jesse and Aiken's boys were making their way north along the lake shore. It was late in the day, the sinking sun hidden by heavy gray clouds in the west. The air was pregnant with moisture.

"Why do we have to report to a colonel?" asked Judd Peters. "I thought we were supposed to report to Captain Aiken."

"We report to whoever they tell us to," replied Jesse. "If the Captain tells us to report to Colonel Appling, that's what we do."

"Sounds like he's trying to shove us off onto someone else," complained Fred Allen.

As they approached the old torn up bridge across the 'crick', Jesse remembered the last time he was there with his friend Daniel, that fateful day that started out so innocently and ended so tragically. He drove the thought from his mind as his small band of riflemen approached the creek.

"Sir," he said approaching the man in charge, "Aiken's rifle company reporting for duty, Sir."

Appling looked at the pint-sized, raggedy boy as if he had come from another planet. He was obviously not expecting anyone. He sized up the other boys with growing disdain.

"Where are your commanding officers?" he demanded to know.

"Back at the cantonment, Sir," answered Jesse, standing at his best imitation of attention. "Captain Aiken and Lieutenant Flagg ordered us here to help defend the bridge, Sir."

"We've got all the men we need," snapped Appling, pointing to the regulars and militiamen camped around the area. Their fires were already starting to glow in the waning light. "Why don't you boys take your pop-guns and go find a nice spot to camp for the night. I'll call you up if we need you to run some errands."

With that the colonel turned his back, dismissing him.

Jesse stood there for a moment looking at the officer's back then shook his head and walked back to his friends.

"What'd he say?" asked Judd Peters.

"Not much. Just that they don't need us," replied Jesse.

"That's the army for you," observed Fred Allen. "Tell you to go someplace then tell you to go someplace else. I'm sick of taking orders from these jackasses."

"Me, too," said some of the others.

"Everyone's too busy to look out for us, anyway," said Judd Peters.

"I say we make Jesse here our captain," suggested Fred Allen. "We know what to do."

They all voiced their agreement.

"All right, men," said their new commander. "Follow me."

Jesse led them back to the village along the lakeshore road, past large fields and small wooded plots to the mouth of the Saranac. There was a blockhouse at the point overlooking the bay. Peter Sailly's friend, Lieutenant Fowler was there commanding the troops guarding the artillery stationed at the point. It had grown dark and it was starting to rain.

"Well, well, if it isn't Mister Lebow," said the lieutenant, recognizing Jesse as he and his crew walked up. "What can I do for you boys? Why haven't you all left with your parents?"

"We've volunteered to fight the Brits," Jesse informed him. "General Macomb assigned us to Captain Aiken's company, with Lieutenant Flagg. They sent us to Dead Creek, but some of the boys here don't have guns, Sir, and the ones we have aren't that good. I was wondering, eh, if we could exchange them for real army rifles."

"Do you have any requisition orders?" asked the Lieutenant, a little amused but trying not to show it. He knew of Jesse's reputation and what he had done.

"No, Sir," answered Jesse. "But I figure if we're in the army and going to be fighting redcoats the least we can do is have real army guns."

"Well, private, that's good enough for me," said Fowler with a smile.

The lieutenant looked around at some of the old bird rifles and squirrel guns, hand-me-down muskets and vintage pistols the boys were carrying.

"Looks like you boys could use a little re-arming," he observed. "Let's see what you can do with these."

Opening the heavy, thick wooden door to the blockhouse, he reached inside and threw open a box full of the latest army issue rifles and started handing them out. Even Jesse's gun, given to him by his host Mister Sailly, paled in comparison. Soon they were armed to the teeth with the latest model 1812 flint-lock muskets. Their clothes may have been tattered and torn, but their arms were glistening new and shone in the candlelight of the blockhouse.

Something happened to that gang of boys that night as they marched away from the bunker to camp out on the point under the trees, where they found a deserted barn for shelter against a cold, hard rain.. They felt like part of something grand, even though their numbers were quite small, especially in comparison to the huge force bearing down on them, over three times their size. The look and feel of their new weapons … the way they felt in their hands as they hefted them to aim … the awesome silent power of the things, so much more accurate and with so much more range than anything they had shot before. It gave them a feeling of invincibility. With such guns in their hands they could do anything.

Jesse looked around at his little group with pride – Judd Peters, Henry Averill, Ira Wood, St. John Skinner, Jonathan Woodward, Melancton Travis and Freddy Allen. Even little 14-year old Hiram Wadsworth looked bigger with his shiny new musket in his hand. They had come a long way from practicing their drills in the schoolyard.

The next day they awoke, wet and cold, to the news that the British had arrived. Their right flank was within a mile of the west end of the village along the Beekmantown road. The boys gobbled down some hardtack Captain Aiken had given them, grabbed their new rifles and rushed to the area, but there was nothing happening when they got there. Everything was quiet. Not a redcoat in sight. They spent the better part of the morning rushing about following every rumor and glimmer of a redcoat but none appeared. Jesse was getting a little frustrated and called a halt to it around noon. He ordered the boys to forage for something to eat and found a good campsite. So far his first day of command had been less than stellar.

Allen quickly shot a couple of chickens at a nearby deserted farm house and Judd had them cooking over an open fire in no time. A few of the boys grabbed some apples from a nearby orchard and they settled down for their repast. They were just finishing their lunch, talking about what they would do when they finally found the British. Suddenly, gunfire erupted to the northwest only a few miles away. They picked up their guns and rushed in the direction of battle.

As they ran the gunfire increased, then cannon fire could be heard, booming in the near distance. The sounds of battle led them in a northwesterly direction toward Beekmantown where the British right flank was marching down the center of the road at Culver's Hill.

By the time the boys got there the Americans were falling back, firing as they went from behind trees and fences. Jesse and his friends rushed through the retreating militiamen straining to see a redcoat among the fleeing soldiers. Soon they reached the Halsey House, at the corner near the Platt Farm on the Beekmantown road. They were just in time to see two cannons fire three brisk rounds of grape and ball into the advancing British.

Jesse had never seen anything like it. The roar of the cannons, the thick acrid smoke, the screams and cries of the wounded and dying as they were mowed down like stacks of hay by the blasts, shocked the boys into dumb, staring silence. As they watched in horror, a mass of men in red surged toward the now silent guns, and grappling hand-to-hand with the struggling defenders, captured them. Those who could, made a hasty retreat over the bridge to the south side of the river.

"Come on boys!" yelled Jesse, urging his men forward toward a knot of men firing at the British from a small wooded area as the enemy formed up on the opposite bank of the river. Soon Aiken's riflemen were among them, finally getting their chance to shoot redcoats. And shoot them they did.

There were so many of them in their bright red uniforms with their white belts across their chests that they were hard to miss as they stood in lines right in the middle of the road. Every now and then they'd unleash a solid volley into the woods in front of them, but usually with little effect. Their shots were high, and whoever had just fired from that spot had already moved to another. Soon, however, more redcoats came up until the whole north bank was covered with them, along with cannons and cavalry. They streamed toward the bridge and began flanking the defenders, who had to move back to avoid being trapped.

As the regulars and Militia retreated back toward the village and the forts, Aiken's boys crossed the road at the new bridge and Winehel's Mill and positioned themselves behind the mill's old stone walls. As the British formed up on the near bank, the boys began firing into them at will, their shots seldom missing the mass of red coats.

Even Jesse, who had already killed a man, felt sickened at seeing his bullets hit their mark and a man jerk and fall to the ground, not to move again, or even worse, to wiggle and spasm in his death throes. He soon became immune to it. The British had come half way around the world, uninvited, to invade his home and try and take it. "Well, this is what you get," he thought, taking aim and killing another, shooting him right between the eyes. Some of the other boys weren't taking it too well and had stopped shooting altogether. Some vomited on the ground. Some were scared and looking behind them for a place to run as the British balls whizzed over their heads and got closer. Some, like Fred Allen, had a demented gleam in their eyes and seemed to enjoy the killing. Jesse just thought it was necessary. They were defending their country against invasion. Suddenly he heard one of his boys cry out and they stopped shooting altogether.

He rushed to the sound of the cry with the others to find his friend Judd Peters lying on the ground. He was always the best dressed of the group, in his new clothes with the latest style, always the best looking with his fresh haircut and trim figure. Now he lay on the ground his arms stretched over his head, his eyes closed, as if sleeping off a late night binge, except he had a small red hole in his new white shirt right over the heart.

"No!" cried Jesse. "Not Judd!"

He knelt over the body, trying to shake him awake. "Wake up Judd! Wake up!"

"I don't think he's going to wake up," observed Fred Allen. "They shot him clear through the heart. He's dead."

They all stood around the body in shock. In their youthful exuberance they hadn't considered their own mortality, their feeling of invincibility bolstered by the British army's obvious inability to effectively deal with them. It was like shooting partridges at a fair. They had lost all respect for their enemy only to now realize that all it took was a lucky shot from a single musket to end it all. Death suddenly became all too real, all too close.

"They're coming," said one of the boys, looking down at the river where the British were now moving up the bank toward the old mill where they were hidden. "We better get out of here."

But Jesse wouldn't go. "Leave him," cried Allen, trying to tug Jesse away from his dead comrade.

"No," said Jesse, shaking Fred off violently. "We're not leaving Judd here. Help me."

With that, even as the British were at the water's edge, he had the others help him lift Judd's body and carefully carry it back to the village. It was hard going, the dead weight of their comrade making him seem twice as heavy as he was. They carried him back through the trees, managing to avoid the British who came on in hot pursuit. The English were irate at being shot at by a foe that wouldn't show itself or stand and fight, a foe that fought like a bunch of savage Indians.

Jesse and the boys eventually made it back to the cantonment with their dead friend in their arms. Jesse reported Judd's death to Captain Aiken, who sorely regretted hearing the news. All their exuberance, all their lust for war, had gone, at least for the moment. None of the boys slept that night. They all thought of poor Judd, cold and dead at the age of sixteen. Some cried, but not Jesse. As the night wore on, thoughts of sadness turned to thoughts of bitter revenge. Before daybreak, with hardly an hour of sleep, they took their rifles and stalked off into the damp morning mist bent on retribution.

Chapter 19

Dead Creek, Village of Plattsburgh, NY, September 6, 1814.

The British advanced toward Plattsburgh along two parallel lines, their right flank on the Beekmantown road, the other along the lake shore road. When the left column approached the creek about a mile north of town at the northern most end of the lake, it halted. As the men milled about the dismantled bridge, more soldiers arrived from the rear until the road got quite crowded. Suddenly a cannonball landed in the middle of the crowd, dirt and body parts flying everywhere.

Someone pointed toward the lake, where a puff of smoke could be seen at the front of a gunboat. Another could be seen floating next to it. A minute later another cannonball crashed among the terrified British.

For a moment there was widespread panic and confusion, as everyone tried to find cover in the confined and crowded space.

"Bring up the artillery," yelled the officer in charge at the bridge, a major. "If they think they can shoot us down with impunity, they will have to think again, by George."

Soon half a dozen 6-pounders were taking aim on the two gunboats, which continued to fire sporadically, but now from farther away.

"How about it, Sir, should we give them the rockets?" suggested his artilleryman.

"That's a good thought Lieutenant," said the major, resplendent in his red officer's coat on top of his white charger. A few moments later, a bank of Congreve rockets were raining down on the gunboats, which because of the choppy water could not return fire. They beat a hasty retreat. Soon after that, the British had the bridge repaired and were marching across it like a conquering army, spreading out on the north bank of the Saranac river like marauding red ants.

While his troops bivouacked along the lake, Prevost, the Governor-General of Quebec and commander of the British invasion forces, surveyed the scene from his headquarters at the Allen Farm. Located on the crest of a hill about a mile west of the mouth of the river, it had a perfect prospect of the whole bay with Macdonough's ships in the middle. The disposition of his troops as they occupied the village and the surrounding districts was also clearly visible. His headquarters was in the middle of a roughly four square mile area occupied by his forces, which stretched another three miles to the west and two to the north, all the way from the river and lake.

His second in command, Major General de Rottenburg, surveyed the enemy positions with him. He had nothing but disdain for the Americans and their army.

"I can see the American forts and the positions of most of their troops," he observed, looking through a field glass. "It is not an impressive sight. Two or three small sand berms faced with wooden boards and open interiors, and a few trenches thrown around them. Nothing like the fortifications our lads had to overcome in Spain and Portugal or France. I see no problem in taking the place. We will either drive them out or flank and destroy them. Give me a couple of days."

Prevost's glasses were trained on the lake where Macdonough's ships were strung in the middle of the Bay, right next to the village.

"What about them?" he asked with concern. "Their gunboats caused quite a disruption on the lake road, I'm told. Several of Brisbane's and Robertson's men were killed and wounded. Our troops will be within range of their ships' guns while attacking the forts."

"Don't worry, General," said de Rottenbug. "We will have our artillery drive them from the bay. In any case, our fleet will take care of the American ships soon enough. With the new frigate we should have a distinct advantage. It will not matter. In the end their fleet will not avail them."

Prevost wasn't so sure and looked at his plans again. Soon the sound of cannon and musket fire erupted near the river.

"Our troops must be arriving," observed de Rottenburg.

Prevost looked at his map, which was laid out on a table next to him with the remains of his midday meal.

To the west of him was General Power, a veteran of Wellington's army, whose forces formed his right flank outside the village. De Rottenburg's own forces occupied the left division, east of Power and in the main part of the village. Brisbane was in the van along the lake shore and in the lower village. Robinson was just north of him. Brisbane's forces started building batteries on the north bank of the river near its mouth soon after occupying the Delord House overlooking the Bay. Macdonough's fleet was in plain view a few hundred yards away.

De Rottenburg jabbed at the map. "We need to find a ford or several such places and get our men across the river to flank them and come upon their rear. Then we will have them, Sir, trapped like the rats they are."

"We don't even know how many men they have," replied the Governor-General.

"They cannot have even half our numbers," said his second in command. "We have reports their General Izard is in Sacket's Harbor. Our diversions have worked."

"Yes, as has Cochran's wonderful diversion in their Capital," said Prevost.

"Yes, Sir," replied de Rottenburg. "These Americans will be taught a lesson they will not soon forget."

Prevost seemed not to hear as he stared out at the distant bay.

"We have to get rid of that blasted fleet," he said again to no one in particular.

Plattsburgh Bay, NY, September 6, 1814

Macdonough surveyed his line of ships as they sat in the bay near the shore, lost in thought. His second in command, Lieutenant Joseph Smith, who had been transferred back to the *Saratoga* from command of the *Eagle*, watched the shore where the British were building batteries on the point near the mouth of the river. Macdonough had done as Macomb had asked and stationed his ships near enough to the village to cover it during an

178

attack, but they were now in danger of being bombarded themselves.

"They're placing batteries on the Point, Sir," observed Smith. "We will be in range of their guns by morning."

Macdonough said nothing, still lost in thought.

"We will move them tonight," the Master Commandant said finally. "When the moon has gone down and it is darkest. Although I have no word of their movement, I expect the British fleet any day now. With their new ship, their strength will be equal to ours, maybe a little stronger."

"Will you meet them in the open lake sir, where we can maneuver?" asked his 1st Lieutenant, assuming Macdonough would follow longstanding naval wisdom.

"I think not," replied Macdonough, having other ideas. "Why give them the advantage of the winds and currents, which will be from the north. No, I'll wait for them at the mouth of the Bay. We will move into position tonight, here, about a half mile from our present position."

He pointed to his charts on the table beside them.

"But sir, we will not be able to maneuver," protested the Lieutenant. "Won't that give them all the advantage? They will be able to bear down on us as they like. We will be sitting helpless."

"That's just what I'm hoping they will think, Mister Smith. Mister Williams' scouts have reported that their fleet has a large complement of long 24's. If we remain out in the lake they'll smash us to pieces. Our carronades won't reach them. We'd not be able to maneuver either. But I know these waters quite well now. He'll lose the wind as he turns south around the 'Head' and stall, in irons, right within range of our guns. It is they who will find they can't maneuver. We will block the approach to the bay from the south and they will be within range of the guns on Crab Island. It is our best chance."

Smith thought long and hard, and looked dubious but said nothing, trusting his commander's judgment.

Later that night, they silently warped the ships a half mile south to take up their position at the mouth of the bay and out of range of the British guns on the point.

The next day, with no British fleet in sight, Macdonough let some of the men go ashore to see their families. Since Sam's was

179

20 miles away in the western mountains having little news of their son, Sam remained on board in a semi-depressed state, which was unusual given his sunny disposition.

"Why so glum, Mister Turner?" asked Smith, who was the officer on the watch.

"Oh, no reason, Sir," answered Sam. "It's just that most of the men got to go ashore and I'm left here alone."

"Not entirely, young Mister Turner, I am here with you as well, for I have no family here in the village. I have a note for you that might cheer you up though. It just arrived. Seems someone wants to see you after all."

"Who?" said Sam, jumping to his feet. If he'd had a tail, it would have been wagging.

"Let me see," replied the Lieutenant, pretending to read the note, but feigning poor eyesight. "I can't quite make it out. A Mister, ah, no, a Miss…"

Unable to bear the suspense any younger, Sam snatched the note from the Lieutenant's hands and scanned it quickly. Smith laughed and looked on smiling. It was from Sam's fiancée, Sarah Nichols. She was visiting her uncle again and waiting to meet him.

After getting a pass Sam took the ship's gig to shore. Because of the shelling along the river, he was landed a half mile south of the boat dock, at a small sand beach used as the landing for the makeshift hospital on Crab Island. Sarah was there waiting for him. They could hear the incessant cannon and musket fire along the river as each side took random potshots at the other.

"Oh, Sam, I thought I'd never see you," she said on greeting him.

"Things have been pretty tight," he replied, not showing his emotions. "The commander has let a few men off the ship to see their families. The rest of us had to remain on duty. The British fleet's expected any day now. How did you manage this?"

"My uncle has some influence in these matters," she said cryptically. "I just had to see you. I'm so scared."

"Why have you not gone home where it's safe?" asked Sam, concerned for her safety. "What are you doing here all alone?"

"My father has come to take me home, but I want to stay here with you," she answered.

"No, that's impossible. It's not safe. You must go."

"I can't leave you," she said, throwing her arms around him.

They were still standing in the middle of the landing, which was crowded with men in uniform bustling about. Sam wasn't used to public displays of affection, having enough trouble showing it in private.

"Come," he said, taking her by the elbow and walking her to a more secluded spot near a row of young trees a short distance away along the shoreline. "You should not have come here alone," he commented when they were by themselves.

"I had to see you. Anyway, my uncle is with me. He's seeing your commander for one thing or another. As I said, he seems to have some influence in these matters. He says the British have a big new ship and possibly an advantage in fire power. Oh, Sam, I'm so afraid for you. I wish you could go away with me."

"Maybe later. Now it's my duty to stay and fight. They need me."

"So do I. My uncle says he might be able to get you assigned to the hospital on his island."

"How dare you meddle in my affairs!" yelled Sam, afraid she had already gotten him reassigned. "He had better not!"

She seemed hurt and surprised.

"I'm sorry," she said.

Sam instantly regretted his outburst.

"I'm sorry dear, but being on that ship means more to me than anything, more than life itself."

"More than me?"

"In a way. If I don't do this now I could never live with myself. I would be letting all my mates down. I would feel half a man, unworthy of you, unworthy of anything."

"But you may die. Then what would I do?"

"Marry another and remember me with a smile. But I would loathe the person who stood between me and this chance, so please don't."

"So here you are," came a voice from behind them.

"Oh, hello Mister Nichols," said Sam, greeting Sarah's Uncle Caleb. "I was just telling Sarah how much serving on the *Saratoga* means to me."

181

"Yes, my boy, your Master Commandant was just saying the same thing. If spirit and intention mean anything, the British are in trouble, even if they outnumber us three to one. But on the lake, my boy, from my reckoning, you're dead even."

"I was just telling Sam you might be able to get him reassigned," said Sarah. She seemed oblivious of Sam's recent words, so caught up was she in trying to protect him from harm.

"There will be no talk of that my dear," replied her uncle. "Sam is where he belongs as are all the brave lads who have come here this day to fight. God bless them all."

Sam stood there not knowing what to say. Sarah looked ready to cry.

"Say, I have an idea," said Nichols. "You have a few hours. It's a splendid day. I had my man fix a picnic lunch, but I have another engagement and can't eat it. Why don't you kids have a picnic for yourselves. The top of the bluff has a splendid view of the lake. It will do you good."

He pointed south through the trees along the shore where the land rose to a high bluff overlooking the lake. Caleb Nichols took Sam and his niece to the top of the hill in his buggy and left them off at a grassy knoll, where they had a picnic lunch as if it were any late summer day and 10,000 British regulars weren't camped across the river a mile away. Sam looked out over a scene that would have been peaceful without the constant bombardment and rifle fire in the distance.

There to the left, at the mouth of the bay formed by the protruding piece of land known as Cumberland Head, not a mile away, was the fleet in line of battle. The *Eagle* lay furthest away to the north, with the *Saratoga* next to it. Then came the *Ticonderoga*, with the small 7-gun *Preble* next to her and closest to Crab Island. The gunboats and galleys sat to the left of the larger ships, along the western shore. Crab Island, where Sarah's uncle lived and a hospital had been established, was to their immediate right, not more than a half mile away. The spot was deserted, just the two of them, though they could still hear the booming of artillery and the popping of muskets in the distance along the river."

"I wish they'd stop," she said. "They've been shooting all night and day."

"I know, ever since the British army arrived."

"It's just terrible," she complained.

"Let's try to forget it for a little while and enjoy our picnic. Anyway, you should have left long ago. I'm surprised your uncle is so nonchalant about it."

"Oh, he's not. Both he and my dad want me to go back to Whitehall, but I refused to go without seeing you."

"Well, you've seen me, and after we've had a chance to spend some time together, you have to promise me that you will go home."

She looked out at the ships in the bay.

"Your ships look beautiful out there," she said.

"You should see them when the sails are unfurled, as they look taking the wind together. It's magnificent."

"I can see why you love it so," she continued, looking at him with pride and admiration, which was a big part of her love for him. Yet she was afraid for his safety as well. "It's just that I don't know what I'd do if anything happened to you."

"Nothing's going to happen to me," Sam assured her. "I've been in battles before, you know. This is not the first time I'm going to have some balls shot at me."

"Why does this have to happen?" she asked, clinging to him. "Why are they doing this?"

Sam had asked that same question many times, of his father and his friends, of his comrades and officers on the ships, of anyone who would answer, and the answer was more or less always the same.

"Well, for one thing we declared war on them," he said, stating the obvious. "I guess they didn't quite learn their lesson from the last war. They lost it but still think they own us and can tell us what to do. Now that they beat Napoleon in France, they're coming back to show us who's boss and try to take it back. We have to finish what our fathers started and show them once and for all we're a country to be reckoned with, to be respected as such."

"Well, if you are brave enough to stay and fight," she said, standing with her feet apart and her hands on her hips. "Then I'm going to stay, too. I'm going to stay right here with you."

Chapter 20

Village of Plattsburgh, NY, September 7, 1814

Jesse and the boys had spent the night at the Salmon River Settlement where there were also large contingents of New York and Vermont militia arriving continuously from morning to night. They had spent the preceding day at the blockhouse at Gravelly Point at the east end of the docks taking pot shots at the British as they streamed into the village.

They still hadn't recovered from their loss yet, but were thirsting for revenge. They spent the day running up and down the river skirmishing with whatever redcoats would turn their way. At one point they joined up with a group of regulars who seemed to have a good firefight on their hands.

"Can we be of service?" Jesse asked the lieutenant in charge.

"We're engaging the troops of Wellington's Grand Army of the Peninsular War, young man," answered the officer. "You had better let the 6th infantry handle this and go back to school."

The insult stung him. "There's no call to be rude," he replied. "We're volunteers. General Macomb himself assigned us to Captain Aiken and Lieutenant Flagg."

"Then I suggest you go find them and play soldier with them," said the lieutenant. "We have a real battle on our hands."

Jesse was about to say something rude when there was a thud and the lieutenant grabbed his groin, falling to the ground at Jesse's feet writhing in pain. Several of his men rushed to his side. He had been it by a musket ball in his private area. His white pants were covered with blood in no time. Jesse and the boys laid down a covering fire as the lieutenant's men brought him to the rear, but they were soon all driven back by the enemy's superior numbers.

"What's his name?" Jesse asked, as they moved back to cover the infantrymen's retreat.

"Lieutenant Runk," said one of his men, a sergeant named Nate Peters, as he helped carry the fallen officer away. "He was a good man."

184

"Will he make it?" asked Jesse.

"I doubt it," answered Nate. "He's lost a lot of blood. He'll be lucky if he lives through the night."

He died the next day, the only army officer killed in the battle, but by then Aiken's boys would be burying one their own.

Demoralized and tired, still reeling from their loss of the previous day, Jesse and his friends returned to the settlement. That evening after a desultory supper, someone made a surprise visit to their camp.

"Hi, men," said General Macomb, showing up unannounced and attended only by their sponsors, Captain Aiken and Lieutenant Flagg. "I'm hearing good things about you boys. I'm sorry to hear about Judd Peters. He was a good lad. He died defending his country. His name will live on in this nation's memory for generations. We are going to have a ceremony for him at the cemetery tomorrow. He will be buried with full military honors. In the meantime, I want you boys to rest and take things easy. We have some new uniforms for you at the fort. You can stop by there before the ceremony and pick them up."

The General's words lifted their spirits, especially those of Jesse, who was feeling quite low. The news that his friend would be buried with full military honors and remembered as a hero was a boon to him. His feelings of sadness changed to pride with the knowledge that Judd's death would have meaning, not like that other death on the bridge not so long ago.

Village of Plattsburgh, NY, September 8, 1814

Prevost inspected his troops, walking his large white horse down a broad street from the hillcrest at the west end of the village east to the lake, the whole mile's distance filled with his army. Both sides of the road were crowded with British troops as far as the eye could see. Every field and orchard, every lawn and hillock, the landscape was dotted with their campfires and tents. His generals rode with him, all on their thoroughbred stallions, impeccably groomed and harnessed. Troops at attention lined the road the whole way.

185

Sporadic gunfire could be heard in the distance along the river, which increased as they approached the village. The entire layout of the battlefield, including the lake, was in view as they descended the low hills to the water. The valley was as fertile and lush as any in the country, farmland and grazing land and woods for hunting, a veritable paradise to English eyes. Prevost nearly salivated when he thought of the possibilities for his nation. He could also see the lake, however, and the evident possession of it by the American fleet was the only annoying feature disrupting the perfect picture.

His entourage took a left when they reached the main street of the upper village, and followed the Saranac. Keeping back behind the hilltop overlooking the river near its mouth, they stayed out of range of the incessant musket file and occasional cannon ball. The English fired back in turn, neither side doing much damage, but keeping up the firing all the same for appearance sake if nothing else. Ignoring the warnings of his junior officers, the Governor-General made his way to a point near the river's mouth to get a better look at the situation in the bay, stopping at the Delord house where a command post had been established.

"Sir, you are within range of their guns here," observed his adjutant.

"That can't be helped, Captain," responded Prevost. "I have to see the situation for myself if I am to direct this attack."

A diversion had been staged further up the river, where they could hear the firing increase, so they hadn't yet been noticed. "We're safe for the time being," the Governor-General assured him, satisfied.

He asked for his field glass and scanned the bay from his vantage point. The mouth of the Saranac River was below him, the western shore of Cumberland Head a mile and a half away across the bay to the east. Macdonough's ships were right in the middle of the Bay blocking its entrance.

"We established the battery on the point as you ordered, Sir," said General Brisbane, whose troops occupied the left flank closest to the lake and river. "But they must have towed their fleet further out during the night. They're out of range now."

Just then a cannon ball thudded into the yard in front of the house a short distance from where they stood, showering it with dirt and shattering windows.

"Where did that come from?" exclaimed Prevost, ducking instinctively.

"Must have come from across the river," replied Brisbane. "I don't think the naval guns can reach us here. It's no longer safe, General. I think we should withdraw."

"That's all right," said Prevost, whose descendants would one day place a commemorative granite block on the spot where he stood overlooking the bay. "I've seen all I need to."

Back at his headquarters at the Allen Farm, on the hillcrest west of town, he received the dispatch he had been awaiting. The news did not make him happy.

"Blast it!" he exclaimed on reading it.

"What is it General?" his adjutant asked in alarm.

"It's Downie. He says the fleet won't be ready for another two days. I'll be blasted if I'm going to attack and waste time and good men with that bloody American fleet sitting out there within range of my troops."

A short time later a rather stunned and miffed General de Rottenburg conveyed the Governor-General's orders to the other commanders.

"What?" objected General Power, whose forces occupied the British right flank, which stretched to Hammond Farm three miles outside the village. His forces had already started to reconnoiter viable crossing places where he could ford the river and flank the enemy. "I'm already starting to probe the north bank of the river. We can have them flanked and surrounded in a couple of days, captured in two more. Why have us stop now?"

"I believe the Commander wants to wait for Downie to clear the American fleet from the bay."

"He seems to be obsessed with that bloody fleet. Damn the boats!" swore Power. "We have an assured victory here. All we have to do is press on."

"The General has his reasons. Anyway, what have you got against a little rest, heh? We've been marching and camping for days."

"My men are tired of all this and want to get things over with so they can go home."

"We all want that, Manley, but there's no reason to take chances," said Prevost's second in command. "We don't even know their real strength or position. They say there are troops and volunteers streaming in from all the states in their country, even with our diversion in Washington."

"So much more reason for us to press on," replied Power, one of Wellington's best.

"Don't let your emotions get the best of you, Manley," said de Rottenburg. "What happened to Lord Wellington's nephew is not your fault. It's the chances of war. He fell leading his men in the vanguard of our forces. It could have happened anywhere, to anyone."

"It has nothing to do with Colonel Willington's death, General," answered General Power, somewhat annoyed by de Rottenburg's reference. "It is just plain good soldiering. We have the advantage. By all estimates we outnumber the enemy three to one. There is no reason to stop now and every reason to continue our operations. Why give the Americans time to assemble more troops and build more fortifications? Tell me, Sir, what is the logic in that? Would Wellington wait here like this? Would the great tyrant Napoleon do so? I think not."

"I would be careful what you say to the Governor-General right now, Manley," suggested the division commander. "He is under a lot of pressure. Much rides on the outcome of our mission. He knows this country as well as any man and sees the big picture."

"He is afraid to lose men," said Power flatly. "Lord Wellington would have known what to do with these troops. He is not afraid to lose men."

"Neither was Caesar, or Napoleon for that matter, and look how many thousands upon thousands of men they are responsible for slaughtering, on both sides. After the calamities in Europe we might all pause before we throw more men into battle."

"That kind of thinking is no way to win a war," replied Power.

"Perhaps not, Manley, but we are all tired of it after so many years. I pray for an end of it."

"And so do I, Sir. So let us do our job and finish it."

"I will do what I can to recommend continuing your flanking activities, General Power, but in the meantime, you will obey your orders and hold you current position. Is that understood?"

"Yes, Sir, General, and let me respectfully thank you for letting me speak my mind."

"I always want you to speak your mind to me, Manley," said de Rottenburg. "That is something I value much."

General Power and the others obeyed their orders but none of them were happy about it. Power, for one, had grave misgivings about the consequences of delaying the attack.

Village of Plattsburgh, NY, September 8, 1814

Sergeant Nate Peters was at Fort Brown where the noise of the cannon and rifle fire was deafening. It had been going on all day. To what effect, Nate and his men did not know, for although they could see the enemy in the distance on the opposite bank, they could not tell if their individual shots hit their mark or not. All that could be seen were the small puffs of musket fire as the enemy shot back, and the concussive "thud" of the American cannonballs as they landed amongst them.

What Nate saw did not look good, however. Their numbers were staggering, more than he ever thought possible. He had never seen so many soldiers in one place, and the fact that they were the enemy made Nate feel very small. He had all he could do to keep up his bravado and spirits in front of his men in the face of such overwhelming numbers. He wondered if his side had done all it could in building their fortifications, which now seemed quite pitiful. Their own forces, spread thin along the south bank of the river from its mouth to Pike's cantonment, a few miles west of town, now seemed terribly inadequate.

"It doesn't look good, does it Sergeant?" observed the lieutenant in charge of the berm, an agreeable fellow who Nate respected for his commonsense attitude and experience. All the men, including Nate, were still reeling from the loss of the popular Lieutenant Runk.

"No, Sir," replied Nate. "There sure are a lot of them. I don't see how we can stop them, Sir."

"We can't, but we can make them pay for every inch of our soil they walk on. Have you heard about Washington?" he asked his sergeant.

"No, Sir. What happened?"

"They burned the capital is what they did," answered the Lieutenant, still not believing it himself and finding it hard to live down the insult. "They burned the nation's capital and got off Scott free. Not only could we not defend our own capital, we let the enemy get away without so much as firing a shot. It's downright disgraceful, I say, almost enough to make you ashamed to be an American. Well it won't happen here, not if our General has anything to say about it. Macomb is a crafty fighter. He'll think of something."

"I sure hope so," said Nate, surveying the mass of troops in red on the other side of the Saranac.

"They'll be probing along the river, looking for likely places to ford," observed the Lieutenant. "We won't stop them by sitting up here."

He ordered Nate to take a dozen men to march west along the back roads, then circle back east along the river in full view of the enemy. Nate gave him a questioning look, then saluted and did as he was ordered.

"And don't stop marching until I tell you to stop."

"Yes, Sir," answered Nate, walking back to his platoon with a frown.

By his estimate, Nate and his men had been marching up and down this road in circles for the past six hours. It had been a cold, blustery rainy day and it was now almost six at night. Of course, he knew what Macomb was doing and told the men as much, but that didn't make the incessant traipsing up and down the road any easier to take.

At points on their circuit Nate would get a good glimpse of the north side of the river, where the land rose gradually to the crest of the western hills. There he could see thousands of the enemy with their red uniforms and their white tents. They covered the ground from east to west like locusts as far as he could see. Their numbers made Nate's own forces, which had only a few days before given him comfort, now seem pitifully small in comparison. They stretched for miles while the Americans clustered in little knots around their forts and bunkers.

"I am getting tired of this endless marching around," complained one of his men, marching in line near him.

"It's for a good purpose, I assure you," said Nate. "The more men they think we have the more cautious they will be and slow to attack. That will give reinforcements time to arrive."

"You think General Izard will return?" asked the man, hopefully.

"I don't know, but let's make them think every citizen in the state has come to our defense."

"Yes, Sir," replied the private. "If it means not having to fight."

"Oh, I'm afraid we will have to fight," Nate assured him. "At least I hope so. Isn't that right men?"

They all grunted their agreement, but it was half-hearted and doubt-ridden, affected as it was by the sea of British across the river.

"Let's make some noise then," he yelled. And they all yelled back. As they marched Nate shouted out phrases to ignite their martial zeal and they recited some equally violent sentiment back in unison, raising the hair on the back of his neck. Sometimes he just loved the army.

A little while later, while they were marching out of town again on the back roads out of sight of the enemy to come back in on the west road in full view, Nate got talking to his lieutenant, Nathan Hammock, who was riding alongside the platoon on his horse.

"There sure are a lot of them, eh Sergeant?" observed the Lieutenant, again, expressing the same observation he'd made earlier in the day.

"I can't deny that, Sir," replied Nate. "But will they know what to do with them?"

"From who I hear they have commanding them, I reckon so," said the Lieutenant.

"Then what are we going to do?" asked Nate in concern. "Do we even have a chance?"

"Oh, there's always a chance. The fortunes of war are fickle. The Brits don't appear to be overly aggressive. As a matter of fact, we aren't seeing much of a concerted effort to cross the river at all. Perhaps they are waiting for their fleet before they attack."

"The longer they wait the better for us. Right, Sir?" reasoned Nate.

"That's right, Sergeant, and the more we can deceive them the better as well."

"That's why all the marching, right?"

"Right. It will inflate our numbers in their eyes and make them all the more cautious. It's always darkest before the light, Nate, but General Macomb has a few tricks up his sleeve, I assure you. He'll bamboozle these British if anyone can."

Nate looked across the river and let out his breath in a loud exhale. "I don't see how the General is going to hold his position. There're too many of them. They'll flank us easily and get to our rear. With our backs to the lake we'd be in a tough position."

"That's just what Macomb wants them to try," said Hammock. "He has an idea and we, Sergeant, are going to help carry it out."

"What do you have in mind, Sir?" asked Nate, happy to do anything other than march.

"See this road we're on?" Hammock said pointing behind him.

"Yes, Sir, the one we been marching on," replied Nate.

"Well, as you know, it leads east right back to the village. Now what if we sort of disguise it say, and make it turn and go in a more southerly direction, say a mile and a half to the Salmon River. That might cause them a little confusion, wouldn't you say Sergeant?"

"Yes, Sir. That might lead them astray a bit," said Nate, getting the idea and a good chuckle.

A short time later, after dark and without fires or torches, Nate and his men threw off their jackets and traded their muskets for axes and shovels. They were covering one road and making

another where there had been none, following General Macomb's
new orders.

Chapter 21

Village of Plattsburgh, NY, September 9, 1814

Jesse stood at attention with the other boys of Aiken's Rifle Company in their new uniforms, their heads hung low, as they buried their fallen comrade, Judd Peters. They had all said their silent goodbyes, all except Jesse, who had the most to say but couldn't find the thoughts to form the silent words. His mind was empty, a deep black pit that he was afraid to look into. Instead he saw nothing, felt nothing.

Judd was gone, just like his friend Daniel, never to return and that's all there was to it. He knew his mother would have told him they were in heaven and at peace, but Jesse had little concept of such things, hardly having gone to church since his eleventh birthday. Jesse didn't look back. There wasn't much there for him to remember except playing on the barroom floor, getting cuffed by his father and losing his friends. Instead, he looked forward to fighting redcoats.

He felt badly about what had happened to Judd and wanted to pay his respects, but most of all wanted to get back to soldiering. He knew he would never get another opportunity like this again, for wars come only once or twice a century and this one had already seen two. This would be the last chance for many a year for a boy to become a man in the heat of battle, fighting to defend his home and country, and he could think of nothing better than to die a hero in battle. He envied Judd for that and fantasized constantly about it, and the tears everyone would shed. And if he lived, he would become like his Uncle Benjamin, Sam's father, and others like him, respected war heroes, patriots of the first order. It was all the same to him. After that, nothing much mattered.

With the village cemetery on the other side of the river in enemy hands, they buried Peters beside Fort Moreau. The sound of the honor guard firing their guns was drowned out by the constant booming of cannons along the river.

The firing from the American side was just as deafening, a loud percussive, continuous roar of artillery and cracking of muskets, as sharpshooters and batteries fired at anything that moved on the opposite side of the river. Jesse and most of the boys, as badly as they felt about their fallen friend, couldn't wait to take part in it. Some, however, had had enough, and returned to their families living like refugees at the Quaker Union,

All through the day there had been skirmishes at the bridges and fords along the river as the British tentatively probed the American defenses. Despite their commander's orders to hold their position, they couldn't prevent clashes as they established sentry points and outposts.

Volunteers from Vermont had been flowing into the village like a spring-fed stream, while a small British force at Wait's Mill to the west had been driven off again. So far the Americans were holding their own, but wherever the enemy moved in force the Americans had to give way. It seemed that it was only a matter of time before the enemy's numbers would overwhelm the defenders, but yet they did not attack.

As soon as the ceremony was over and the officers had left, the boys took off on their self imposed mission to avenge Judd Peters. No one told them what to do or where to go. Captain Aiken gave them a few words of encouragement. Lieutenant Flagg smiled. They knew the twenty odd boys from the Academy were armed and dangerous. They knew what Jesse could do when riled. The boys had already showed their mettle and mauled the British with their guerilla tactics. Their sponsors were hoping for more of the same, although they also prayed they wouldn't be burying any more of Aiken's boys.

As they collected near the fort Jesse spoke his thoughts. "I don't know why we're hanging around this side of the river waiting for the redcoats to come to us. We should be on the other side where they are."

"Yeah," agreed Fred Allen, hefting his musket. "Let's go shoot us some more redcoats."

"It isn't quite that easy," replied Jesse, thinking of their numbers. "We've got to figure out some way to get over there and back without being seen."

"There's a good shallow ford at Pike's Cantonment, right at Rugar's woods," observed B.L. Skinner, one of the more intelligent of the group. "From there, we'll be in woods we know. They go all the way north clear to Tom Miller's farm."

"Yeah," said Freddy Allen. "I've been hunting in there for years."

"Perfect," agreed Jesse, not knowing the area as well, but getting the idea. "We can spy on the redcoats all the way out and shoot at them all the way back."

Later that night, back in their old buckskins and homespun woodsmen's jackets, they stole across the river into the woods on the north bank about two miles west of the river's mouth. Easily eluding the sentries who patrolled the river bank, they ran along pine carpeted trails through a long line of wooded hills. The British were all around them along the banks of the river and in the surrounding fields, and camped along the roads. The boys could see their campfires and tents between the trees, where they were hidden in their dark, leaf-shrouded depths.

They stayed in the woods that night, without a fire and not far from Prevost's headquarters at the Allen Farm. They ate hard biscuits and beef jerky, and shared a few canteens of spring water. Some of the boys picked apples along the way, which they shared out for desert. They took turns standing guard while the others pulled their coats about them and slept on the ground. It was a warmer than usual, almost balmy night, after the cold windy day before.

They had no fear. Despite, or maybe because of the death of their comrade, they felt even more invincible. It was the invincibility that comes with naive thoughts of glory and heroism, and an unrealistic romantic notion of death. That and a youthful, exuberant acceptance of fate, that one throw of the dice - fame and glory or death. They felt like they were fighting against a great red tide that was engulfing the country like a giant pestilence, and only they could stop it.

Just before dawn the next morning they sneaked across the west road, unseen by two pickets who stood within sight of each other, into the woods behind the crest of the western hills. From there, from different vantage points, they could spy on troops from Power's and the rest of de Rottenburg's forces.

They stayed together and moved about constantly, keeping in the middle of the woods. They followed paths they knew well. At intervals along the way, one or two of them would crawl to a knoll and look out, or climb a tree and peer through the branches. They did this all day, finding good vantage points and visiting them repeatedly as they followed a large circle around the inner perimeter of the woods, making mental notes of all they saw. What they saw stunned them, for not only did the British cover the whole village along the river a mile deep, they extended north and west for as far as the boys could see from the tallest trees.

Jesse had a difficult time restraining his men from shooting redcoats, who were sometimes only a few dozen feet away, well within range of their army issue muskets. They hadn't eaten a good meal since the night before, so he had all he could do to prevent the group from taking aim at the game around them as well. The British didn't seem to bother with hunting and they didn't seem to be foraging either. It was getting late, almost dusk.

"Those redcoats seem to be eating pretty good," said one of the boys crawling back from one of their lookout areas. "They've got a whole beef cow cooking on the open fire "

"I say we shoot 'em and take their beef," said Fred Allen only half joking. "I'm starving."

"This is as good a place and time as any," announced Jesse seriously. "But forget the meat. We'll eat when we get home. Tonight we'll have some fun. You all know the drill."

They crept forward on their bellies through the trees with their weapons extended before them until they were at the edge of the woods looking out at the British camped along both sides of the road. They were at the lip of a knoll overlooking the highway. Each took aim, and on a nod from Jesse, fired, almost simultaneously. Several British fell instantly. The alarm was sounded and hundreds of troops were mustered to attack the area where the shots were thought to have come from, but of course there was no one there by that time.

The boys had disappeared before the bluish smoke from their muskets blew away in the breeze. They moved like panthers through the woods. swiftly and silently, striking without warning, only to disappear again into the gathering night, working their way back toward the river.

To the British, the woods, which seemed like a backyard to Jesse and his friends, were like a forbidden maze. Troops would venture in once in awhile on patrol only to get lost and eventually return discouraged or not at all. So the British avoided heavy wooded areas as much from fear of desertions as fear of the enemy. Jesse and his friends could pass through them easily, and knew all the switch-backs and side trails, and where they led. They could walk to places using the wooded trails in a half hour, which would take three times as long using the roads. They could pop up in any number of concealed spots to fire into the flanks of the unsuspecting British without fear of anyone pursuing them. They made good use of this knowledge, causing havoc all the way down the line, until they were finally back at Rugar's woods just north of the river where they had crossed the day before.

Flush with the exhilaration of their recent success many of the boys wanted to continue shooting redcoats, but Jesse, despite sharing their excitement, had other plans.

"Hopefully we've drawn their attention away from the crossing area," he said when Fred wanted to continue the game. "Let's keep it that way. They'll be on high alert. No sense letting them know where we are. Let them think we're still back at the hillcrest."

"Ah, Jesse, I don't see why we can't keep shooting them all night," said Fred Allen. "They don't seem to know what to do."

"Just the same, I'd rather not let them know we're here so we can make a clean getaway."

As they were arguing, one of the boys stumbled upon something interesting.

It was well known that in times of trouble like the current invasion, folks would sometimes bury their valuables, this in a time before banks were common or safe. Knowing this, some of the boys had been on the lookout for signs of buried treasures as they crossed the landscape on their foray.

"I found something," said Jonathan Woodward, a heavy-set lad with wire-rimmed glasses who was standing by a pile of leaves and dirt. "A crate of some kind, half buried in the leaves here."

"Whoever hid it there didn't do a very good job of burying it," observed Skinner.

198

"They must have been in a hurry," replied Jesse. "What is it?"

Jonathan Woodward brushed the leaves away and dug a bit with his hands. Then some of the boys helped him pull the heavy crate out of the ground.

"Wow!" he exclaimed, opening the lid. "It's spirits. Someone buried their whiskey."

"Great!" said Fred Allen, pulling out a bottle eagerly. "Just what a man needs after a long hard day of fighting redcoats."

Woodward joined him in uncorking a bottle and took a swig. The other boys gathered around eagerly, even the ones like Jesse who had never drunk hard liquor.

"I think we should wait to drink until we get back," suggested Jesse looking around with concern. "Things could get rough. We'll need our wits about us."

Just then there was a shout of alarm and a volley of gunfire directed their way. The British were not totally hapless and the alarm had been sounded all the way down the line. The forces along the river at the forest's edge were on high alert. A couple of them, hiding in the shadows had heard the commotion when the boy's found the stash of spirits and sounded the alarm. There was now a detachment of about 40 British regulars carefully making their way through the edge of the woods, firing as they came.

"Quick," ordered Jesse, ducking and looking about for the source of the gunshots. "Forget the whiskey. Let's get out of here!"

Only half the order was obeyed as four of the boys grabbed the heavy crate before fleeing toward the river. The others formed into groups of five, one group retreating, while two others laid down a covering fire from behind the trees. They loaded and shot their guns so fast, the pursuing British thought there was twice as many of them than there really were. In this way, they were able to make it through the woods to the ford even though more and more British converged on the area.

At the ford, Jesse and ten of the boys, Fred Allen included, lay on the ground and behind rocks and kept up a tremendous barrage as the others made it across. When those boys reached the other side, they covered the retreat of the Jesse and the rest, who waded across the rushing water. As they did, more of the British emerged from the woods on the north bank and proceeded to fire at them in the dark. The combined return fire of the entire rifle company, however, kept the British back.

Jesse and the boys made their escape back to the fort where they celebrated long into the night after reporting what they saw to Captain Aiken, who then told General Macomb. With the free spirits to be had, the boys' told and retold their story long into the night.

Jesse and the rest of Aiken's Rifle Company felt better than they had in days and slept well that night, for besides quenching their thirst for spirits, the boys had quenched their thirst for vengeance as well.

Plattsburgh Bay, NY, September 9, 1814

Waiting for something to happen was the hardest part of battle, thought Sam. One was on constant alert, at one's station, ready for action, but there was nothing to do but sit and wait. One couldn't leave the ship or relax. One could hardly eat or sleep for the suspense of it, a long, tedious, anxious period of relentless stress and little action. Sam, for one, wished the British fleet would come. He wasn't the only one, as the British commander, General Prevost, fretted over the delay as well.

The tedium was somewhat relieved when Sam got to help train a group of 40 men lent to Macdonough by General Macomb, but he was greatly disappointed when he saw them - mostly prisoners just released from the brig or black New Englanders from the Pioneer Corps. Sam got along well enough with the latter, however, most of them being carpenters like him and eager to learn. Most of these men were assigned to the gun crews on the *Eagle* after Macdonough transferred a number of his old crew back to the *Saratoga*.

They expected the British fleet any day. It had recently been sighted at anchor at Chazy. It was not the British Sam was worried about, however.

Despite his most strenuous objections and pleading, Sarah had refused to leave the area. She insisted on staying south of town with her father and uncle, who was still spying for the State

Department. Sam thought they were being downright irresponsible where Sarah was concerned, but was apparently outvoted. They all seemed more confident in the situation than he did. The thought of Sarah being in possible danger drove him to distraction and made him almost forget his own jeopardy.

The musicians were practicing the beating and fifing of commands, which Macdonough insisted upon right up until the time of battle. Lieutenant Raymond Perry, Oliver's brother, had been drilling the *Saratoga's* gun crews relentlessly, although he had recently fallen sick. When the fighting finally came, they would all be ready. They were as good as any crew afloat as far as their Master Commandant was concerned, and he had seen more than his share. While he longed for command of a frigate on the high seas, the small but heavily armed brig would do for now. He knew he would be an even match for the British fleet. He hoped his knowledge of the lake and bay would be enough to give him the advantage; that, and Divine Providence.

"Remember what I told you," said the chief surgeon to his young assistant. He hoped he wasn't being overly optimistic assigning someone so young and inexperienced to the task, but assistant surgeon mates were hard to come by in these parts, and Sam had shown much aptitude. He had handled everything they had thrown at him this past year. He was confident Sam would conduct himself well. "When the time comes you will have to make quick decisions of who to help and who to let be. If you can help them, then do it quickly and move on."

"I understand," said Sam, trying not to register that they were talking about the lives and deaths of his mates, men he knew and had lived with closely over the past year and a half. "Stop the bleeding where I can. Move those who can be moved below. Put the dead overboard."

"I know it sounds heartless Sam, but it's the only way." The surgeon had a far off look in his eyes as he remembered other shipboard battles at sea and shuddered inwardly at the horror of it.

"I'll do my best, Sir," promised Sam.

"I know you will, Sam. By the way, how's your father? Have you seen him lately?"

"Yes, the other day when I was granted leave to see my fiancée. I found out that he was in the village. We had dinner together at the fort."

"That's nice. He must be very proud of you."

"He's more worried I'll mess up."

"No chance of that, I'm sure."

"I'll do my best," promised Sam again, wondering what it would be like and wishing it would all be over soon.

Chazy, NY, September 9, 1814

Captain Downie, the commander of the British Fleet, under intense pressure from the Governor-General to support his attack, had finally moved his ships from Isle aux Noix to anchor off the mouth of the Chazy River. There, about twelve miles from Plattsburgh, he began fitting the cannons on the new ship.

"Blast that man," said Downie speaking to his second in command, the unflappable Captain Pring, the only constant in Britain's constantly changing policy on the lake. "Prevost pushes me to support his troops, even before the paint is dry on the ships."

"He does make it seem urgent," replied Pring. "He just wants to ensure an easy victory, I suppose."

"I've got crews who don't know their ships, and officers that don't know their crews and I know neither. Commodore Yeo rushes me here then leaves me hanging in the wind to be at the beck and call of the Governor-General, a man, in my opinion, who has no business leading this affair. He has no current experience in battles of this nature and no mind for strategy."

"Be that as it may, Commander, he has been here a lot longer than we have. He is the man in charge and the one that we must obey."

"I'm doing all I can, but he's not even given me time to train my crews properly. What's the rush, I wonder? The Americans aren't going anywhere."

"He wants to move down the lake before winter, I suppose," said Pring, who had long experience on the lake.

"What difference can a few days make?"

"I don't know, Sir, but the General's man is topside waiting for an answer."

"An answer he shall have then," replied Downie, striding out of the cabin and up the short ladder to the main deck.

The British army officer in his bright red jacket stood near the gangway with his hat under his arm, waiting. Downie strode up to him and saluted. The officer, a tall light-haired man with blue eyes and captain's insignias, saluted back.

"Tell the general I shall weigh anchor tonight at midnight," he said to Prevost's messenger. "I will arrive at Plattsburgh and engage the American ships wherever they may be tomorrow morning at dawn. Tell the general that I have not had time to complete my crews and am using army personnel to make up the shortages, but the fleet will be there to support his attack as ordered."

The British captain saluted and returned to shore with his message, riding directly to Prevost's headquarters twelve miles away, where the Governor-General had been waiting impatiently for Downie's reply.

"Ah," said Prevost on hearing the news, finally showing signs of the confidence an army needs from its commander. "Downie will be ready tomorrow. We attack at dawn."

Village of Plattsburgh, NY, September 9, 1814
(Evening)

Gerald St. Denis, like many Green Mountain Boys, had taken his horse, his sword and his musket and volunteered to fight. Although he saw nothing especially wrong in his family selling cattle across the border to long time clients and relatives, he wasn't about to stand by and watch the English invade his country, even if it was a part of the country called New York. If they took Plattsburgh, his own state would not be far behind. So in spite of the fact that the Vermont State militia was not called out, here he was defending the village.

He had joined Captain Farnsworth's Company of Vermont riflemen in patrolling the south bank of the Saranac River, taking turns firing potshots at the enemy throughout the day. He knew the Captain, who was also from St. Albans and had joined him for mess at the fort. While they were eating, Eleazer Williams, who had been consulting with the General, approached him.

"Excuse me, Mister St. Denis," he said. "I was wondering if I could have a word with you."

"Why yes, Mister Williams," replied Gerald, surprised to see the Indian spy master. "It is nice to see you, Sir."

The last time they had spoken had been about the smuggling of spars for the British ships. He wondered what it could be this time.

Captain Farnsworth excused himself to go back to his troops. Eleazer Williams took his place at the table.

"What is it you wish to talk to me about?" Gerald asked once they were alone.

"I have news of your brother," said Williams looking Gerald straight in the eye.

"Louis? What of him?"

"You are not going to like what I have to say," said Williams, approaching the subject with caution. "Your brother has been spotted with the British."

"Louis? What are you talking about?" asked Gerald, suddenly all ears.

"He was conveyed in a British ship from Vermont to Chazy. Then he was spotted in the village talking to a number of British officers. I'm afraid your brother is aiding and abetting the enemy. He has contracted and delivered a large shipment of beef across to New York through Champlain. They have apparently been planning this for some time, as it has all happened before my people could even report it. It is being done as we speak."

"They told me they were stopping," muttered Gerald, hardly believing it but knowing it to be true. "They lied to me. What a dupe I have been to believe them. I should have known."

"There is nothing you could have done," responded Williams, knowing enough about men to know Gerald was telling the truth and had no part in it. "You have volunteered to come here and fight. You have been fighting since you got here, as have all your gallant and fine Vermont men. I only wish there weren't those few who were conspiring against us. Things are bad enough without our own people feeding their army as it invades us."

"That is the very thing General Izard said," said Gerald, burning with indignation. If Williams knew, then it was certain General Macomb knew as well, which meant he knew Gerald's family was involved in the smuggling. How could he ever look the great man in the eye again? He felt humiliated, used by his brother and friends.

That evening after Williams left, Gerald milled about the fort, staying to himself, morose and agitated. The feelings he felt for his brother left him sullen and angry, afraid of what he would do if he met and confronted him. How could Louis do such a thing? How could he stab his country in the back at its hour of extremity and consort with the invading enemy? No argument or reason could explain it to him, and he thought of them all. It was just pure greed and selfishness, and it made his blood boil.

As he walked about the fort he passed a group of volunteers from the 15th Regiment. They were led by a flamboyant captain named George M'Glassin and they had volunteered for a very dangerous mission. Gerald walked over and volunteered on the spot.

"Good," said Captain M'Glassin. "We can always use another man. Glad to have you, but you may have second thoughts when you hear what we're going to do."

"No, Sir," replied Gerald, thinking only of the humiliating knowledge that General Macomb knew he was from a family of traitors. He knew of only one way to make up for that fact. "I'm not backing down from anything."

"Good," said the Captain, not surprised. Volunteering had become downright contagious since the British had arrived. Men young and old were volunteering for the most dangerous of missions without a thought or a question, just wanting to do their part to defend their homes. It made him swell with pride and honor that he was to lead them.

"There's a British gun and rocket battery being built across the river that is within range of Fort Brown. We are going to take it out with a night attack. It's a risky endeavor, but I figure we'll have surprise and speed on our side. We can ford across near the printing office, surprise the batteries and spike the guns. Maybe take a few prisoners in the process. Are you men still with me?"

They all yelled "aye" to a man. Soon after that, they left the fort. About fifty strong, they snaked their way along the high south bank of the river, to a ford a few hundred yards above the fort. They crossed unobserved, while another detachment set up a diversion nearer the fort. Soon there was a heavy firefight in progress, which covered the advance of M'Glassin's volunteers.

Gerald, who had done most of his training and fighting on horseback, was having a little trouble keeping up with the regulars. What he lacked in stamina, however, he made up for in enthusiasm and intention. He was going to redeem himself and his family's name or die in the attempt.

They made their way unseen through a long line of trees and brush along the bottom of the cliff bank on the north side of the river, back toward the fort. When they were directly under the battery of cannon and rockets, they fanned out and rushed up the long, steep riverbank in silence.

Gerald found himself in the middle of the line and was the first one to crest the hill, coming upon the British gun crews before they were aware of the attackers. Then pandemonium broke out. Gerald, who was breathing hard, had his pistol in his left hand and his saber in his right.

As he came over the lip of the hill, he found himself facing the muzzle of one of the big 12-pounders. Next to the cannon was a soldier who was just lifting his rifle to shoot him. Without stopping, Gerald shot the man in the face with his pistol. At the same time another man came at him with a ramrod. He parried the attack with his sword and brought it down blade first on the man's collarbone. He dropped the ramrod and fell, crying in pain and holding his neck. Gerald stepped over him and moved to the next man.

There was shooting and screaming all around him, but Gerald was only dimly aware of it, although he sensed their attack had taken the enemy completely by surprise. They were pushing them back away from the guns and rocket batteries, leaving the ground littered with the dead and wounded, some of them his own men. Still he pushed on.

In no time, M'Glassin's men scattered the enemy away from the batteries and quickly destroyed the rockets, spiking the guns before enemy reinforcements could arrive. Then they vanished as quickly as they had appeared, back across the river to the fort. All accept one of them.

Gerald lay where he had fallen staring up at the clear night sky. He was aware of a small white light, growing bigger and brighter until it filled all his vision. Then a voice said to him, "You have done well, my son. You have upheld your honor and the honor of your country. You will be beloved in the memory of those who will come after you. They will remember your brave deeds for generations. You will be loved and honored by those who never knew you as if you were a dear friend. Sleep well young warrior, and dwell in the halls of the immortals. All those who have changed the world through their bravery and deeds welcome you."

His eyes stayed open even as his heart, which had been pierced by a mini-ball, ceased to beat. They saw not the light of the stars, but the inner light of the soul, that radiance which can never be dimmed, not even by death.

Chapter 22

Macomb was a whirlwind of activity, sending out orders and dispatches to his far flung positions. He proved the ancient adage that in times of crises great men are apt to think that after everything has been done, there is still something more to do. Just when most would have thought themselves strong enough, Macomb continued to order the strengthening of fortifications and bunkers. When his soldiers were dog tired and scared, he continued to show unflagging confidence and ordered his men to continue marching in circles, feigning new arrivals even as real volunteers flooded the area from Vermont and New York. Soon he would have as many of these rough hewn patriots as he had regulars, most of whom could shoot just as well as any soldier.

General Sam Strong had arrived with more Vermont militia and was camped on the sand plain next to Pike's old cantonment, next to the river a few miles west of the village. Tom Miller had mustered another 243 men of the New York 36th Regiment at the Salmon River settlement. It wasn't enough to offset the huge numeric superiority of the British, but it was something, and every little bit helped.

Macomb expected the attack any minute, yet none came. "What could they be waiting for?" he wondered out loud to his subordinates. The British fleet had finally been spotted off the mouth of Chazy River, but Macdonough had reported the winds were contrary today, so unless they towed them, which was extremely unlikely, there would be no British ships arriving today. Did that mean the British army would not attack as well? Were they waiting for their fleet? That would certainly explain their actions and the less than aggressive tactics. It might also be a weakness in their strategy that could be exploited.

Could Macdonough win the lake battle? Many thought not, but the Master Commander himself and most of his officers seemed confident that they could. The War Department spy, Caleb

Nichols, thought the numbers favored the British slightly, due to their new frigate. Eleazer Williams on the other hand, thought the British gun crews were inexperienced and the officers new to the ships and men. That could prove an advantage as well in a gun for gun pitched battle.

There were some who thought the American fleet should meet the British on the open lake, where there was room to maneuver and perhaps withdraw to regroup if things went badly. Many thought waiting for the slightly superior English fleet in the bay, with their backs to the land, was a big mistake. It gave the British the advantage of the initiative and left Macdonough with no room to maneuver or escape. Many said they would be helpless, like ducks in a barrel. When Macdonough explained his strategy to Macomb, however, it had made perfect sense. The man knew the lake and he knew sailing. Macomb would bet on him any day no matter how many people disagreed.

British Headquarters, Allen Farm, Village of Plattsburgh, NY, September 10, 1814

Things on the north side of the river were not going well. Prevost had just received word from Downie that due to contrary winds, the fleet was still stuck at Isle la Motte and would miss the planned dawn arrival. They would not arrive until the following day.

Prevost was beside himself, letting the stress of his responsibility get the best of him for a moment.

"How do they expect me to undertake this operation if everyone and everything contrives to oppose me?" he said to no one in particular, although his top aides and generals crowded around the map table at his headquarters. "Downie will not make his promised arrival today. I want you all to stand down and hold your current positions."

No one said a word, although it was easy to tell that they were not happy. Power looked quite agitated.

"What is it, General Power?" asked Prevost, noticing his expression. "We can do nothing until the fleet arrives, hopefully tomorrow. I wish they had never transferred Fisher. He would not have delayed so."

"I understand the new ship was not yet ready, nor the crews," observed de Rottenburg who knew Downie and thought well of him. "It is not entirely the Captain's fault. He is a good man."

"That may be, but it has been one excuse after another since he has been here," complained Prevost, not to be denied a scapegoat. "In any case, I am not doing anything until they arrive. It will be a coordinated attack of combined naval and army forces. I will not have my men bombarded at will by those American ships."

Power was about to say something, but held his tongue. Again Prevost noticed his subordinate's agitation.

"What is it, Power?" he asked. "Speak up man!"

"Sir, I understand wanting to wait for the fleet and coordinate our attack with them, but there is a lot we could be doing in the meantime, Sir. I believe my troops can envelop their left flank in the west. If I can be allowed to continue our flanking maneuvers in that area, I'm certain I can get around their lines and come up on their rear. If we can capture their guns, we can turn them on the ships and drive them out of the bay, Sir."

"That is exactly what I want you to do, General, but only when the fleet arrives. I want this to be a coordinated attack, not a bunch of piecemeal skirmishes. We won't accomplish anything that way. When I give you the word, I want you to do precisely as you have described. Send your western most troops across at this point here."

Prevost stabbed at the map in an area marked by Colonel Murray and known to the American's as Pike's Ford.

"Flank the enemy and come up on their rear here."

The map they had was rough and years old, but gave the general lay of the land around the village and the Saranac River. He pointed to a location just a half mile south of the American forts, directly in their rear.

"Your attack on their rear will signal the advance of our whole line," said the Governor-General. "But you will wait until the lake battle commences tomorrow morning."

"Sir, at least let me probe the area, reconnoiter a bit," said Power. "Try to at least establish a bridgehead and stage my troops for the crossing."

"No," replied Prevost, folding up the map. He was done arguing with his men. They would hold their position for the day. "We can't let them know what we intend to do and give them time to adjust their forces. This must be a surprise. We will make our move in the midst of the confusion and fighting on the lake. When the Americans see their fleet destroyed in front of their eyes and then find your troops in their rear, their defense will collapse. We may not have to fire a shot. It has happened so in the past."

His generals, the best in the world by the opinion of many, including those who had fought against them, were less than convinced but said nothing. A short time later they were back with their troops where some of them gave vent to their feelings with a bit more honesty and a lot more emotion. However, they all obeyed their orders and held their positions.

Lake Champlain, NY, September 11, 1814 (Morning)

A light breeze from the north finally enabled Captain Downie to meet his commitment to the Governor-General. Early that morning, they left Isle la Motte off the mouth of the Chazy River, and sailed the twelve miles south to anchor off the north shore of Cumberland Head. Their spies had told them that the 'Head' no longer contained any batteries. They had all been stripped for the defense of the village.

A short time after arriving, Downie ordered the fleet to scale their guns, shooting them off with cartridges alone, to signal their arrival to Prevost. It was the sign to commence the attack. The sun was just rising over Mt. Mansfield in the east, casting a golden glow over the water.

Downie himself scouted the American position in a small boat accompanied by a few men and his second in command, Captain Pring, who commanded the 16-gun *Linnet*. He ordered the boatswain to take him around the south end of the 'Head' so they could view the bay.

"Just as I thought, Captain," observed the fleet commander to his second in command, Pring. "They are lined up waiting for us."

"Perhaps we can lure them out of the bay and fight them in the open lake where our long guns will be more of an advantage," suggested Pring.

"No," replied Downie, observing the American fleet's line of battle with satisfaction. "This is just as well. He is conceding the initiative to us, and blast him, Daniel, I am going to oblige him. We will come into the bay along here." He pointed to the Cumberland Head shore. "We'll run north and deliver our broadsides as we pass, then we'll turn in on them and rake their sterns. They will be sitting in the water like beached whales."

Pring, who knew the lake better than Downie, had his doubts, but he didn't think much of Macdonough's strategy of sitting with his back to the land either. Both captains were confident in the outcome regardless of the tactics used.

A short time later, the mainsail trimmed on Downie's *Confiance*, she turned windward to gain speed. Her sails filled with the northerly wind as she led the other ships into battle. She was followed by Pring in the *Linnet*, with the smaller *Chub* and *Finch* following, along with ten of their gunboats. Then, as Downie reached the south end of Cumberland Head and the mouth of the bay, he braced the yards and trimmed the sails. Putting the helm hard over, he beat his ship back against the wind to turn into the bay where the Americans waited.

Village of Plattsburgh, NY, September 11, 1814 (Morning)

"Finally, we're moving," observed Sergeant James Fenwick of the 88th Foot, as the general order was given to move out.

"It's about bleeding time," said another man in his company. "I'd about given up on an attack."

Fenwick was stationed with his men to the west of Brisbane troops, which held the Americans' attention along the lakefront and eastern end of the river. On the command to attack, they began to cross the river at several fording spots that had been scouted out.

Rushing down a steep embankment to the wide, shallow, rock-strewn river, they splashed across in knee-deep water. Many lost their footing on the slippery rocks in the fast-moving stream. When they were halfway across, the Americans opened up a blistering fire from trees on the opposite bank and from the bluffs above. A few of Fenwick's men made it across only to be pinned down and captured. The rest fled back to the north bank and ran for cover, most of them, including Fenwick, making it back to the top of the high bluff from where they had started.

"This is bloody crazy," complained the man crouching with him behind an old chicken coop near a deserted house. "They're as thick as fleas over there. I thought we were going to wait for the bleedin' fleet to finish them off. Wasn't there supposed to be some sort of flanking action?"

"We need to hold their forces in the front here," answered Fenwick, understanding the strategy perfectly well. "It's to be a coordinated attack. So you just stand your ground and when I tell you to charge again, you do it. Do you understand, Private?"

"Yes Sir. But, Sir, can you find us a better spot to get across where there aren't so many of them waiting for us?"

After leading his men further down the river bank to a spot seemingly devoid of cover on the opposite bank, they made it across the swift, waist-deep water unopposed, and fanned out to establish a small bridgehead.

Moving back up the river toward the firing, they encountered a group of militia, which Fenwick's small detachment of 100 men soon drove off. The skirmishing attracted more defenders, however, until Fenwick and his men were outnumbered and things became quite desperate. Before long more British crossed the river and drove off the Americans, only to withdraw again. Fenwick and his men followed.

Fenwick and his commanding officers all knew the task was not to attack the enemy or storm their forts, but to demonstrate in front of them and hold them in place. Fenwick added his own orders to those of his superiors'.

"Let us kill as many Americans as we can."

Chapter 23

Sam woke to the sound of a cannon booming in the distance, as the officer of the deck signaled eight bells. Rolling out of his hammock, he hurriedly dressed in the small cramped cabin he still shared with the ship's other carpenter's mate.

"What was that?" he asked in a hurried whisper, but his bunkmate just turned and went back to sleep. Sam ran up the ladder to the deck where he met the ship's Boson's mate, an old sailor who supervised the deck hands.

"What was that?" Sam repeated anxiously, looking out at the dawning light. The water in the bay splashed lazily against the ship's hull.

"A British signal gun, I suppose," replied the mate. "They're letting their army know they're here. I reckon they'll be coming around the 'Head' any time."

A short while later, Macdonough himself appeared at the rail of the quarterdeck looking at the mouth of the bay with his glass.

Sam's throat was dry and constricted. His breath came in short gasps. He face was etched with agitation. Others ran aloft to get a better look. Everywhere men were shouting or obeying orders, although what could be done had already been accomplished.

Macdonough's fleet was anchored in the middle of the bay about a mile from the western shore. His northern most ship, the 20-gun *Eagle*, under Lt. Henley, was just southeast of the mouth of the Saranac, with the 26-gun *Saratoga* next to it. At the southern end of the line was the 7-gun *Preble*, commanded by Charles Budd, sitting northeast of Crab Island at the mouth of the bay. The 17-gun *Ticonderoga*, under Stephen Cassin, floated between the *Preble* and the *Saratoga*. The American gunboats and galleys were aligned between Macdonough's battle line and the western shore of the bay.

Macdonough had springs put on the ships' cables and stern cables deployed so they could turn about without using their sails, which were furled. His ship was equipped with a kedge anchor off the bow, with a hawser attached to the quarter side. It could be used to wind the ship so it could turn to bring either port or starboard batteries to bear on the enemy. They had shot and powder aplenty, and their sails and rigging were in perfect order. They were ready.

Just then Macdonough had his drummers beat to quarters and the ship was cleared for action. The men ran to their appointed stations, their faces sober with anticipation. As Sam looked on, Macdonough knelt in prayer. His officers, who surrounded him, did the same. In the dead quiet of the morning, with seagulls and the lapping of the waves making the only sounds, the commander's words came to Sam clearly in the crisp morning air.

"Oh Lord," intoned Macdonough. "Protect us in our hour of need. Be a sword in our hand that we may conquer our enemies. Be our shield and protect us from those who come to take our homes. Guide our hands that we may smite Thy enemies, for surely those who invade our land, who come to burn our homes and enslave our children, can find no favor with Thy Divine Grace. Lord, watch over us and lead us to victory. Amen."

They all echoed the last word, and many stayed on their knees with their heads bowed, adding their own silent supplications. They were in this position when the enemy ships rounded the bay and came into sight, sailing in a line straight toward them, their sails trimmed to beat against the wind.

Sam stood transfixed, staring toward the enemy ships that seemed to be flying over the water at them, the lake breaking on their bows. His face was ashen and creased as if he had aged ten years. The Boson's mate patted him on the shoulder and gave him an order, pulling Sam out of his state of shock with familiar words and routine. He looked up to see his commander standing on the gun deck. He had the mizzen shroud grasped in his left hand. The cannon's lanyard was in his right. He was leaning over the barrel of the gun aiming it at the first of the enemy ships, which bore down on them speedily, looming out of the morning mist.

Just as it looked like the biggest and closest of the ships would sweep past them to unleash a broadside, their sails began to

215

luff, flopping as the erratic wind in the bay gave out just as Macdonough predicted it would. Like a fish out of water, their sails gasped for air. Soon the giant English frigate coasted to rest, bow on, not two cable lengths away. As she did, the *Saratoga* let loose a devastating broadside with its four starboard side18-pounders and half a dozen 32-pound carronades. The whole deck shook as if it would fly apart, rattling Sam from his teeth to his toes, right down to his very bones. The sound blocked out all senses for the moment. The ship was instantly enveloped in thick acrid smoke. It wafted over the decks and lingered, obscuring everything around them, before rising up the masts like a ghostly shroud to be blown away by the wind. A moment later the *Confiance* responded in kind, with a broadside of its own 14 double-shotted 24-pounders, rending the *Saratoga's* bulwark and railings into a thousand deadly splinters and shards. Several men at the guns were sent sprawling to the deck.

Macdonough, who had been standing at the rail next to one of the guns, wheeled to the other side of the deck to avoid the splintering wood. It seemed like nothing could survive such a blast, and for a moment Sam lost all sense of where he was and what was happening. When he finally could see again, as the smoke slowly blew away, he regained his senses and saw men strewn about the deck all around him - bodies covered in blood.

He got up and staggered toward the nearest body, one of the gun crew who was only dazed like himself. He helped the man to his feet and sent him back to his station after checking him over. The next man he came to was not so lucky, with a large splinter of wood stuck in this throat. Sam came to him just in time to see him sputter his last words in a spray of phlegm and blood. He left him on the deck for the loblolly boy, the surgeon's aid, and went to the next. By this time the *Saratoga's* gunners had reloaded and run out their guns for another broadside at the stationary *Confiance*, which had dropped anchor several hundred feet away. The ships stood at close action, beam to beam, blasting each other at a frenzied pace.

A shot passed through the mizzen mast a dozen feet above Sam's head. Another thundered into the hull amid-ship just above the water line below him. The high jagged screech of 18-pound balls cutting through the air all around him filled his ears. The noise alone seemed lethal. Still, he went about his work helping the wounded with calm and poise.

The *Confiance's* sheet anchor had been shot off, making it impossible for Downie to maneuver his ship. Over twenty percent of Macdonough's crew had been killed with the first volley. Macdonough himself had been momentarily knocked unconscious by the concussion of a blast. It was a desperate life and death struggle, but Sam, who was right in the middle of it, was oblivious to the chaos around him. All he could remember when he tried to recall that terrible two hour battle was the constant line of wounded and dying men, a series of faces and medical procedures, which he attended to one by one.

Sam would later be able to recall every tourniquet and sling tied, every wound and injury treated, every compress and bandage applied, but nothing of the battle that waged around him.

Then, fifteen minutes into the encounter, the hand of Providence smiled on the Americans, although none of them knew it at the time. A cannon ball shot from one of the *Saratoga's* guns hit a cannon on the British frigate, behind which Downie was standing. The gun carriage exploded, forcing the gun back into Downie, killing him instantly. His First Lieutenant gallantly did his duty and took command for the remainder of the battle, but the British fleet was virtually rudderless. Unable to locate the ship's signal book, Lt. Robertson could not notify the fleet's second in command, Captain Pring, of the commander's death. In the confusion and noise of the engagement, without the fleet commander to lead them, the British ships were on their own.

Although the ships stood blasting each other, their big guns booming, there was a slight difference in the sound and a larger difference in the effect. The volleys from the British ships were ragged and sloppy, without discipline, many of their shots passing harmlessly over the heads of the Americans. The sound from the American ships in contrast was fast and uniform, their fire smashing into the enemy ships' hulls and bulwarks with murderous accuracy. Macdonough's gun crews didn't have to think, but only repeat what had been drilled into them for months…fire and load…fire and load. They worked like machines, while chaos reigned around them.

Western Shore of Plattsburgh Bay, NY, September 11, 1814 (Morning)

While Sam tended to the wounded, bandaging cuts and mending broken bones, sending those who would live below and throwing those who had died overboard, the battle raged on about him.

The stationary ships blasted each other at close quarters for an hour, filling the decks with carnage and the lake with smoke and debris. A crowd of three hundred stood watching from the Cumberland Head shore, only a mile from the battling ships. The sound of cannon blasts filled the air like one continuous peal of thunder, while the bay filled with smoke, obliterating all but the vaguest image of the ships. Others watched from the New York shore. One of these was Sarah Nichols.

Sarah, true to her threat, had not gone home to Whitehall. Her uncle's farm on Crab Island had been turned into a hospital and she volunteered to help organize the place. When the British fleet arrived off Cumberland Head she and her uncle had gone to the mainland, where they were now standing on the bluffs opposite the island watching the engagement.

Arriving at the hilltop above the small sand beach where she had sat with Sam, she remembered their last time together and wished more than anything that he was with her now. When she looked out at the ships lined up before her in the clear morning light, her heart filled with pride and not a little anxiety. Pride that her man was part of that splendid sight, defending her country in such a glorious way. When she saw the English ships coming around the head of the bay, however, their sails billowing, so big and with so many guns, her heart leaped to her throat and she could hardly breathe. She wanted to cry out a warning but her throat constricted and tears came to her eyes. She was terrified, not only for Sam but for all the poor men on those ships. It was a terrible but beautiful sight and it almost overwhelmed her.

"Don't worry," said her uncle sharing her fear and anxiety. "They'll be all right. They've trained long and hard for this moment. They'll come through, don't worry. Perhaps we should

218

retire. Your father awaits and I promised I'd take you to him when the battle started."

But Sarah would not go. When the battle began she stood rooted to the spot like an ancient stone statue, unable to turn away. Each broadside shattered her heart. Her worst nightmare materialized, right before her eyes. The biggest enemy ship bore down on Sammy's ship like a giant iceberg. There was an eruption of fire from the smaller ship, the lack of sails on her masts making it look even smaller and more vulnerable against the larger ship looming before her. Then, with another bigger blast from the larger ship, the whole terrible scene was engulfed in smoke and flame. Only the fire from the mouths of cannons could be seen, like something out of Hades. She screamed and threw her hands to her mouth, but the sound was swallowed by the din of the cannon blasts. It seemed that every ship in the British line was firing at Sammy's ship. No one could live through that infernal, she thought. It was the last thing she remembered from that morning. Sara Nichols fainted dead away.

Her uncle, who still reported to the War Department after Armstrong had left, had a bird's eye view of the entire engagement and recorded it all. He blamed the outgoing Secretary for the whole fiasco of leaving the entire strategic lake and village undefended. Although he didn't say as much to his distraught niece, now being tended to by several local women, he did not feel confident in the outcome of the lake battle, on which, in his opinion, everything hinged. The English have the preponderance of firepower, regardless of Williams' assessment of their ability to use it effectively, he thought.

While it was hard for him to make out the details in the smoke filled bay, the general outline of the ships and the progress of the battle were discernable. The bigger ships immediately grouped together into two clusters. The *Saratoga* and *Eagle* fought the *Confiance*, *Linnet* and the smaller *Chub* on the northern end of the battle line. The *Ticonderoga* and the *Preble* battled the *Finch* and four gunboats. The American gunboats and galleys gave what support they could.

Most surprising of all, seven of the British gunboats hung off the mouth of the bay and did nothing. Perhaps they were waiting in reserve, but it surprised the war department spy and gave him hope; perhaps they were not well commanded. As he watched, one of the ships battling the *Saratoga* and *Eagle*, the smaller one called the *Chub*, had its bowsprit and main boom shot away. Nichols watched in fascination as it drifted down Macdonough's battle line and struck her colors. It was quickly boarded and taken to shore as a prize. Things were looking up, and Nichols quickly changed his assessment. It looked like the Americans were gaining the upper hand.

A short time later another British ship, the *Finch*, being pulverized by the *Ticonderoga* and the *Preble*, drifted out of the line of battle and onto the rocks of Crab Island directly across the narrow channel from where the war department spy stood. After exchanging fire with the island's six-pounders, the crew of the sinking ship was forced to strike her colors. The four gunboats fighting by her side soon gave up as well, while the seven remaining gunboats stayed out of the action.

"Two down, two to go," Nichols said to himself. Things were looking up.

Aboard the *Saratoga* on Plattsburgh Bay, NY, September 11, 1814 (Morning)

Macdonough watched as his gun crews delivered another broadside into the stranded British ship - boom, boom, boom - it thundered, echoing off the mountains that ringed the 100-mile-long lake. The British frigate shuddered as the double-shotted balls tore into her. One shot hit her top mast, which tumbled to hang momentarily in the rigging before crashing onto the ship's deck.

"Aim low!" bellowed Macdonough, "at the waterline and her hull!"

He didn't have to worry. His men were working as a well-oiled machine. Even though their leader was sick and his replacement had been killed, they worked quietly, without supervision, each doing his job as he had been trained. He made a point to mention young Mister Perry's excellent instructions and drilling.

He also made a point to mention young Sam Turner as well. It was Sam who had seen to the cut over his eye and many of the other men's injuries as well. He was impressed by the way Sam was able to treat the men and care for their wounds. He admired the presence he commanded on the deck during the battle; and the cool way he worked amid the explosions and chaos. Even though he was not an officer and had no medical training to speak of, Sam was one of the best assistant surgeons Macdonough had seen. He would make it a point to mention young Sam in his after-action report; that is, if any of them lived to dispatch such a message.

The two big British ships were giving back as good as they got, although their shots seemed not to be as well aimed. It was the sheer number of them and their tonnage that had Macdonough worried.

Right at the peak of the battle, after the ships had been blasting each other for almost two hours, Henley in the *Eagle*, who was getting hammered by the two remaining British ships, cut his cable and drifted out of the line of fire, dropping anchor between the *Saratoga* and the *Ticonderoga*. The *Eagle's* maneuver caught Macdonough off guard, for he had given no such signal. He had ordered all his ships to hold their position in the line. As he watched the *Eagle* sail by he found his ship completely exposed to the deadly fire of the *Confiance* and the *Linnet*. His flag ship was in a desperate state. For a moment the Master Commandant faced disaster.

"Blast him!" shouted Macdonough, ducking for cover, as several of his starboard guns were hit in the volley.

"Sir," yelled his First Lieutenant, Joseph Smith. "All our starboard guns are disabled or unmanageable. They have set us afire, Sir, with hot shot."

"Let go the stern anchor!" Macdonough shouted over the din. "Cut the bow cable Mister Brum! We'll use the kedge to wind our guns to bear. Mister Beale, see to that fire there!"

The orders were obeyed with alacrity, and the ship wound about to expose her other line of guns. As the deck fire was being extinguished, they unleashed a fresh broadside with devastating effect. Henley and the *Eagle* joined in the barrage from his new position in the line, and fired their own remaining cannons at the enemy frigate. The *Confiance* seemed to wilt before

Macdonough's eyes as he watched intently from the deck of his ship.

The carnage aboard the enemy vessel must have been terrible and for a brief moment Macdonough felt badly for the men aboard that ship. Even as he felt these sentiments, however, his crew was reloading their cannons to fire again.

The *Confiance* was a floating hulk, her masts and hull shattered, her rigging and spars torn and shredded. She was listing sharply to starboard as she took on water. She could not have had one or two guns left in order, although the pivot gun on her bow was still operational. Yet she did not fire. Macdonough ordered his crews to hold their fire as they watched the enemy ship for a sign. Suddenly, the British flagship's colors were struck. The battle was over, or so they thought.

It was nearly eleven AM. The battle had raged for more than two hours and all but one British ship had surrendered. The *Linnet* battled on, firing cannon balls as fast and at whatever she could.

"What are they doing?" demanded the chief surgeon, who had come on deck to get a breath of air after two hours tending the wounded in the cramped quarters of the sick bay. "Can't they see the battle's over and they have lost?"

"Ah, that must be the indomitable Captain Pring," said Macdonough recognizing his antagonist of the last two years. "He won't give up until we blast him out of the water."

"Then I'd do it, Sir," urged the surgeon as a cannon ball whistled by a few feet over their heads.

"I intend to," replied Macdonough. He ordered Mister Brum to wind the ship toward the *Linnet*. This time Sam ran to the capstan as the sailors who were still on their feet and able struggled to haul the ship around and keep their footing on the blood-soaked deck. Slowly but surely they brought the ship around so her larboard guns bore on the stubborn and well-captained *Linnet*.

"Now!" Macdonough thundered. His big 32-pound carronades went off one after another with a deafening roar. The broadside shattered the smaller ship. She was pushed backward by the force of the blows hitting her hull in multiple places, crashing gun carriages and their crews, rending bodies apart like sliced butter. A moment later Pring surrendered. The battle was finally over and the sudden silence was deafening.

A dead calm stole over the battle scene as the smoke slowly drifted away like the ghosts of the dead. Only the groaning of the wounded and dying could be heard, the seagulls having all fled. The lake was littered with debris and corpses. They would be floating up on beaches on both sides of the lake for weeks. Macdonough looked about the gore-strewn deck, so wet with blood it was hard to walk on, and shook his head. He could only imagine the scene on the enemy ships.

"Tend to the wounded," he said to his surgeon, who went back below deck. He didn't have to remind Sam, who immediately returned to helping the injured.

"Give me a damage report," ordered Macdonough to his First Lieutenant Joseph Smith, who was standing by his side. "And see if you can keep us afloat long enough to accept Pring's surrender."

Chapter 24

Pike's Ford, Saranac River, NY, September 11, 1814 (Morning)

General Power had been ordered to hold his position for an hour after the battle on the lake began. He waited for the Quarter-Master-General's guides as he listened to the booming of the guns on the lake. Eventually, General Robinson's column and the guides arrived at Power's encampment. The combined force then set out for Pike's Ford. Because of their lack of maps and inability to scout the terrain ahead of time, the going was slow and they lost their way in the maze of logging roads and byways. All they knew was to keep going until they got to the river, which they eventually did. They could hear the deep rumble of the naval cannons on the distant lake, echoing over the surrounding hills. The lake battle preoccupied the minds of many of the troops, as did the strangeness of the country and the thickness of the woods. Eventually they reached the river at Pike's old cantonment and started wading across.

Knowing the British were likely to try and flank his forces and come upon their rear, Macomb had sent a contingent of regulars and militia to meet them. If they couldn't stop them they were to try to divert them to the south and away from the forts, inflicting as many casualties as possible. Nate Peters and his men were among those sent out from Fort Brown. They were joined by Aiken's Rifle Company, the boys who seemed to operate without a commanding officer, but managed to show up wherever there was the scent of an Englishman. They were now hiding in the underbrush along the south bank of the river at Pike's Ford, together with four hundred New York militiamen.

Jesse's heart was pounding. No matter how many times he had shot another man, the anticipation was still difficult to control. That and the fear aroused by seeing so many of the enemy pouring across the river. They seemed to stream out of the woods like red, oozing lava. It was hard to hold fire when there were so many of the enemy getting so close. The British skirmishers would have no problem enfolding the small pocket of defenders and cutting off their escape if they weren't careful. He wondered if some of the other boys like Fred Allen could control themselves enough to hold their fire until the order was given. None of them were that good at following orders. Jesse wanted to let the enemy get as close as possible before they unleashed their volley. He'd beat them with the butt of his rifle if he had to.

A moment later the order came. The riverbank erupted in an explosion of smoke and shot. The English advance, midway in the river and only twenty yards away, slowed, then halted, then withered in the face of a second volley. Many fell and were carried away in the shallow rapids. The troops massing on the other side of the stream began firing back in turn, making the trees and rocks around the defenders crack and ping from the strikes of the flying musket balls. Soon 6-pound shells from their field guns joined the fray and the Americans had to pull back slowly, firing from under cover as they did.

Jesse and his friends were experts at fighting while moving backwards, and Sergeant Nate Peters and his regulars had plenty of practice as well. They continued to offer stiff resistance as they kept up an incessant fire, shooting from behind every tree, rock and wall they could find. Their marksmanship and tactics were a distinct advantage in fighting the British, who formed in straight lines on the roads and in the open. Despite all their experience fighting Americans they still didn't seem to have learned their lesson.

With their overwhelming numbers, the British were now stretched over a mile from the south bank of the river, pursuing the withdrawing Americans. Without the knowledge of their scouts, and without firm intelligence, they had no idea where they were and no organized plan. They were like a blind colony of insects groping in the darkness for the light, their regimented strategy outdated in the face of the American guerilla tactics.

As they withdrew, Nate led his men in a southeasterly direction along the new roads they had constructed earlier leading to the Salmon River Settlement. They were about a mile south of the ford, in an area of thick woods that pressed upon the road on both sides.

"We'll make a stand here," said Nate to his men. Jesse and Aiken's boys were standing nearby.

"Why don't we line up in the woods on both sides of the road and shoot them as they come down?" suggested Fred Allen, always thinking up ways to shoot redcoats. Nate looked at the large, big-boned seventeen year-old and laughed.

"That would be good," he said, "for the British. We'd shoot each other in the crossfire."

"Don't mind him," chuckled Jesse. "He's big on brawn but small on brains." He looked at his friend who smiled back sheepishly. "We'll do whatever you want us to."

"We'll line up behind that ridge," said Nate, pointing to a rocky protuberance a few yards back in the woods, hidden in the shadow of the trees. "It will offer a good vantage point overlooking the road. It's protected by the rocks and boulders. It will be like a fortress."

They all scampered off the road and into the woods to take up their positions on the right flank of the approaching British, who came marching down the way a short time later in long columns of four with their drums beating. The column seemed to go on forever.

Some of the boys ran along wooded trails back down the road to cover more of their line, while some of them ran ahead. All were hidden behind the rocks and trees. Nate waited while the head of the line marched by, counted to ten, then aimed his musket at an officer on a horse and shouted the order to fire. The woods exploded with musket shots and several men in red fell to the ground. The British formed a defensive perimeter and fired back into the woods. Their shots ricocheted harmlessly off stone and rock. The Americans reloaded and fired again at the British who still stood in the open roadway. Then more English formed up and their skirmishers attempted to flank the Americans, who fell back into the woods, only to form up again further down the road.

They were performing a strategic retreat as General Macomb had instructed. "Retreat as the enemy advances," he had ordered. The British were being lured away from the village.

Eventually, Nate and his men arrived at the location of Lieutenant Sumpter's artillery and a force of the Essex Militia, near an old stone wall at the road's entrance to the Salmon River

Settlement. The British were stung and angry at the ungentlemanly tactics, and desperate to get to the forts, which they estimated should be less than a mile away. They hadn't noticed that the sounds of the lake battle seemed to be receding into the distance.

The vanguard of Power's regiment was now at the Salmon River Settlement, about two and one-half miles southwest of the village, instead of being just south of the forts. Sumpter opened fire with his two 6-pounders. The British decided to use their numbers and storm the guns. They rushed forward with a yell, using their bayonets and small arms. Nate's men held their ground as the Vermont militia began to fire on the enemy's left flank from the woods. Aiken's boys came out of the woods on the attackers' rear cutting them off from the rest of their forces. Instead of capturing the guns, an entire company of the British 76th Regiment became prisoners themselves. Jesse had captured his first redcoat, though he almost got bagged himself, when the British counterattacked and drove the defenders back again. Then the British began to retreat.

The boys were firing at the retreating redcoats, when through the smoke and din of battle, Jesse took bead on a drummer boy standing in the middle of the road beating out what must have been a retreat command. Jesse steadied his musket and took aim but didn't fire. Instead, he rested the barrel of the musket on the fence post he was crouched behind. As much as he enjoyed shooting redcoats, he didn't have the heart to shoot the little drummer boy. Fred Allen who was crouched next to him had no such compunction, however.

Jesse saw Fred lift his musket and take aim at the boy out of the corner of his eye. Without thinking, he jammed the barrel of his rifle down on Fred's, knocking it downward so that his shot went into the ground. Jesse looked up to see the drummer boy finally being led away to safety.

"What'd you do that for?" griped Allen.

"He's only a kid," said Jesse, recalling how small Daniel looked lying in the gutter by the side of the bridge. "There's no call to shoot him."

"Ah, since when have you gone soft on redcoats?" complained Allen, taking bead and shooting at the last of the retreating British.

Jesse sat by the fence he had been crouching behind and put his rifle up. He was tired of shooting redcoats. As a matter a fact, he would be happy if he never shot anybody again. He'd had enough with killing. He had done what he had to do to defend his home, the place where he grew up. It had been Judd Peter's home as well, a home he would never play or hunt in again.

For the first time since the war started, Jesse felt badly for the people he had killed. He was sorry that they would never return to their loved ones, but then they shouldn't have come and tried to take his home away. He hoped the retreating soldiers disappearing hastily down the road would make it safely back to England, and that no one would ever seek to take their homes away from them.

While they had been fighting the British, the guns on the lake had gone silent. Jesse wondered what that might mean.

Village of Plattsburgh, NY, September 11, 1814 (mid-morning)

Prevost stood on the hill overlooking the river and the south end of the village and bay, watching the lake battle. He was confident at first, when the British fleet appeared at the mouth of the bay like avenging angels. He had ordered General Brisbane to effect a general mobilization of his forces as soon as the lake battle commenced. He was to deploy along the whole mile-and-a-half where the river ran through the village, engaging the forts with artillery, holding the enemy in front of him while Robinson's and Power's regiments circled around their rear.

Instead of focusing on the action in the village, however, Prevost was fixated on the battle on the lake. He had staked so much on it and waited so long that he was obsessed with the outcome, even though technically he had all he needed to take the village and the American forts within a few days at most. Then the unthinkable happened. One of the British ships drifted out of the battle line and struck her colors. A few minutes later, a second British ship floated out of the action and grounded on the rocks at the north end of the island at the mouth of the bay. Two British ships had surrendered in no time.

It seemed to him from his vantage point on the hill that the American ships were better crewed, their volleys sharper and better timed, while those from the British ships were ragged and erratic, almost hesitant, as though they weren't sure how to use the guns.

He peered angrily through his field glass.

"What are those gunboats doing sitting there at the mouth of the bay?" he fumed to no one in particular. "Why don't they join the battle? They're just sitting there."

"They are probably afraid of sharing the fate of their four sister ships, which have just been captured," said de Rottenburg, his second in command. "Let us press the attack, General. Once we take their shore batteries we can turn the guns on their ships and help our fleet."

Prevost ignored the advice and continued to stare disconsolately out at the lake. His plans were evaporating before his eyes. With the lake in British hands and the American Navy destroyed, he would have made short work of the American forts. Perhaps he could have negotiated an honorable surrender without a shot. Once Plattsburgh and the lake were under his control, he intended to move quickly down to Albany and join up with other British forces from the east coast to push down the Hudson before winter set in, and perhaps cut New England out of the war. It would be a large territorial gain for his country and would certainly have a positive effect on any peace negotiations, but it all hinged on a quick, speedy and cheap victory here. That victory, at least on the lake, was slipping away.

Why don't the gunboats attack to support their flag ship? Why does the American flagship keep on firing after receiving so many devastating broadsides from the bigger better armed ship? What are they, demons? These questions and others bombarded his mind as Prevost contemplated the impossible. There was no plan B.

Then, the unthinkable happened, as he and his generals watched, the American commander wound his ship and delivered a devastating volley with the port guns, all fresh and operable. The effect was shocking. The British frigate seemed to disappear in a cloud of smoke and flame. As he watched in horror, the 37-gun *Confiance*, the pride of His Majesty's Navy on the lake, now not much more than a floating hulk, struck her colors and surrendered.

They all stood crestfallen, as if the Governor-General himself had just been shot and killed.

"What are your orders, Sir? Shall we press the attack, Sir?" de Rottenburg asked hopefully.

Prevost did not answer. He watched Pring's fruitless, though courageous attempt to continue the battle, until the American flag ship performed the same dastardly maneuver again, and wound to deliver a fresh broadside on the *Linnet*, silencing her for good.

Prevost stared dumbstruck as Pring's flag was dropped in surrender.

"All is not lost, General," urged de Rottenburg. "Let us press the attack, Sir."

All the guns seemed to stop at once, as everyone who could watched the lake. There was a hurrah from the American forts and the forces lining the lake. Then Prevost heard what he'd been waiting for, gunfire from his flanking attack.

He listened intently for several minutes and then…the unmistakable sound of cannon fire.

"Where is that coming from?" he asked. "Is that Power's men?"

No one answered. They all strained to hear the smattering of small arms and field artillery that rose to a crescendo like distant fireworks and stopped.

"It's too far away," said Prevost answering his own question. "It's too blasted far away."

Aboard the *Saratoga* on Plattsburgh Bay, NY, September 11, 1814 (Late Morning)

Sam watched as what was left of the British fleet's commanding officers were rowed to the *Saratoga*, which, like the rest of Macdonough's ships, was in real danger of sinking. The crew worked the pumps, however, and Sam, with the other carpenter's mate, had rigged some repairs to the damaged hull. Now all activity had ceased as the British officers climbed up the rope ladders to the *Saratoga's* deck. The weather-beaten, but still kicking Boson's mate piped them aboard. Macdonough had what was left of his crew standing at attention with their hats off in respect.

The British officers stepped aboard as smartly as they were able. Macdonough and Pring faced each other, their officers at attention, doing the same. They were all dressed in what was left of their best formal uniforms. They formed a strange looking lot, many with bandages on their heads and with their arms in slings.

"So that's the famous Captain Pring," observed one of the men near Sam. "He doesn't look so great."

Sam thought Pring looked just wonderful; a bit careworn, but dignified just the same, a formidable enemy and excellent leader. His had been the last ship to surrender after all the rest had done so. He probably would still be firing his cannons if there had been any left that were operable. At least that's what Sam thought, and he was sure that Macdonough would have agreed.

"We are here to surrender the fleet in the name of His Majesty's Navy in North America," said Pring, taking off his hat with a slight bow. He removed his sword from its scabbard, and presented it, handle first, to Macdonough.

"Put your sword back in its scabbard, Captain," said Macdonough, touched by the plight of his adversaries and impressed by their bravery. "You and your brave men have earned the right to keep your swords, Sir. It is an honor to finally meet you. I wish it had been under better circumstances."

"Commander, your victory is well deserved," replied Pring, putting his sword back into its scabbard. "You are truly an honorable opponent." His men, who had removed their swords to present them to Macdonough, replaced them as well. It was then that Pring realized why they had been so soundly defeated. This Macdonough was no ordinary man. "Your crews are the best I have ever faced in battle, Sir. Their names will forever resound to the glory of your nation."

"Is there is anything we can do for you, Captain?" asked Macdonough extending his hand, which Pring took and shook, bowing again.

"We have many wounded men," said Pring. "Captain Downie is dead I'm afraid, killed in the first few minutes of the battle. So is our surgeon, Dr. Davis."

"I'm sorry," said Macdonough, suspecting as much when the Commander had failed to appear. That it happened so early in the battle, as he was told, gave Macdonough some pause, and he saw it as a sign that God had indeed been with them that day. "I will ask for volunteers to help attend your injured."

"Thank you, Captain," said Pring relieved. "That is most honorable and generous, Sir."

Pring watched in gratitude as several men, including Sam, volunteered to help the British injured. He was having a new-found appreciation for these strange Americans, aggressive one minute and bristling with weapons more than not, kind and generous the next, the epitome of clemency and grace. He would never understand them and never stop admiring them. He hoped he'd never have to fight them again, at least not any like this bunch standing around him now.

Macdonough was a little surprised when Sam volunteered to help the English seamen, although he shouldn't have been. It was just like the carpenter's mate turned assistant surgeon's mate to be one of the first to volunteer, which he did without thinking. What could Macdonough do? He was a bit miffed that his best medical man next to the surgeon was leaving when there were still many wounded who needed attention, but his sense of honor prevented him from saying so. The surgeon was still below deck completing amputations. Sam had been spared the job of assisting in the gruesome operations because the surgeon felt that Sam's talents were better utilized on the deck where the men needed immediate and intelligent medical attention. Sometimes a few minutes could make a big difference. Now, Sam was about to be ferried to an enemy ship to help with their casualties and there wasn't a thing Macdonough could do about it without losing face in front of the British Commander.

"Let me know if you need any assistance, young Mister Turner," he offered as Sam followed the others to the gangway while the ship's gig was being lowered.

"What do you want to go and help them for?" said a disgruntled crewman as Sam entered the port gangway. "They're the damned enemy. They just killed dozens of our mates."

"They're wounded and need our help," answered Sam. "The battle's over." It didn't really matter to him who he helped, as long as he was helping other human beings.

"What about our own men?" said the angry mate, a man in his twenties who had obviously lost several friends that day. "There's plenty of them wounded. Why don't you stay and help them?"

"The Commander asked for volunteers," replied Sam. "He would have said something if it wasn't acceptable for me to go. You heard the British officer. They've lost their surgeon. They probably don't have anyone who can help their wounded."

"It's down right unpatriotic," growled the man turning surly and blocking Sam's way. No one seemed to notice or offered to help, although it was obvious Sam was in distress. Perhaps they agreed with the disgruntled sailor.

"Let me go!" yelled Sam, fearing he'd be left behind, and trying to move around the man. "Why aren't you bothering anybody else? What are you bothering me for?"

"Because you actually know what you're doing," said the man. "You actually know some doctoring, Those other fools don't know anything about medicine. The British are a bunch of murdering thieves. So what if they're hurt. They should all be dead. That's the whole idea of this stupid war!"

"What's gong on there?" said the Boson's mate, from the other side of the deck, finally noticing Sam's plight.

"Why are you keeping this man from doing his duty?" he asked the surly seaman, moving to the gangway.

"Sorry, Sir," he replied. "But we need him here."

"Suppose you let the Commander decide who's needed and where," said the old sailor. "Mister Turner is going to help English-American relations after we've won the battle. Remember lads," he said pointing to the shore, "There's still ten thousand British soldiers out there."

Village of Plattsburgh, NY, September 11, 1814 (noon)

Sergeant James Fenwick had been demonstrating with Brisbane's regiment across the river from the American forts for almost two hours, making runs across the wide shallow river, ducking behind rocks and trees like an Indian as he returned fire from the Americans. He and his mates were finally getting the hang of fighting these frontiersmen. James Fenwick could be downright ungentlemanly if he wanted to, and he wanted to in the worst way. He was tired of being shot at and ducking cannon fire. He wanted to teach these upstart Americans a lesson and then go home. However, he suspected that if his forces won here they'd be staying awhile. It didn't look like that would be happening now.

Just as quickly as the order had been given to attack - even if only half-heartedly – now they were being ordered to retreat.

"What?" Fenwick exclaimed on getting the order from an officer, an arrogant aristocrat, a lieutenant he could hardly stand.

"Retreat," said the lieutenant, not happy to be repeating himself. "The whole army is moving back to Montreal. The order to retreat is being passed down the entire line. It comes from General Prevost himself."

"But, Sir." objected the dumbfounded sergeant. "We have them on the run. We outnumber them three to one. You've got to be kidding."

"The fleet has been defeated. It would be suicide to try and take those forts now. Move your men back, Sergeant. That's an order."

Fenwick looked around and saw other bewildered men starting to move to the rear.

"What about my wounded?" he yelled after the retreating officer.

"Leave them," came the response. "The orders are to retreat with all haste back to the staging areas, and then back to Montreal."

Fenwick sat where he was for some time, mumbling obscenities to himself. His men looked to him for leadership and finding none, started to wander to the rear on their own accord. The enemy had ceased firing, but the British artillery now opened up a fierce barrage to cover the retreat.

234

"Here we are retreating when we should be attacking," he fumed to no one in particular, "Stupid idiots."

"Why aren't you moving to the rear as ordered?" said the young lieutenant who had returned to make sure his orders were being carried out.

"I have wounded, Sir," Fenwick responded in defense, surprised by the officer who he hadn't notice ride up.

"Blast your wounded, Sergeant! You were ordered to move your men to the rear where they are needed to help with the wagons and ordnance. You will do as you are ordered. Now move or I will have you in irons!"

The lieutenant raised his sword as if to slap him with the flat of it, but James raised his rifle instinctively, sticking his bayonet in the horse's face, which caused it to rear up on its hind legs and start bucking down the road with the Lieutenant holding on for dear life. Fenwick almost laughed out loud despite his sour mood. Then he noticed he was almost alone, the whole British army having moved north out of the village. The artillery would remain to fire all day long and into the evening, shelling the forts on the south bank of the river.

By the time he had reached the staging area in Champlain, only a few miles from the border, the skies had opened up to unleash a cold, hard downpour that drenched him even through his heavy red army jacket. He was walking with his head down, among troops he did not recognize. He never did find his own company, not that he really tried. Instead he wandered unseen among strangers, his mind a seething cauldron of emotions and contradicting thoughts.

He found it unimaginable that this great army and its generals could retreat defeated from a battlefield like this after all their grand victories in Portugal, Spain and France. The disgrace of it stung him to tears, which mingled with the rain to all but blind him as he stumbled along through the drenched countryside.

How could this happen? What did it mean? Why had they shipped them all the way over here just to turn and run at the moment of victory? Why couldn't they have just sent them home like everyone wanted in the first place?

The roads had turned to muck and mire, and moving the supply wagons and ordnance was all but impossible. Some of it was being destroyed, some dumped into the lake. More of it fell into the hands of the locals who came out of the woods following the retreating army to scavenge anything left behind. When he did stop to look up and wipe his eyes, Fenwick was virtually alone in the back of a deserted farmhouse next to a field of unharvested corn.

Disgusted at the decisions of his superiors, fed up with the dithering incompetent politicians and their idiot generals, he had come to a momentous decision.

He took a quick look around and not seeing anyone, ducked into the farm's barn at the far edge of the village. Most of the activity was going on at the other side of the hamlet, near the lake and to the north where troops were already filing out to march the last few miles to the border. The British were not wasting any time. Not only did they leave over a hundred of their wounded behind, they lost hundreds to desertion. One of those was James Fenwick.

It was dark inside the barn. Once he made sure he was alone, he peeked out the barn door to make sure no one had seen him. As he did, he noticed a patrol pass by looking for deserters and rounding up stragglers. It appeared they were going to check the house and perhaps the barn as well.

He looked around quickly for a place to hide and almost cried out in despair, for the barn was empty. There was not so much as a blade of hay to cover the dirt floor, with just a couple of empty stalls and some old clothes scattered about. He turned toward the door and was about to leave when he happened to glance up. About fourteen feet above the entrance was a small loft just large enough to stand on and stack some bales of hay.

He noticed a few boards nailed to the wall that evidently served as a makeshift ladder. Hoisting his musket over his shoulder, he started slowly up, rung by rung. Just as he made it to the lip of the loft and slipped over, the barn door was flung open and one of His Majesty's finest burst into the room with his bayonet pointed in front of him. After a cursory look, he turned and left without so much as an upward glance to where Fenwick was hiding.

He laid there in the dark for a while, relishing the warmth and dryness of the loft, but soon realized that the longer he stayed there, the more likely he would be caught. He had decided to cast all aside and gamble on this lucky new country, for lucky it must be to escape the fate his vindictive government had planned for it.

Looking through a crack in the barn's siding, he saw that a guard had been placed in front of the farmhouse on the road to keep the troops moving and discourage deserters. Fenwick climbed down the makeshift ladder and looked around for something to help his escape. He found two things right away in the clothes left in the barn, an old pair of trousers and an old slouch hat. He quickly discarded his red uniform, burying it quietly in a corner of a stall, and put on the old farm breeches. Donning the hat, he unrolled an old horse blanket and threw it over his shoulder, leaving through a loose plank in the rear of the barn. Ducking through the cornfield, he made his way east toward the lake, staying well out of the way of his own troops, who now seemed to be everywhere. He was aided by the deep woods he found at the edge of the cornfield, and the dark of the late afternoon storm clouds looming above.

Somehow he made his way to the lake without being spotted. He crept through the brush along the shoreline and by luck found an old dory lying upside down on the shore. It appeared to have been hastily covered with weeds and bushes, but the wind and hard rain had blown most of that away. Thanking his lucky stars, he turned the small boat over and pulled it to the lake.

Even though it was old, it appeared to be seaworthy. He looked out across the water to the opposite shore not far away. He wondered if he could make it. Finding an old plank to use as an oar, he shoved off into the marsh, the high cat-tails and overhanging willows concealing him from view. Slowly, he made his way across the lake. Beyond the marsh and in the open, he could sense the water was quite shallow. Luckily for Sergeant James Fenwick, the distance across at this point was not far and the water protected from the wind. The surface of the water was flat but rowing with the plank was difficult and painful. His hands were blistered and his arms ached by the time he made it to an equally-marshy Vermont shore, just before sundown. Sergeant James Fenwick, late of his Majesty's fighting 88th Foot, was about to become an American.

Crab Island, Lake Champlain, NY, September 11, 1814 (Late)

It had been a long, terrifying, exhausting day for Sam Turner. The endless series of sorrow and suffering still hadn't ceased to torment him. As tired as he was, however, sleep eluded him, as did his peace of mind.

After volunteering to help the wounded on the enemy flag ship, he had been ordered to the hospital on Crab Island to assist the injured, both British and American. The carnage on his ship had been terrible, but that on the British frigate was even worse. Sam hardly knew where to begin, the deck had been so strewn with mangled bodies. Some were mere boys of ten or twelve, musicians and powder-monkeys, who carried gunpowder from the powder rooms deep in the ship to the gun decks. There were even a few women among the injured on board the British ship, who assisted the ship's cook and surgeon.

At first, Sam and his mates were greeted with hostile stares, but after they started seeing to the wounded, those looks turned to ones of gratitude and respect. He tended to those he could help and had the dead collected for burial. Those with serious injuries were transported to the hospital on Crab Island at the entrance to the bay, where the hapless 11-gun *Finch* still lay grounded, now manned by an American prize-crew.

It was at the hospital later that afternoon that Sam had his worst experience of the day and came closest to losing his faith in human nature. Although the Nichols' house was large, it was reserved only for the injured officers and these soon filled the place to overflowing. Large tents had been thrown up around the house, where operations were performed, mostly amputations, which went on all day long. The severed limbs were piled high outside the tents waiting removal and burial. Most of the American surgeons, joined by a few of their British counterparts, were now on the island. Sam reported to his chief surgeon and tried to ignore what was happening all around him. It was hard not to hear the screaming and smell the stench of the slaughterhouse, as the surgeons sawed through human bone and sinew. Sam clenched his jaw and fought down the nausea only to be told he was being assigned to tend the British wounded outside.

The fields, lawns and gardens about the house were covered with the wounded, the British and Americans separated into two groups. Most of the Americans tended to their own. Sam noticed that there were few British surgeons about, and wondered if they had all been killed, which many of them had. The British wounded were lying on the ground with only two or three attendants and those did not seem to know what to do. Sam surveyed the situation and then took charge, issuing orders and seeing to the enemy wounded as if he were on the deck of his ship tending to his own mates. His actions did not escape notice. Unfortunately, it was from those who didn't like what he was doing.

The only other Americans in the area were three sentries who had been detailed to guard the enemy injured in case some were only feigning their wounds or had somehow gotten by the inspecting doctors. They watched Sam for awhile with disapproving stares. Then, as he was busy bending over a seriously wounded British sailor, they sauntered over to Sam and started taunting him in much the same way the sailor on the *Saratoga* had when he volunteered to help on the enemy ship, only this time it was even more belligerent.

"What do you think you're doing?" asked the biggest and meanest looking of the three. "Who told you to help these prisoners?"

The men were army regulars, not navy men. Sam didn't know who had authority here, although he assumed it was himself.

"The chief surgeon from the *Saratoga*, Doctor..."

"This here's an army hospital," interrupted a second man, a little smaller but just as mean looking as the first fellow. "We say what goes on around here, and we say you ain't helping no damned Englishmen."

Sam ignored them and went on with his task, talking as he did so.

"Gentlemen, this is a naval hospital." He pointed to the tents and the house as he worked stitching up the wounded man's leg. "Those are naval officers working in those tents. The house is owned by Mister Caleb Nichols who reports to the Secretary of War. These are naval prisoners taken in battle and deserve all the care specified in the..."

239

"Don't give me any of that crap," said the biggest of the three, stepping forward as if to hit Sam. Sam stood and turned.

"You men are interfering with my work. If you have any objections to my being here, I suggest you take them to your commanding officer."

"I'll take you to my commanding officer, you little toad," declared the army man, stepping forward to grab him. Sam slapped the man's hands away with unsuspected speed and strength. Surprised, the army man took a step back, but it only made him angrier. He came at Sam again with a whistling right that just missed Sam's head as he ducked to the left. Without thinking, Sam drew his pistol, which he had tucked in his belt, and pointed it at the man's head, only three feet away.

Sam had brought it at the last minute, as he left the ship for the hospital with his belongings, not thinking he'd have much use for it at an American hospital. He had seen most of the enemy wounded and doubted if twelve of them together could cause much harm. Many of them wouldn't survive the night. He thought he'd have more need of a shovel than a gun where he was going, but he took it anyway, tucked in his belt, more because he didn't know what else to do with it rather than that he'd actually need it. Now here he was pointing it at one of his fellow countrymen.

The three sentries instantly brought their rifles up and pointed them at Sam. He didn't flinch. It was a matter of who would blink first, and Sam was determined it wouldn't be him.

"What's going on here," rang out a deep, commanding voice with a distinctive accent. Several of the enemy wounded who had been lying nearby strained to stand to attention. Sam turned and recognized the man from earlier in the day. It was Captain Pring, the commander of the British fleet.

"Haven't you killed enough men without killing each other?" said Pring. "What seems to be the trouble here?"

The three army men looked over their muskets not knowing what to think. They were being confronted by a very high ranking enemy prisoner and they suddenly were uncertain what to do. Adding to their discomfort, the British officer was accompanied by a civilian in expensive clothes. They lowered their rifles. Sam did the same with his pistol.

"This man is here without orders," said the biggest of the three, a corporal. "He refused to identify himself."

"I was busy seeing to this wounded man," replied Sam, pointing to the man lying on the ground who he had just stitched up. "They were trying to interfere with my work. I'm trying to help these men."

"Is that true?" asked the civilian, Caleb Nichols. He had been talking to the British commander as they walked the grounds observing the injured. Pring had been very forthcoming and Nichols was learning a lot that might be of use to the Secretary of War. The lack of American doctors among the British wounded was embarrassing enough, but this current incident was downright humiliating. No one answered his question.

"You men get back to your posts," he ordered. The three men stood there sullenly looking at Sam as if they weren't finished with him.

"We don't take orders from you and some captured redcoat," said the biggest of the three.

"I know your commanding officer, boy," responded Nichols losing his patience. Sam gripped his gun a little tighter. "Who is it, Colonel Storrs? Or is it old Melancton Smith at Moreau?"

"Major Vinson at Fort Scott," volunteered one of the men, who immediately got a dirty look from his companions for his trouble.

"Well, Major Vinson would not be happy to hear three of his men are interfering with doctors at the hospital trying to do their job. The battle is over gentlemen. We won. Now is the time to show we are generous in victory. The war is not over and our conduct here could go a long way in ending it honorably for our side. Now go back to your posts and let this man do his duty. He is here under express orders from Master Commandant Macdonough who has supreme authority on this lake, including this island."

The men reluctantly shouldered their muskets and returned to their posts.

"Thank you, Sir," said Sam to Caleb Nichols. "I don't know what I would have done if you hadn't come along."

241

"It looked like you were doing all right for yourself there, young Sam," replied Nichols. "You were holding your own against the three of them."

"You are the young man who first volunteered to help on my ship today," observed Pring, recognizing Sam from earlier in the day. "It seems you are paying for your generosity. I'm sorry helping my men has caused you any harm."

"No harm," answered Sam. "I'm an assistant naval surgeon. An injured man is an injured man as far as I'm concerned, no matter what uniform he's wearing."

"That's very commendable of you, young Sir, and I salute you for it," said Pring, taking off his hat and bowing courteously as he did on the ship during his surrender. "I will make a point to mention you in my dispatches back to the home country and to your own country's leaders as well. If there were more men like you, perhaps this war would not have happened."

"I'll drink to that," declared Nichols, taking the Captain's arm and leading him back to the house for more fruitful discussions.

Chapter 25

Village of Plattsburgh, NY, Late October 1814

The British had returned to Canada, and from there the troops were finally on their way home. In Plattsburgh, things had returned to a semblance of normalcy. The militia and volunteers had gone back to their towns and villages, and the locals had come home to their farms and houses. For some though, things would never be the same again.

Sam and Jesse walked up from the docks toward the heights above the village on the north side of the river, an area only a month ago inhabited by over 10,000 British regulars. Now it was covered with fallen leaves, which the townsfolk rushed through to their appointed rounds.

"Mister Sailly said you have yourself quite a nest egg with all that prize money you got," said Jesse, looking at his older cousin enviously. They had both grown quite a bit since that summer day two years ago when they had first heard about the war. But Sam had grown faster. Jesse now had to look up him when they talked.

"Yeah, I made out all right," replied Sam, not wanting the full size of his new fortune to become public knowledge. It would be if his cousin got wind of it. "They gave me double shares, one for being a carpenter's mate and one for being a surgeon's mate. They usually don't do that, but everyone of the crew agreed, so I guess I can't complain."

"I guess not," said Jesse, not knowing how his cousin could stand to be on a ship in the middle of the lake sharing broadsides toe-to-toe without so much as a rock to crouch behind. It just wasn't human, but that's what Sam thought about Jesse and his exploits, which were still the talk of the village. "My old man says they gave out almost a quarter of a million dollars. Why that's almost as much as the whole government spends in a year."

"Not quite," laughed Sam. "But it sure is a lot. You have to remember, the Master Commander gets almost ten percent of that, and it's shared among all the officers and crew."

"Yeah, but my Pa says you're a rich man. He's says you must of gotten a couple thousand dollars. What are you going to do with all that money?"

"Oh, I don't know," replied Sam honestly. "Maybe buy some land. My dad says it may take years before it's finally paid out. I've got to worry about how to make a living in the meantime. Not much call for ship's carpenters or surgeon's mates these days. They say the war may be over soon. They're having peace talks in Belgium."

"Yeah, my teachers told us," said Jesse.

"Oh, you're back in school?" asked Sam surprised. "I thought you hated school. What, you want to be an officer after all? I bet you'd make a good one. I can see it now, General Jesse Lebow."

"No, I don't think I want to be in the army," declared Jesse, turning serious. "I was talking to Mister Sailly and he said there're all sorts of opportunities for a man with a college education."

"College education?" exclaimed Sam, even more surprised. "Since when do you want to go to college?"

"I don't know," said Jesse. "I was thinking of being a lawyer."

"A lawyer?" Sam responded. "Now I know you've flown the coop."

"Yeah, you too," said Jesse laughing. "I heard you're engaged. You thinking of getting hitched to some old hag?"

"Don't call Sarah an old hag," replied Sam. "She's the most beautiful girl I've ever met."

"Good enough then," said his cousin. "You'll have to introduce us."

"If you promise not to call her an old hag."

"It's a deal," laughed Jesse. Despite everything it was nice to spend time with his cousin. They stopped at the Academy where some boys were racing in the field.

"Say, I hear you fellows are going to get a medal or something," said Sam, "for what you all did in that rifle company."

"You mean Aiken's Rifles?" replied Jesse, relishing the way the name sounded when he said it. "I don't know about any medals. They promised they'd give us all new rifles though."

"Oh, that's nice," said Sam impressed. "They should give you a medal too. I hear General Macomb himself commended you all in his dispatches to Washington."

"Who needs a stupid medal. I wish they'd a just given us the guns we had during the fighting. They were real nice pieces. Now we'll have to wait for who knows how long. That must have been some battle you were in," commented Jesse changing the subject.

"I guess so," Sam responded. "I don't remember much. I was mostly helping the injured. It's all kind of a blur, just one big line of blood and bandages."

"Mister Sailly said you got a commendation too, from Commander Macdonough himself, for what you did in the battle. It must have really been something. You could hear it for miles. Even down near the Salmon River where we were."

Sam was silent. Jesse could see his jaw tighten with the memory of his ordeal. Despite his words, Sam remembered all too well. He hadn't had a chance to talk about it to anyone until now.

"It was terrible," he said finally, tears forming in the corners his eyes. "I never want to go through anything like that again for as long as I live. We were throwing the dead overboard. People I knew, mates, some younger than you and me, just kids, musicians or powder boys. The bodies are still floating up along the lake. There was a pile of legs and arms by the tents at the hospital, where the surgeon performed amputations all day. At least I was spared the worst of that, but what was happening all around me was just as bad; bodies being blown apart, heads blown off, people with large spikes of wood sticking in their throats and eyes, screaming and bleeding. I kind of blocked it all out at the time and regarded it as just a series of injuries to be treated. I hardly thought of them as humans. But I have not had a peaceful night's slumber in the six odd weeks since the battle for the nightmares and memory of it, no matter how I try to suppress it."

Finally having a chance to unburden his soul, Sam ended his burst of emotion with a long sob. Jesse reached up and put his arm around his cousin's shoulder.

"I know what you mean," said Jesse understanding. "We didn't have it as bad as you on those ridiculous ships, but I know what you mean. One of our mates was killed, and I saw a lot of other men killed. I did a good amount of killing myself. Got to almost liking it, but then I realized what a terrible thing all that killing was, how many lives it ruins besides just those getting shot, and like you say, sometimes those that's killed are the lucky ones. Your Pa was right. War is a hell of a terrible thing."

The boys had found a quiet spot under a thick old spreading chestnut tree and held each other's shoulders sobbing quietly. They soon composed themselves, however, and straightened up to look around nervously. No one was about or appeared to have taken notice. But when they started walking down the road in front of the Academy, someone recognized Jesse and soon a crowd of excited boys had gathered around them.

"Hi, Jesse," said one of them, a classmate but not one of Aiken's gang. "You get your new rifle yet?"

"No," replied Jesse, a little annoyed they had lost their privacy, but happy to have a crowd of admirers to tell his stories to.

"Hiram said you fellows must of shot more than a hundred redcoats," said the boy who obviously didn't believe such tall tales.

"I reckon that's about right, but I don't know how many the other fellows shot," answered Jesse.

"Who's this?" asked another boy, from a younger class, noticing Sam's sailor garb.

"This is my cousin Sam," replied Jesse proudly, glad to have another family member to brag about. "He's with the fleet. He was on Macdonough's flagship during the battle in the lake."

Jesse didn't have time to finish the introduction when the crowd of boys exploded in a chorus of questions and exclamations.

"On the *Saratoga*!"

"During the battle?"

"What was it like?"

"Was it loud?"

"Did you shoot a cannon?"

"Do you know the Commander?"

"Wait a minute, wait a minute!" shouted Jesse. "One at a time. Calm down."

"Yes, it was all those things, and no I didn't shoot a cannon," said Sam laughing.

"Sam here's a ship's surgeon's mate," declared Jesse.

"Wow," said one of the boys. They were all impressed, all except Fred Allen and a few of the others that had fought with Aiken's rifles.

"How many was killed?" asked one of the younger boys, curious about the size of the battle. Sam, who had seen the casualty report, answered first.

"We had 28 killed on the *Saratoga* and 29 wounded, some seriously. We lost 52 killed altogether in the lake battle. There were another 58 wounded, most of who were brought to the island. It was a long few days caring for them. There were over a hundred British wounded. They suffered double our casualties. I don't know how many were killed, but there must have been 70 or 80 of them from what they say."

"Wow!" exclaimed some of the boys.

"I'm surprised everyone wasn't killed," declared one of the oldest of the group, who had watched the battle from the shore of Cumberland Head. "I've never seen so many cannons all shooting at once so close together. I'm surprised anyone survived."

He looked at Sam as if he were a living ghost.

"It was hell," said Sam, stating what would soon be a cliché of war. "We captured almost 350 prisoners. When I went aboard the enemy flagship, we found almost forty wounded and even more dead. It was dreadful. We were right to help them. They were in dire straights. Many more would have died needlessly."

"Good," said Fred Allen. "We killed over a hundred redcoats and wounded over a hundred more, and no fool American better help them."

Jesse and Sam said nothing, but excused themselves and continued on their way.

"Don't mind them," said Jesse to Sam. "That Allen is a blowhard. I can handle him."

"Oh, I don't mind," replied Sam. "I got it harder from my own mates. Some of them just didn't understand."

Neither did Jesse, but he told Sam he thought he did the right thing.

"You ever think of becoming a doctor?" asked Jesse "You're so good at helping people."

"Yeah, I thought about it," said Sam. "But it would take a lot of schooling and I could never do it. That doesn't mean I can't help folks as they need though. I've learned a lot. What about you, Jesse, are you serious about going to college and becoming a lawyer?"

"I sure am, Sam," answered Jesse. "After what happened, I kind of want to make something of myself, you know, for the ones who didn't make it."

"That's a nice thought, Jesse. Maybe I can help, once I get my prize money."

"Gee, Sam that's a mighty nice thing to do, but I can't..."

"Yes, you can, Jesse. I just might need a good smart lawyer to take care of all the property and businesses I plan to buy."

"You got yourself a lawyer," said Jesse. "I'll pay you back every nickel."

"I know you will, cous," replied Sam, putting his arm around Jesse's shoulder as they walked down the road together. "I know you will."

The End

Epilog

Plattsburgh, NY, 1826

Jesse stood at attention with his comrades-in-arms of twelve years ago. He had indeed gone to college in Boston and become a lawyer, a good one, specializing in land and banking laws, although he wasn't against taking a criminal case once in a while just to keep his skills honed. He was standing in line next to big Fred Allen who had opened a barroom, which a lot of the veterans of the battle frequented. Sam was there too, to see his attorney cousin and all the other boys of Aiken's Rifle Company get the brand new guns they had been promised over a decade ago. A lot had happened in that time.

Sam's prize money finally came in, only four years after the battle. It was a whopping $2,800 and made him a rich man. He immediately bought a farm and some property near his family's place. Then he bought his father's homestead when he retired shortly after the end of the war. He hadn't stopped buying since, and was now one of the more prominent landowners in the district, with several farms, a mill and his own shipbuilding company on the lake. He looked on proudly with his wife Sarah and their two little girls, Jessica, eleven and Julie, ten, both blondes like their mother.

"For volunteering to fight against overwhelming forces in defense of their country," began the commanding officer of the fort. "For bravery and daring beyond the normal call to duty, and for causing significant harm to the enemy in support of the regular forces of the United States, I hereby present these army issue weapons to the men of Aiken's Rifle Company. May there always be Americans who come to their country's call as you have done."

There was a smattering of applause from the family members and local dignitaries in attendance. The Commander began announcing the names of the recipients.

Jesse stepped forward as his name was called and received his rifle. After the ceremony he rushed over to show Sam his new gun.

"It's a brand new 1824 Hall Model breech-loading rifle," said Jesse, joining Sam and his family after the ceremony. He was as excited as a kid. "I'll do some great hunting with this thing."

"As long as you don't hunt redcoats," replied Sam, laughing and admiring the gun. "We'll have to go out this November. I'll let you get the first buck."

"That will be the day you have to let me get the first one," Jesse joked back.

"That's a nice plaque," said Sam noticing the small silver badge on the stock of the gun.

"What's a plaque Mommy?" asked little Danny Lebow, Jesse's five year old boy.

"It's like a trophy," answered Jesse's wife Mary, who he had met in Boston while going to college. "It tells a story about how your Daddy was a hero in the war."

"What does it say, Daddy?" asked Danny, pulling at his father's arm so he could see the small plaque.

"By resolve of Congress, presented to Jesse Lebow for his gallantry at the siege of Plattsburgh in September eleventh, eighteen-fourteen," said Jesse, "Better late than never," he added.

"It's never too late," said Sam, slapping his cousin on the back. "And may they never forget."

Some say the Battle of Plattsburgh was the turning point of the war and had a profound effect on the peace negotiations in Ghent, part of Flemish Belgium. It showed the British could be turned back and defeated. It did not give the opportunist government in London an excuse to prolong the war or trade peace for territory as some would have liked. It showed the British that war in America would be costly and difficult to win, and infinitely different than the one they had won on the continent against Napoleon. It provoked a fundamental change in British policy toward the United States, which together with the stunning victories of her Navy's "blue water fleet", led not only to a peace with honor for the new country and her nascent armed forces, but to a newfound respect among nations.

The small battle in a little village in upstate New York had changed the fate of a nation. Though it has almost been forgotten in the welter of great events of our past, nothing can negate what so few had won with so much bravery and so little cost, in the greatest battle that almost was.

Acknowledgements

This book was inspired by a chapter on the Battle of Plattsburgh in George C. Daughan's book '1812', which put the battle into perspective and emphasized its significance. It brought home to me the relative size and quality of the invading force, one of the largest and best trained armies to ever invade our country, as well as the small number of defenders. What inspired me most, however, was the fact that over 3000 volunteers came out of the woodwork, so to speak, to defend the village and their homes. Where most would run, these farmers and merchants, miners and tinkers, old men and boys, came forward and put their lives on the line.

Unfortunately, inspiration alone does not make a novel. Other than the broad outlines of the battle, I had little idea of what really took place. I knew there was a story there, but I didn't know what it was. Luckily for me, I happened upon Keith Herkalo's wonderful book, 'The Battles at Plattsburgh'. Not only was it filled with the most interesting and fascinating facts, it described the entire war from beginning to end, from our town's perspective. Here was the story that had to be told, with the names and places familiar to anyone from the area. It formed the skeleton on which I hung the meat of my story. Without Mister Herkalo's painstaking research and significant new discoveries this book could not have been written. I also want to thank Keith for his careful reading of the book for historical accuracy and his encouragement in pursuing publication. Any remaining errors or inaccuracies, however, are entirely my own.

I am indebted to Joy A. Demarse as well, and her book 'Nine Days a Soldier', which recounts the story of Aiken's volunteers. In her research for the book, she uncovered the names of several of the boys, which I make use of in my chapters on these colorful and interesting young men.

We are fortunate to have such an untiring servant as Keith and people like Joy, to keep the spirit and memory of those days alive. Although perhaps less significant and costly than many of the battles in our country's illustrious past, what happened in our small town on September 11, 1814, has a special meaning to our nation's history. It was a turning point, a time when a new young nation earned the respect of that older, larger one from which she sprang, a respect earned with the blood and lives of her patriots, however few and long ago.

To my Father with love, an ex-marine who could shoot the head off a snake. Gone but not forgotten.

46169678R00142

Made in the USA
Lexington, KY
25 October 2015